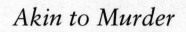

Akin to Murder

By Alanna Knight

Akin to Murder

An Inspector Faro Mystery

ALANNA KNIGHT

Allison & Busby Limited
12 Fitzroy Mews
London W1T 6DW
allisonandbusby.com

First published in Great Britain by Allison & Busby in 2016.

Copyright © 2016 by ALANNA KNIGHT

A CIP catalogue record for this book is available from
the British Library.

First Edition

ISBN 978-0-7490-1919-8

Typeset in 11/16 pt Sabon by
Allison & Busby Ltd.

The paper used for this Allison & Busby publication
has been produced from trees that have been legally sourced
from well-managed and credibly certified forests.

Printed and bound by
CPI Group (UK) Ltd, Croydon, CR0 4YY

For Niamh,
with love

CHAPTER ONE

1864

Before the full horror of a situation in which his family became involved in a murder, Detective Sergeant Jeremy Faro had not envied policemen who were unmarried. He knew nothing of his wife's early life and a sense of delicacy forbade him to raise the subject, knowing only her story that rape by a guest in a great Highland house had resulted in Vince, and parents who speedily disowned her.

Serious crimes had been at a low ebb that year, only one homicide. A young railway worker in East Lothian who had murdered his faithless wife. According to the Edinburgh City Police a domestic open-and-shut case. At the trial the jury agreed and ignored his not-guilty plea. The judge donned the black cap, and pronounced a sentence of death.

Faro had missed most of the trial, away on a complex Edinburgh fraud investigation with tentacles reaching out to Glasgow, Dundee and Aberdeen; a case Inspector Gosse considered beneath him. When Faro returned it was all over and in the railway station the newsboys were shouting: 'Guilty local man to hang.'

Ignoring that misinformation, since Musselburgh could hardly be described as local, he sighed. The newspapers would have their day and return their efforts to arouse interest in international affairs, like the American Civil War where brother fought brother and sons fought fathers, or in Denmark where the enemy was Prussia. Not since Culloden and the bloody history of the Stuarts had such emotions stirred Scotland and now readers' only concern was with local issues regarding the expansion of the city boundaries southward, a situation involving heated letters to the editor.

As Faro walked up the High Street past St Giles' Cathedral, his future seemed to stretch out offering little excitement beyond the normal daily routine, waiting for something to happen beyond the trivialities of lost or stolen animals, drunken assaults and enlivened by the occasional burglary. Duties which seemed rather boring after the sensational murder involving the legendary 'curse of Scotland' two years ago, not that he longed for homicide or violent crime, especially as he was now a happily married man expecting his first child.

Strolling into the Central Office, however, he was met by pandemonium and an almost apoplectic Inspector Gosse shouting that he couldn't believe what had happened.

John McLaw, the man whose trial had just ended, was on the way back to Calton Jail where he was to be confined awaiting the death sentence to be carried out. And he had escaped.

The prison van had been struck by lightning in a

thunderstorm that Faro had witnessed from the railway train. The horse unhurt but terrified had run amok, the carriage overturned and in the resulting confusion McLaw had got his handcuffs unlocked and vanished.

A search party of constables was already out. A sighting of the escaped prisoner heading towards Leith, where departing ships were being alerted, while other police forces up and down the country were telegraphed to be vigilant. There had already been incidents, an assault and an attempted burglary in the New Town, the victim giving a description of the man he had wrestled with. It fitted McLaw.

The general conclusion was that he would be heading north and west to his homeland in the wilds of Argyll, among familiar hills that, once covered in an early snowfall, would be impossible for searchers and provide a natural sanctuary, with the glens closed until the spring thaw. Skimming the details of McLaw's trial as Gosse ranted on about his spectacular escape, Faro handed him back the papers.

'I'm surprised at the verdict.' He shook his head. 'There are too many loose ends in this case.'

Gosse seemed surprised at this observation. 'Indeed. Pretty obvious to me, as well as most intelligent folk.' He shrugged. 'Just one of our usual sordid domestics.' He paused and added sarcastically, 'And what makes the clever sergeant think he knows more than the judge and jury?'

'Right at the beginning, I would have liked to interview the victim, get a few explanations from him. I gather he was appealed to, to come forward. Pity he didn't do so.'

'What do you mean, pity he didn't come forward?'

'Might have helped McLaw, even if he was guilty.' Faro said weakly.

'No, no.' Gosse stared at him in astonishment. 'Come on, Faro, you're hopeless. For God's sake, use whatever wits you have about it. No wonder he wanted his identity concealed. Discretion, Faro, that's why. Can't you see it at all? It's all there in front of you, a jealous husband and a cheating wife. Happens all the time. I will give it to McLaw, he made a good try, but imagine expecting any one in their right minds swallowing that yarn. An unseen lover who, instead of scarpering, knocked him out and when he came to, there was his wife lying beside him, with a knife stuck in her chest. He just invented the whole situation. As for the other man who preferred to remain anonymous . . .'

Pausing, he grinned. 'If it was true, then I should think he had some very good reasons for remaining silent. Come on, Faro, you're a married man yourself, surely you understand this sort of thing.'

Faro shuddered, hoping he would never have that particular crisis to cope with, glad that it was very unlikely with his dear devoted Lizzie, whose whole world went round and stopped with him. He sighed thankfully. The most unlikely woman in the world to deceive him or ever be unfaithful.

'Anyway, too late for that now. And McLaw was just a bloody savage. John McLaw – we had to call him that with a first name nobody could pronounce,' growled Gosse, raising his head from the latest report. 'We lowlanders aren't like that. Not like those damned highlanders, thank God. We know our place.'

10

Faro's eyebrows raised at that somewhat sweeping statement, typical of the man, as he continued:

'Can't trust them. Damned villains, the lot of them.'

'Not all of them; my wife is from the Highlands,' Faro said quietly.

Gosse ignored that. 'A sleekit lot. Wait till you've had as many dealings as I've had with them.' He paused to shudder expressively. 'Aye, you never knew what was going on in their heads, what they were thinking when you walked into a public house, like as not weighing up the possibilities of sticking a knife in your back. Aye, sleekit, that's what. Man, they don't even speak the same language. Foreigners, the lot of them.'

And that included Lizzie. This was true since their first meeting here in Edinburgh five years ago; he had never heard her speak Gaelic.

As is often the way with those who become dear to us, he thought later, it was as if she had come into his life complete and ready-made, waiting for him, and with that, her world before they met had ceased to exist.

Yet he could not pretend that Lizzie was the love of his life; there had been Inga St Ola in Orkney. Inga, whose memory was bitter – a knife in the heart, for she would not have him. So accepting the bitterness of truth, he had compromised, taking Lizzie, content to know nothing about her except that he was exceedingly fortunate having found someone to love him so much that he owed her marriage, especially in regard to her tragic early life. How he respected and admired her courage in keeping and bringing up Vince.

Listening to Gosse ranting on, he realised he was

11

learning almost more about the criminal McLaw than he knew about his own wife. He had never questioned her. After that first kiss, a whispered account with eyes closed like a confession, to shut out the terrible vision. No, she was not really a war widow with a son, and then the full awful story, quickly told with little detail, anxious to get it over with. Some tears, too, but Faro had not wanted to pry, his heart wrenched, deeply touched by her tragedy, he decided never to mention the incident again.

There was a further flurry, a nasty moment later when Vince, resenting Faro's intrusion into their lives, proudly told him his father had been a brave soldier, killed in India, and he seemed determined that his mother remain faithful to his memory. It had taken their lives threatened in a murder to convince him good things occasionally come of bad, and he had transferred his devotion from his heroic non-existent father to the detective-sergeant who had saved their lives, thereby removing himself as the one just cause and impediment to their marriage.

Faro sighed. Was Vince to be the only son he would have? Lizzie had miscarried twice and now, pregnant again, past the dangerous early stages, they had both sighed with relief and begun to hope anew. Perhaps it was as well to pretend the past was a ghost that had been laid for ever.

'And what do you think of that, Faro?' barked Gosse.

Faro realised that he hadn't been listening, the tirade going over his head. He was tired of Gosse's endless moaning, how he had arrested McLaw and, making it his business to see him to the gallows, he had been humiliated by his escape. The prison van accident had robbed Gosse of his final triumph. No one did that to Gosse and got away

12

with it and Faro was well aware once again that Gosse was quite capable of bending the evidence to suit the crime, and here there was something even stronger, the personal element. Gosse was a man devoid of pity: he would kick a lost dog in the gutter, laugh at the misfortune of beggars, asserting that men's misfortunes were their own doing and that being harsh and strong, without pity, was what made a true policeman, a great detective.

'You'll never make it, Faro, you have too much heart, a great big softie, that's what you are. You'll never get beyond the mentality of the policeman's beat.'

Gosse had been wrong, of course, when he was promoted to inspector to find that his hated detective constable had also been elevated to sergeant. He told himself that was doubtless due to the good word put in by retired Chief Superintendent Brandon Macfie, who looked kindly upon Faro, another bone of contention.

Nothing was ever going to rid him of Faro it seemed. He was especially bitter that Faro's fancy woman, his juicy widow, had not fallen into his arms when she had the chance, captivated by what he fondly believed was his charm, his irresistible allure to women.

She had married Faro. He would have been surprised to know that Lizzie had been completely unaware of his intentions, of his pursuit of her. He was Faro's boss, his wife meanwhile away from Edinburgh caring for some sick relative (Lizzie believing the story he gave out, she had in fact left him for ever). But Lizzie was without vanity and never saw her reflected image in the mirror as an attractive woman. Life did not owe her anything. All she asked was a safe future for her adored Vince, and, grateful for a marriage happy beyond her imagination, she was content to love and serve Jeremy Faro for the rest of her life, provide him with a comfortable home and bear his children.

Her idea of a comfortable home, Faro discovered, also included offering it to others not so fortunate. Lizzie could not resist waifs and strays – fortunately only a stray cat and dog.

As yet.

CHAPTER TWO

Faro bought a newspaper on his way home. A paragraph stated that the searchers were out for McLaw and reminded readers that this was a dangerous man, a murderer on the run. For the rest, the world might be in turmoil across the Atlantic and in Europe, but the only emotions stirring Edinburgh were less to do with an escaped prisoner and more about a frenzy involving builders demolishing old dwellings and developing the open countryside, involving outraged discussion and constant appeals to the council.

The city was stretching its sides. First northwards, with the New Town in the last century, now it was the turn of the south side beyond Arthur's Seat. From ancient times, on this land once owned by the abbots at Newbattle, early farmers had left the marks of their runrig fields still visible. At its base, medieval families with crops and animals had made a drove road heading south through East Lothian, carrying their sheep and cattle beyond the massive boulder-strewn heights with its bracken-lined gullies and hidden caves, haunted by legends of King Arthur with his knights, their hounds at their sides, awaiting the trumpet call that would awaken them to ride out and fight for Scotland.

'Is it true, sir?' asked Vince.

Brandon Macfie was telling him the story on one of their Sunday afternoon walks with Faro, explaining that Arthur's Seat was a corruption of the Gaelic name Alt na Said, Height of the Arrows.

'King Arthur missed his chance, I fear. And Prince Charlie would have welcomed his knights' assistance. He needed all the help he could get.'

'Still lost the throne and changed the course of Scotland's history,' Faro added grimly.

Edinburgh was growing rapidly since the Industrial Revolution. The greedy eyes of developers had been turned to the countryside surrounding that long road, leading stagecoaches as well as drovers to the Borders and eventually to England.

For centuries past, the old drove road far below them, still the main road south, had seen its share of history, watched over by the heights of Samson's Ribs on the lower reaches of the extinct volcano. King James had ridden at the head of his army of clans raised and lairds with their banners, riding out confidently with their tenants to fight and die on the bloody field of Flodden. And in another disaster, the army of Prince Charles Edward had ridden victorious, before that last desperate attempt to reinstate the Stuarts had ended with Culloden.

Macfie loved history and the open country beyond the southside of Edinburgh. He sighed deeply as each day a little more vanished into bricks and mortar, and great terraces, rows of houses, some of them very ugly indeed, rose on those once peaceful meadows to accommodate Edinburgh's rapidly increasing population.

No trumpets, no hunting horns, but hammers. King Arthur and his knights still slept undisturbed apart from the builders' hammers (respectfully silent on Sundays) echoing across the hill as the suburb of Newington extended its boundaries. The developers had moved in and the area on either side of the old drove road was transformed by monstrous scaffolding as vast terraces four storeys high, a more modern version of the tenements of the Old Town's closes, arose to house Edinburgh's artisans who could not afford the grand Georgian New Town but wished for a speedy exit from association with the notorious slums of the High Street, between the Palace of Holyroodhouse and the lofty castle.

Soon there would be nothing left but St Anthony's ruined chapel where once a light had glowed to keep sailors safe at night as they negotiated the waters of the Firth. And at the base of Arthur's Seat, Solomon's Tower, an ancient pele tower, almost a crumbling ruin and owned by some noble family who, they were informed, refused to give permission for its destruction.

Pausing to light a pipe, Macfie looked up at the lazy cloudless Sunday sky. It was an idyllic scene with only the distant sound of church bells calling in the worshippers.

He smiled down at Vince. 'On a day a like this, lad, you could imagine anything, if you were that way inclined.'

Faro walked at their side and he looked at the tall Orcadian policeman. There were still unmistakable traces of his origins in high cheekbones, the wide mouth and slightly hooded, dark-blue eyes. As for that thick, fair hair, all he needed to complete the image of a warrior was the horned helmet.

He chuckled. 'Your stepfather might have been one of King Arthur's knights.'

'Not really, sir,' Vince said firmly. 'He's a Viking.'

Faro laughed. 'Yes, Vince, but the knights came from everywhere.'

Macfie regarded the boy fondly. His devotion to Jeremy had extended towards his stepson, seeing both as the family he had been destined never to possess, the son he had lost in a tragic accident – Sandy – who would have been Jeremy's age.

A very popular man as chief superintendent of the Edinburgh Police Force, although his affection for Faro had been sneered at, especially by Gosse, since nothing but a coldness had ever existed between Macfie and the now inspector. The reason for this was that Macfie was an honest policeman. He did things by the book but he would never put a foot wrong by inventing or planting evidence on a criminal and he suspected and distrusted any officer, like Gosse, who did so.

'It is just a legend, I'm afraid, that has come down the ages, lad,' he said firmly. This was a clever youngster, and he was always keen to hear how he had done in exams, and as he knew some of the teachers at the school, he had excellent reports of Vince's progress from the Royal High School where he had long been a governor. He decided to ensure that the boy went on to university. Aware that Jeremy could not afford such fees on his salary he had made sure, if he didn't live long enough, that Vince was included in his will, for as a widower for many years before Sandy died, this was the family he had chosen.

'So the legend isn't really true, sir?' Vince, disappointed, turned to Macfie who shook his head.

'Very unlikely, lad. And one should always tell the truth, remember.'

Vince regarded him proudly. 'I always do, sir. My mother insists on it.'

Faro felt a prickle of unease, a shadow on that cloudless day, like a premonition of disaster.

What would happen when Vince was told the truth and learnt that his very existence was based on a lie?

CHAPTER THREE

The slopes of the hill were throwing dark shadows into the fading autumn afternoon as they walked back down to Faro's cottage. Even in the diminishing landscape it was heartening to know that the cottage would survive, for a time anyway. This once remote area had seen small pockets of land owned by the wealthy, and part of the rapidly disappearing Lumbleigh estate, the former gamekeeper's cottage, had been gifted to Lizzie by her grateful employer Mrs Lumbleigh before her disgraced husband Archie sold out to the developers. They departed Edinburgh for ever, into what they hoped was a warmer and impersonal southern England where Archie's wealth might make a stir in Bath and Brighton, which had never heard of the Lumbleigh scandal. The large, ugly house had nothing to commend it and was being speedily demolished to the delight of schoolboys like Vince playing amongst its ruins.

The sound of church bells was long silent. The sunlight

fading into a mellow autumn dusk had advanced down the hill, enfolding them within the daily drama of the twilight gloaming. Below them the road out of Edinburgh to Dalkeith, now languishing under mud and builders' debris, was once bordered by a few windblown trees, a lot of boulders and occasional stray sheep. Now its magnificent view of the lofty pinnacles of Arthur's Seat would be hidden for ever behind a long line of grey-faced tenements four storeys high, Faro thought sadly.

Macfie came back with them, to a cheery fire with the crackle of logs, candles already lit and a snow-white cloth on the table, an appetising smell of cooking with tea and scones prepared by a welcoming Lizzie Faro. Macfie regarded her fondly and a trifle anxiously, for although she looked well, he hoped this time she would carry her baby full term, the dangerous early months over.

Thanking them both for their hospitality, he said he must be going home soon. He smiled, for home was no longer at Nicolson Square, the police-owned house he had lived in most of his career. He was moving to Sheridan Place, a handsome, newly built villa, an extension of the original Georgian-built Blacket Place, private and exclusive behind handsome pillared gates locked each night by the lodge keeper as an extra protection against roving gangs from the High Street closes, who eyed the outer reaches with their wealthy citizens as fair targets for thieving.

Macfie said almost apologetically that he had inherited the house. Faro knew he had rich relatives over Glasgow way but he had never talked of them beyond specifying that with the new house had come an abundance of rooms and an excellent housekeeper.

The previous Sunday, instead of their afternoon ritual, Faro with Lizzie and Vince had been invited over to view the premises and were suitably impressed by a modern house on two floors with attics for the servants and handsome bow windows overlooking front and back gardens. Lizzie was also very impressed by Mrs Brook who had already moved in and taken up her duties by producing tea and scones – quite excellent – for them.

Looking out of the window, Macfie said: 'I know nothing about growing vegetables or anything like that. I'm no green fingers either, but have always fancied sitting outside my own place in the sunshine. None at Nicolson Square, but now this has me wondering whether I've taken on more than I can manage and help will be needed to keep it all in order and stop that fine lawn turning into a jungle.'

Faro laughed. 'Lizzie has green fingers, if that's what you're looking for.'

'I'll come and help you dig in the summer holidays, sir,' Vince said eagerly. 'Me too,' said Lizzie. 'I love my flowers and vegetables.'

Macfie smiled. 'You'll need to bring the wee one with you, Lizzie.'

'I'll do that, sir. I can push the pram across.'

As he was leaving, he reminded them that he would not be with them for Sunday walks for the next two or three weeks. He was guest speaker at a London conference and then planned to visit two of his retired professors from university days, one in Paris, and the other in Vienna.

Vince was very impressed and sighed deeply. It must be wonderful to be grown-up and so famous. He had been working at weekends, earning a shilling in an antiquarian bookshop on the High Street that also specialised in medical textbooks, a popular place for browsing medical students. Vince, already an avid reader, was intrigued by the stock, especially the illustrations, and when Mr Molesby was out seeking business, negotiating the sale of his most valuable books or buying new ones, with no customers in the shop needing his attention, he took every opportunity of reading medical history.

Approaching fourteen, he had already decided on his future. His goal in life was to go to university and become a doctor like his first grown-up friend Dr Paul Lumbleigh, whom he greatly missed since after his parents' departure, he had also moved from Edinburgh. Vince had no idea where the money would come from, certainly not his stepfather's salary, but he had infinite hopes.

'I'm working at the weekends now, in Mr Molesby's bookshop,' he told Macfie proudly.

Macfie nodded eagerly. 'The old antiquarian shop. I know it well.' He added with an approving glance, 'Lots of splendid reading for you, lots to learn about many things in your spare time.'

'Plenty of that, sir.'

'Used to go in myself for bargains in law books when the shop was owned by old Molesby's uncle. He died childless, a bachelor, and left it to his nephew.'

'I'll be working this Sunday as well. The stock is in a bit of a muddle, I can tell you, and Mr Molesby said he would pay me extra if I could go in, and with the shop closed, we could catalogue some of the books.'

As he was to state later and tried to prove to Inspector Gosse, when he went that Sunday morning, Molesby had just poked his head round the door and said there was a change of plans. He was going to church and then out to lunch.

Could Vince come on Monday instead, as he remembered that it was a school holiday for Founders' Day at the Royal High, his old school. Vince was delighted.

'Of course, sir. I'll be along in the morning,' he said.

'Very well, but don't be late.' Molesby smiled, but there was no Monday morning ever again for the old man. He was to die sometime that day.

CHAPTER FOUR

Faro walked back to Sheridan Place with Macfie, thinking how large it seemed after their tiny cottage. Dining room and housekeeper's apartments, kitchen, parlour, bedroom and a wash house outside, with a rather grand staircase that wound its way upstairs to a handsome drawing room and four bedrooms, all empty and echoing at present.

'The furniture arrives next week, but I'll only be needing the one room and perhaps another for a friend or an occasional guest.'

They had been talking about Orkney recently and how rarely Faro managed to see his mother Mary.

'We would love to have her, of course,' he told Macfie, a slight exaggeration but no matter. 'But the cottage is too small. A day or two, but weeks . . .'

And that gave Macfie an idea.

He turned to Faro and smiled. 'I have it. Your cottage is close by, so your mother can stay here with me. Mrs Brook will put her in the guest room and take good care of her.'

That Mary Faro would regard being taken care of as a pleasure, her son doubted exceedingly, while feeling guilty with Kirkwall too distant for more than a yearly visit and his mother's deep-rooted dislike and fear of Edinurgh, never forgetting that her beloved Magnus, a constable on beat duty, had been killed by a runaway cab on the Mound. This she regarded as deliberate murder, for reasons unknown, leaving her a widow with four-year-old Jeremy, who she had promptly taken back to Kirkwall.

Mary Faro had never forgiven him for leaving at seventeen to join the police force in Edinburgh, following in the footsteps of his father, destroying her dream that he would be content to stay in Orkney for the rest of his life. None of this policeman nonsense but a crofter married to a local lass with grandchildren she could see every day. After despairing if he would ever find a wife, she had been reconciled and even glad that he had found Lizzie Laurie. She approved of this widowed Highland girl who had all the qualities she admired in a young woman, and they had much in common, both good, conscientious, competent housewives, with no ambitions more than to look after a good husband.

Now Mary Faro was looking forward to grandchildren and had been dismayed that so far, after two years' marriage, there had been no hint of any baby. They had kept the early miscarriages from her but her delight that Lizzie was pregnant at last had overcome her reluctance to visit Edinburgh and she had immediately suggested that she come and look after Lizzie in the later months. A fact that made both Faro and Lizzie (secretly) groan.

And so it was to be arranged. Mary Faro was to travel by ship from Kirkwall to Leith where Faro would meet her off the boat. Lizzie was anxious that their cottage should meet with her mother-in-law's approval. It had two large rooms, one a bedroom, the other a living room, which at one end housed the traditional Scottish box bed, comfortable, warm and private from the rest of the family, suitable for an elderly relative or a couple of small children. Vince had been delighted at the prospect of this warm nest that he would have to relinquish once the new baby outgrew the bedside cradle in his parents' bedroom.

An extension to the length of the cottage was a barn that had in former days housed cattle. The gamekeeper's family had turned it into a wash house, an enviable addition with its ceiling of drying rails, a boiler which could be heated from beneath by a log fire and a tin bath, for this wash house-cum-laundry was also a boon, where newly built houses for working-class Edinburgh could not boast of such a luxury. There was also a loft above the kitchen, used for storage. It was quite large, with a skylight window and access by a wooden ladder.

Faro and Lizzie loved their cottage nestling at the foot of Arthur's Seat, hating the thought of moving into the town or living in one of the four-storeyed houses in the terraces now under construction. But with the children she hoped for, a growing family, there was only one solution. Lizzie decided that the loft could become a bedroom and Jeremy agreed. It was a good idea – anything that turned their little cottage into a family home for years to come, as they visualised the garden echoing to the shrill delight of children at play. Children still to be born.

Faro had already mentioned the loft to Dave, foreman of the builders who greeted him warmly each morning and thought it could be carried out at the same time with little difficulty and not too great an expense, slotted in with their weightier project of the terrace houses.

As Dave was almost certain that the cottage was safe from the developers' plans, Faro and Lizzie realised that with extensions and adaptations, hopefully this might remain their home for the rest of their lives. But in the meantime, the loft was out of the question for his mother's visit. They could hardly expect an elderly woman to leap up and down stepladders.

And that raised another problem. Mary had never met Vince. Macfie had decided that when Jeremy and Lizzie got married, they should have their honeymoon in Orkney unattended by twelve-year-old Vince. Lizzie was anxious about leaving her son but Macfie had insisted he would take good care of him. There was always a room in the police house at Nicolson Place for an occasional guest.

Vince had enjoyed staying with Macfie and a bond was established between the two. Jeremy wondered if his mother had ever forgiven him for leaving Orkney and as the years passed without any signs of him taking a wife, Mary had been relieved when he married a foreigner, a war widow with a young son. She had got over her disappointment about a dream daughter-in-law – but not that Inga St Ola, God forbid – and she made a particular point of asking about the boy, Vince, in her letters.

Now Faro had a new fear. There was no doubt in his mind that she would like Vince. She would certainly be most sympathetic and question him about his father, who he could not remember, having been a soldier killed on duty in India. She had a natural empathy for young widows left with a small son. She had been through that herself so painfully.

And Mary always wanted to know everything about everybody: 'leave no stone unturned' might have been invented by her – every small detail was of interest, a curious turn of mind that she had passed on to Jeremy. It had evolved as observation and deduction. That she would employ these powers on Lizzie and Vince, Faro had not the least doubt. Somewhere a thread of suspicion, a misplaced word and the lie they lived would be revealed.

And it was the consequences for Vince that Faro feared most: the fact that not only the father that he boasted about to his schoolmates so proudly, but indeed his whole life, was based on a lie.

As he retraced his path to the cottage, walking past the disembowelled Lumbleigh House, he saw their happy existence tumbling like a house of cards, as steadily as the ruined estate before him, and he thought of all he had to lose.

It was heart-warming to push open the door and see two smiling faces welcoming him, as Lizzie and Vince sat at the kitchen table, the lamplight making haloes of their bright, fair hair, curls so attractive in Lizzie but, alas, such a blight on Vince's early schooldays until those who teased him found he also had a strong pair of fists.

Faro sighed deeply. It was always so good to come home and their cottage was an enviable luxury to his colleagues, with windows gazing across the extinct volcano that was now Arthur's Seat, magnificent and unchanging. To their left, Salisbury Crags, two remnants bequeathed by one of the many ice ages that had shaped Edinburgh's seven hills. Their beauty never failed to move him, with the changing light of the seasons, and they were a favourite walk with his stepson, accompanied by a new member of the household.

Coll was a stray mongrel that had wandered in, starving, shivering, one cold night and had been promptly adopted by Lizzie. With a weakness for waifs and strays, she already had a feral cat, inadequately named Puskin, a very large, striped creature and quite ferocious enough to keep her natural enemy, the dog, at a safe distance.

Wrapped serenely in the comfort of a family, Jeremy Faro had forgotten his early misgivings, how he had once considered taking the step into matrimony out of a sense of duty having slept with Lizzie after a party where they both drank too much, then realising that she loved him with a passion which scared him, for it was far beyond his capabilities of returning. He did not know what that kind of being in love meant, always having his emotions under tight control; he knew only that this was far from the love one would die for, like Shakespeare's Romeo and Juliet, or to a lesser extent, his boyhood passion for Inga St Ola.

During their brief two years of marriage, he had learnt how readily Lizzie's emotions could stir – tears over a broken cup, a ruined stew (more often than not, since Jeremy's hours were unpredictable and liable to delays and changes at short notice). She was still to learn that nerves of steel were a requirement for a policeman's wife, nerves that had been shattered if he was a few minutes late home, and as the clock moved on another half-hour and became an hour, she still trembled at an unexpected rap on the door, expecting a grim-helmeted policeman bearing 'bad news, Mrs Faro'. Usually it was the milkman wanting his pay or one of the many gypsies camped on the far side of Arthur's Seat roaming the residential areas, their men mending pots and pans, their women selling clothes pegs and telling fortunes.

Faro, too, had learnt patience and daily gratitude for a comfortable existence and an excellent housewife after years of non-tolerant landladies. With Vince as a shining example, she was also a devoted mother, although motherhood of Faro's babies had not been so easy to achieve.

Pregnant within months of their wedding day, she had miscarried, more of a bitter grief to her than to Faro who decided that he would have been content with an almost grown-up Vince rather than a crying babe and sleepless nights interfering with his police duties.

At the supper table in the midst of his family, violence seemed to belong to another age, a far-distant planet as the sunset of violet and rose made its dramatic exit and the moon crept up over the hill, not moonlike white and shining but in the likeness of a huge orange. Strolling into the kitchen that evening, he cast out the tormenting demons of his fears and told himself that he was suffering from an overdose of imagination.

They could never happen. He was a happy man.

CHAPTER FIVE

In the days that followed no progress was made in recapturing McLaw, and Faro, besides the usual daily routine, was faced with an increasingly angry and frustrated Gosse. The searchers had more or less given up after racing triumphantly to one or two sightings in Edinburgh and East Lothian with negligible results.

They were always too late or had been misinformed and the general assumption so infuriating Gosse was that McLaw had taken a ship from Leith after his daring escape, and although ships were searched, he had doubtless stowed away. Gosse wasn't satisfied and never would be until he had his man safely in handcuffs and saw him hanged. That there had been no reports from police alerted up and down the country also put him in a rage, although Faro guessed that as the McLaw case wasn't in their territory, other forces had more things to do other than to take an obligatory but cursory look around.

Meanwhile the demolition of Lumbleigh House

continued, the developers daily creeping closer to the cottage, the noise increasing, axes as trees were felled, along with the louder thud of hammers on scaffolding as the new long line of terraces took skeletal shape.

Vince was one of the many sufferers from the effects of this constant disruption. It was still daylight and the builders working long hours were at work when he came home from school. The noise outside made it difficult to concentrate on his homework. Lizzie appealed to Jeremy, but what could he do? He was sympathetic but suggested Vince plug his ears and get on with it.

A school week had flown by for Vince, who was doing well and not hating every lesson at the Royal High or the daily walk up to Calton Hill.

'I have exams coming up soon, and I won't be able to work this weekend,' he reminded his mother. 'I'll be at the bookshop both days,' he added proudly. However he arrived on the Sunday morning to be told by Mr Molesby that there was a change of plans and agreed that he should come on Monday instead.

It was with some disquiet that when he arrived he found the shop door ajar, but Mr M (as he called him privately) was not in evidence. A quick look round confirmed that although most of the books remained on their shelves, there was an untidy scattering of papers on the floor, evidence that drawers had been opened, their contents searched.

His heart pounded in sudden fear. These were unmistakable signs that there had been a burglary. The real treasures, the rare and valuable books, however, were kept with the cash box containing the day's takings, locked away by Mr M each evening. The cupboard door hung open.

But where was Mr M?

He lived upstairs above the shop. Vince called his name but there was no answer.

Still calling: 'Mr Molesby. Are you all right, sir?' he made his way up the steep ladder, leading to the attic above. The premises and the bookshop itself had once been a family home, often as many as twelve to a room. Two doors, a kitchen sink and some shelves with a few provisions occupied one corner of the one-time sitting room, crammed to overflowing with books from the shop. and through a half-open door with shutters, the outline of a bed.

Vince peered in, tapped politely on the door.

'Are you there, Mr Molesby?'

Had he perhaps overslept, had a poorly turn as old folks sometimes did and that was why he had forgotten to lock and bolt the shop door?

Vince cleared his throat, called 'Mr Molesby!' loudly this time.

All was silence but in the streak of light from the shuttered window, a pile of bedding lay on the floor. With a scalp-tingling feeling of apprehension of what he was to find, Vince pulled open the shutters, let in the light and cried out at the appalling revelation.

The bedding was in fact Mr Molesby. Kneeling down, Vince whispered his name. There were bloodstains on his head.

Vince touched him gently but there was no movement, no breathing.

Mr Molesby was dead. And had been for sometime, Vince guessed, his face cold, grey and waxlike.

Vince sat back on his heels. What to do now? He had read and heard plenty about corpses from his stepfather and the medical books downstairs, but this was the first time he had ever seen a dead person.

He looked around. Had Mr M hit his head? After a bad turn, had he fallen and this had been an unfortunate accident?

Or was it . . . murder?

He stifled a gasp of terror, put his hand to his mouth and looked around helplessly. Stepfather would have to be told. He hoped he would be at the Central Office.

After covering the dead man's face respectfully, he slid down the ladder. In the shop he paused. Was there anything he should do, anything to remember from what Stepfather had told him about police procedure at the scene of a murder crime?

Still feeling as if this was all a nightmare and he would soon wake up, he rushed uphill towards the police station at the Central Office. On the other side of the road was Inspector Gosse hurrying along hoping for any news from the latest sighting at Liberton of a suspicious character who answered the description of McLaw.

'Looking for the sergeant, are you? He isn't here.'

And without waiting for a reply, the inspector headed towards the office door, Vince out of breath at his heels. Turning, Gosse demanded, 'What are you doing here? Did your ma send you? Tell her that's not allowed, during working hours. She should know better, sending you—'

'A minute, sir, if you please,' said Vince trying to think

of the right words to describe the scene he had just left. 'This isn't anything personal . . . I'm here to report an accident.'

Gosse paused, his hand on the door and pointed. 'Then go to the desk over there and give the constable the details, then. I'm a busy man, if you didn't know that already—'

'Actually, sir,' Vince interrupted, 'it might not be an accident. Might be, well,' he gulped, 'foul play.'

Gosse stared at him and repeated, 'Foul play, eh?' That had got his attention. 'And how do you know that?' he demanded suspiciously.

'Well, I . . . I found him. I think he was dead.'

'Where? Where was this?' barked Gosse.

'At the bookshop. Where I work, Mr Molesby's . . . down the street—'

'Yes, yes, I know where it is.'

'When I came this morning the door was open—'

'Why weren't you at school?'

'It's Founders' Day, sir.' Vince sounded surprised. He thought everyone knew that. As he spoke, Gosse was signalling a constable and said to Vince, 'You come with us. We'll need you.'

As Vince needed all his breath to keep up with the two men, he gasped: 'Mr Molesby wasn't in the shop, and looking round, a few things . . . had been disturbed . . . and I immediately thought there had been a break-in.'

'Why?' shouted Gosse.

'Because he always makes sure the door is firmly locked, last thing every night.'

They had almost reached the shop. 'I found him in the bedroom, upstairs.'

36

At the door, Gosse and the constable pushed him aside and he said bleakly, 'He's dead, sir. I think he's been robbed and murdered.'

'Aye, and I'd bet even money that this was McLaw's work,' was the grim response.

At that moment Faro appeared on the other side of the street. Surprised to see a scared-looking Vince with Gosse and the constable, he came over.

Gosse, ignoring him, had disappeared into the shop while Vince retold his stepfather the whole story over again, what there was of it, and that didn't take long.

Telling him to stay in the shop downstairs, Faro followed Gosse up the ladder, murmured conversation, then a grave-faced Gosse looked down and told the constable to go back and summon the mortuary carriage.

Faro came down, returned to Vince's side and put an arm around his shoulders. 'Sorry you had to see all this, lad.'

'Did someone kill him?'

'We don't know that for certain, yet. But you go on home now.'

'Yes,' said Gosse, overhearing. 'And don't go too far away.' Then to Faro, 'We'll be needing him later.'

A hard look from Faro and he grinned, saying jauntily, 'First on the scene, Faro, you know the rule. Often as not that's our main clue to the murder.'

And Faro remembered this preposterous assumption, which was Gosse's favourite much-played theory. That the one who notifies the police is in many instances also the murderer. This particularly applied in domestic murder cases, where husband or wife was the victim.

As Gosse and Faro proceeded with an examination of the bookshop, they discovered that the lock on the cupboard had been broken and the key had disappeared. When Vince, with an air of triumph, produced it with the empty cash box in the privy behind the shop where it had been overlooked in the police search, Gosse decided this was highly suspicious and pointed to evidence against the lad as prime suspect.

He rubbed his hands together at the thought that this could be an easy investigation. Although this was undoubtedly McLaw's work, to condemn and accuse the first person on the scene need not be limited to the criminal world of Edinburgh. That Faro's stepson was not to be excluded appealed to him greatly. He had a natural antipathy to anyone or anything relating to his detective sergeant and sought to put him in his place and keep him there. A desire that could be interpreted as jealousy in any other context.

Children of the poor in Edinburgh were often criminals and at almost fourteen, had Vince belonged to that unhappy breed, living in one of the verminous tenements or closes nearby, he would already have been earning or procuring a living, a few coins to hand over to his starving siblings. And Gosse had another reason for questioning him by virtue of his one-time friendship with Dr Paul Lumbleigh, son of the infamous rogue, Archie Lumbleigh, now safely out of the country and living in luxury abroad on the small fortune he had made by selling his house and land to the developers.

So Gosse decided to tackle Vince with some searching questions, see how Mrs Lizzie Faro's clever lad would stand up to a little police grilling. Questions such as how did he know about where to find the cash box? How was he so certain that the old man was dead? What did he remember of suspicious customers? What about the old man's relatives?

Faro was also questioning Vince, who shook his head. 'The only one he ever mentioned was a young fellow, a cousin of some sort, who was a sailor with the mercantile marine. He looked in to see his uncle, as he called him, when his ship came into Leith.'

Gosse had scribbled a note. It was a forlorn hope, even if the name was correct, and he secretly hoped that enquiry would fail as he had set his heart on this as McLaw's work.

'We need you to make a statement,' he said with a stern look at Vince. 'Come back with us.' And handing him the note, he said, 'See if there was a young seaman called Molesby on any of the merchant ships docked in Leith.'

With a helpless and despairing look, Vince followed Gosse. He didn't care for the inspector, thought him too pompous and opinionated, and was well aware that he didn't like his stepfather or his mother. However, he tried always to treat him with the respect due to policemen and upholders of the law.

At the station office, Vince was asked to turn out his pockets. Gosse watched the contents emptied on to the desk. Pieces of string, a pencil and a clean handkerchief, unusual for a school lad. Then the coins.

Gosse counted them carefully, then whistled. 'Ten shillings and four pence?' he exclaimed. 'That's a grown man's earnings,' he said sharply. 'An exceeding amount of money for a lad to be carrying on his person.' Pausing to give Vince a hard look, he demanded suspiciously: 'And where, may one ask, did a lad your age come by all that money?' Was he pocketing the last book sale, for instance, or was it one of many?

'Do you get pocket money from your parents?' he added.

'Yes, sir. Sixpence a week.'

Again Gosse whistled. 'That would keep a poor family down the road there from starving for a while,' was his acid response.

'I have been saving for some time, sir, since I got weekend work with Mr Molesby. He pays me sixpence for that, so I've been saving up.'

'Saving? Is that what you call it. And stealing, no doubt—'

'Not at all, sir,' Vince interrupted shortly. 'I did not need pocket money once I got a job, so I've been saving, oh, for months now, to buy my mother a birthday present.'

Gosse snorted disbelief, watching Vince pocket the coins again. 'You can go now, but remember you might be called on when the official enquiry begins,' he added sternly.

On hearing this account of Gosse's inquisition of Vince, Faro was both outraged and indignant. How dare he? He tried to console Vince, whose nerve broke down in the retelling, thereby also upsetting his mother and ruining their appetites for supper that evening.

'He has nothing on you, lad. You were telling the truth.'

Faro had had a shrewd idea that this was the work of McLaw, after a week on the run, now starving and desperate for money. Certain that this must have been the first thought that occurred to Gosse, it also made it unforgivable to have subjected Vince to this questioning.

40

'The inspector is just doing what he thinks is his job, Vince.'

But Vince was not to be consoled. He was scared. This was his first taste of crime, of being at the centre of a murder investigation, and he was left in no doubt that he was the prime suspect, especially when the inspector was waiting for him in the headmaster's study next day.

Although he shuddered at what the summons meant, his classmates were most impressed that he was helping the police with their enquiries regarding the bookshop owner's murder. They, at least, never doubted his version that had circulated like wildfire round his class.

Gosse beamed on him, an avuncular greeting to impress the headmaster that there was nothing but his pupil's well-being at heart.

The headmaster smiled. 'Of course, Laurie, you have my permission to accompany Inspector Gosse back to the police station.'

'This won't take long, sir.'

The headmaster waved a dismissive hand at Gosse. 'As it is a fair distance, Laurie may take the rest of the afternoon off.'

Vince bowed. 'Thank you, sir.'

Holding his arm firmly as if he might have escaping in mind, Gosse led him back through the main gates on to Calton Hill. He indicated one of the seats and grinned.

'Got off lightly, didn't you? You went as pale as a sheet when you saw me.' A chuckle. 'Guilty conscience, eh? Bet you thought I had come to arrest you.'

Vince sat down and managed to say lightly, with a confidence he was far from feeling, 'As I haven't done anything wrong, sir, that never occurred to me.'

It wasn't quite the reaction Gosse had hoped for. Somehow it showed the influence that his damned sergeant had on the lad.

'At least I got you the rest of the afternoon off.' And taking out notebook and pencil, he shook his head and said sternly, 'I'm not altogether satisfied with your statement. There are some details that need filling in.'

'Glad to help you, sir.' It was a lie, of course, but still very pleasant sitting in the sunshine with its splendid view over the city, even though he would have preferred more agreeable company.

'You discovered Mr Molesby's body on Monday. That is correct?'

'Yes, sir.'

Gosse gave him a sharp look. 'According to the pathologists he had been lying dead on his bedroom floor since sometime on the Sunday.

'And you found the cash box in the lavatory outside. Correct?'

'Yes, sir. It had been opened and the money taken.' And Vince said Mr Molesby told him once that the keys never left his person. At night he kept them along with his false teeth on the table at his bedside.

'The cash box was large and unwieldy, not the sort of thing that a thief on the run would wish to carry. That was why I decided he would have opened it with the key and stolen the contents, but not wishing to linger in the bookshop, the privy would be a likely place.'

'Ah-ha.' Gosse seemed to find this significant and made another note. 'You said first of all you were in the shop on Sunday with the intention of helping him to catalogue books.'

Vince shook his head desperately. 'No, sir. I was never inside the shop on Sunday. I served in the shop as usual on Saturday and when I went back on Sunday morning, he unlocked the door, looked out and said he had another engagement after church and that we had to delay the cataloguing until tomorrow—'

'Wait a minute, did you see anyone inside the shop. Hear voices, for instance?'

Vince gave him a despairing look. 'The shop wasn't open on Sundays.'

'So you didn't see anyone inside?'

'That was unlikely, sir, that he had a visitor. When Mr Molesby opened the door he was only half-dressed.'

'You went back on the next day as promised – so you said in your original statement.' Gosse frowned and consulted his notes. 'At his request, you said. Is that true? Did he expect you to stay off school on a Monday?'

'No, sir,' said Vince patiently. 'It was a school holiday. Founders' Day, you know.' Gosse grunted. The Royal High had that kind of reputation of keeping up its ancient traditions and in his opinion making its boys soft. Not what this lad would have got at the ordinary school in the Pleasance.

He said slowly, 'So, if Molesby didn't have a visitor and he was killed that Sunday afternoon, you were the last one to see him alive.'

'Except the killer, sir.' Vince said brightly.

Gosse growled. 'Don't you get smart with me, young

fella.' And jabbing a finger at him, 'That won't do you any good. All that is required of you is to prove to the police that you didn't kill him.' He added smoothly, 'And give us a lead to find out who did.' He thought for a moment. 'Which church did he go to? The minister might know who he was friendly with.'

Vince said, 'St Giles', sir.'

'St Giles',' Gosse repeated and shook his head. It was very doubtful, in what he imagined was a vast congregation of the cream of Edinburgh society, that the minister would know who Molesby was having lunch with that day. He sighed. A detective inspector now, he was expected to mark his respectability on the social ladder by being a churchgoer. He didn't go to St Giles', considering it too high class, in fact he rarely set foot in any church, which was the one thing he and Faro had in common. Faro wasn't even sure about God, sometimes, although he would never admit that to Lizzie who went regularly to the church in the Pleasance, taking a somewhat reluctant Vince along with her.

'So that Sunday morning you went straight home again, and how do you usually spend the rest of the day?'

'Stepfather and I have a walk on the hill with Mr Macfie but he wasn't with us that time.'

A sharp look from Gosse. The retired superintendent was no friend of his. And only Faro could vouch for his stepson's presence.

'So you were at home the rest of the day until you went back on Monday morning and found the door open. Is that correct?'

'Correct, sir. And Mr Molesby was upstairs lying on

his bedroom floor. Vince paused. 'Exactly as my statement says, sir.'

It was the arrival of a police carriage on the road behind, patrolling the area for a possible sighting of McLaw, that put an end to the interview. Gosse flagged it down and without another word left Vince to make his way home.

CHAPTER SIX

Faro had returned from the dockland office following Gosse's instructions for information on any merchant ships in Leith around the time of the old man's death.

'I'm looking for a young man, name of Molesby.' Even as he said the name he realised the futility of such a search. If the lad was a remote relation, possibly Molesby was not his name, even more unlikely was that he had gone into the shop to rob and kill his uncle.

The clerk shook his head. 'There were no merchant ships in dock at the weekend. One came in on Monday morning, though,' he added hopefully.

Faro shook his head, thanked him and left feeling angry. This was a prime waste of his time – such enquiries were a constable's routine tasks – and yet another of Gosse's attempts to humiliate him.

Reaching Princes Street and heading for the Central Office, a woman was hurrying in his direction, looking very distressed and wiping her eyes.

It was Mrs Brook, Macfie's housekeeper.

He put a hand on her arm, said her name. Looking startled, he realised she hardly recognised him at first.

'Can I help you, Mrs Brook?' he asked and his immediate concern was his friend. 'Superintendent Macfie, is he all right? Is all well with him?'

'Oh, Mr Faro, it is you,' she sobbed. 'Yes, yes, the superintendent is well. I had a postcard from him just yesterday. Oh dear, dear,' she paused, dabbing at her eyes again. 'I've just been to a funeral. And it was awful, awful.'

She seemed considerably shaken and as there was a cafe nearby, he said, 'Come along, let me get you a cup of tea and you can tell me all about it.'

As they waited to be served, she apologised for talking on so, 'But this was the second funeral in just a short while of two sisters. Both dying like that so close together and in such awful circumstances.'

The waitress put down the tray and Mrs Brook, recovering her composure and despite a somewhat shaky hand, poured out the tea and with it the story of two sisters, devoted to one another until some twenty years ago they fell out. Over a man. He had been courting Celia, the younger sister, but chose to marry Agatha. This was a terrible shock, a dreadful betrayal and Celia never forgave, not him, but her sister. She never spoke to her again and although Agatha's husband had a long illness and finally died, Celia still refused to forget the past and comfort her.

Mrs Brook paused and sighed. 'Poor Agatha. Peter had been well off, but after he died they lost everything and he left a lot of debts. There were no children and last year she had to go into the poorhouse, in East Lothian.'

47

The poorhouse she named was highly thought of, Faro remembered. It was also known as a retreat for widows and orphans, who were well treated, and those who were sick and dying but had no families were gladly taken in and cared for in their last days.

Mrs Brook went on: 'Agatha was happy there, it suited her fine but she was always a bit of a recluse, and she never had or wanted any visitors. Then a couple of months ago she took ill, and by a mere chance, at the women's guild in our local church, one of the nurses I knew told me about this poor dying woman who wanted only one thing on earth, and that was that her sister should forgive her.

'It was Agatha, and I remembered that Celia had lived in Liberton and probably still did, as there were often stories in the guild about this eccentric old lady. Anyway, Liberton isn't all that far away and the nurse went to see her with a message that Agatha wanted to see her once more. Her last wish was to take her sister's hand and to be laid to rest in the family vault in Gifford.'

Mrs Brook paused and, refilling their cups, she sighed, 'Celia decided the time had come to make amends and she went to the poorhouse, only to find that Agatha was not only dead, but had already been buried. Not in Gifford but in a pauper's grave. That was terrible. Seeing the grave with its tiny wooden cross upset her dreadfully and she was prepared to make a great fuss. She wanted to know all about this hasty burial and insisted that her sister's coffin be exhumed and taken to the family vault as she had wished, and that she would, from her own meagre savings, pay all the necessary money involved. The poorhouse refused, of course, but Celia was not to be defeated. Agatha was to have her dying wish, so she hired a gardener she knew well. He was also a gravedigger and had a pal who would help, if he was paid enough. It seemed that he was no stranger to this kind of work, and would arrange for a carriage to take the coffin to Gifford.'

There was a pause, a shuddering sigh, before she continued: 'It must have been horrible, I can't imagine. Scary, too, but Celia was determined. And she wanted to look on her sister's face, kiss her for the last time.' Pausing, she regarded Faro in wide-eyed horror, and whispered:

'But . . . but when they opened the coffin . . . Agatha wasn't there. It was empty.'

'Empty?' Faro asked, for this as well as the friendly gravedigger and his pal brought back memories of a time in Edinburgh that he had thought was laid to rest. The notorious body-snatchers of thirty years ago, culminating in the horror of Burke and Hare, not robbers but killers who took in the old, poor and defenceless, murdered them and sold their bodies to the doctors at Surgeons' Hall.

'There were a few stones inside, but no sign of poor Agatha,' Mrs Brook continued. 'Celia was shocked, horrified and very, very angry. It was too late to do anything, no point in taking the empty coffin to the family vault in Gifford. They replaced it, she paid off the two men and, determined to find out what had happened, she went early next morning to the poorhouse where Agatha had lived and died, to insist on an explanation. Where was her sister's body?

'They said that she had made a mistake about the pauper's grave and that they would look into it, but they also reminded her in no uncertain fashion that what she had done was illegal and she could be charged for grave robbing.

'Poor Celia was distraught. It was scandalous and she wasn't going to let it go at that; she would take it to the police in Edinburgh, who would advise her if there was a higher authority to deal with it. Celia's maid went with her, and as they needed some shopping, it was agreed that Tibbie should meet her in an hour with a hiring cab to take them back to Liberton—'

Mrs Brook stifled a sob. 'But Tibbie never saw her mistress again. She came with the hiring cab and was in time to see a carriage racing down the Mound and to learn from a group gathered there that an old lady had been knocked down and had died before they could get her to a hospital.'

Mrs Brook clasped her hands in anguish. 'Oh, Mr Faro, I am sure there is something wrong here. I just can't believe that all this was a coincidence, the empty grave and the other sister killed.'

Faro nodded. He had his own reasons for believing that Mrs Brook was right. The runaway cab struck a chill in his heart. So had his own father been killed – or murdered – by the same means some thirty years ago, and on the Mound. The treacherous steep thoroughfare was a useful means for getting rid of someone whose information was dangerous.

'There was something else too, Mr Faro. Agatha was already dead when Celia received her message.' She paused and shook her head. 'I'm in despair, really I am. Something awful has happened, I'm sure of that, and meeting you like this has been like . . . providence. Is there anything you can do to help?'

Faro leant across the table and took her hand. He was doubtful about that, but managed a reassuring: 'I'll do what I can.'

This account of the burial of an empty coffin was shocking and almost unbelievable. Seeing her safely back to Sheridan Place, as they parted he said: 'A moment, Mrs Brook, if you please. Who told you all this?'

'Oh, did I not say? It was Tibbie. She was in despair, said she'd never forget the scene on the Mound or the sight of that runaway carriage that killed her mistress.'

'Have you her address? I'll have a word with her, if you think that would help?'

'Oh, I do indeed, sir. I'd be so grateful. I expect she'll be at Liberton, at Celia's. That's her only home, where she has always lived. She hasn't anywhere else to go. She was an orphan, from the poorhouse, and Celia took pity on her. A pretty young girl, she was, but lame – a club foot. Mind you, she managed very well, in spite of it.'

With the address of the late Celia Simms, Faro went on his way very thoughtfully. If this was not just a hysterical account from a scared woman exaggerated in the telling, the only person who might have witnessed the runaway carriage incident was Celia's maid.

He sighed, wishing Macfie hadn't been away just now. He would certainly have looked into it. But in his absence – again, if the story was true – it needed urgent attention and as far as Faro was concerned, third-hand hearsay couldn't be described as official police business. He could imagine the eyebrow raising and scepticism if Mrs Brook or anyone else had reported this at the Central Office.

At the moment, however, all his concentration was required on speedily finding the old bookshop owner's killer and freeing Vince from his role as Gosse's prime suspect.

Resuming his walk, he thought about the East Lothian

poorhouse at Belmuir, which had a high reputation. Could it be that they were selling bodies of dead patients to the doctors who were urgently in need of corpses for their medical students, especially since the Anatomy Act of 1832 after the notorious Burke and Hare killings? Recent years had seen a steady increase in the number of poorhouses. A good thing, but it also could have its sinister side.

Doctors would claim that corpses were needed in the interests of the progress of medical science, and since the Industrial Revolution populations had exploded. There were rumours that in the overcrowded midlands of England, with the introduction and spread of the railways, bodies were speedily transported in fresh condition to medical schools far and wide in special carriages, designated as market produce.

Faro considered the possibilities, the options. He could tell Gosse, who would not be in the least interested, completely absorbed by tracking down McLaw; the sale of dead bodies, however illegal, would not have a killer to track down. What use are they to anyone else, anyway, when they are dead, he would ask? At least they are performing some useful purpose.

No, Faro sighed. This was one case he would have to investigate on his own. But where to start? A more subtle approach was needed than his arrival at the poorhouse, asking questions. First of all he would speak to Tibbie.

CHAPTER SEVEN

He intended to go to Liberton immediately but domesticity intervened. Lizzie was in the kitchen, looking near to tears and wringing her hands.

'You've got to stop him, Jeremy. He's been at Vince again.'

For a moment, still immersed in police business, Faro had no idea what she was talking about.

'Who?' Had the dog bitten him, was that the trouble?

'Oh dear, you know perfectly well. It's that Inspector Gosse again – asking him more questions.'

'Where is he now?'

'Out with Coll, I expect. But he's very upset. Seems Gosse was waiting for him – at the school.' She added indignantly, 'This is really awful.' Pausing, she gave him a hard look. 'You have to do something about it, Jeremy. It just isn't fair, questioning a boy like that, making him feel guilty even when we all know he is innocent.'

As well as being very upsetting and scaring for Lizzie,

Gosse's interrogation of Vince was interfering with his schoolwork and that was not to be tolerated. As for Faro himself, although he guessed the real reason was to humiliate him and his family, it was a source of irritation. Aware that his domestic life would continue to be awash with a tide of tearful pleading from Lizzie if he remained silent, there was only one solution. In the now urgent interests of peace at his own fireside, he must tactfully enquire from Gosse why he was wasting so much time continually questioning Vince regarding the details of the bookshop owner's death when they should be pursuing the missing McLaw who was, in everyone's mind, obviously the killer.

Having made his point, which Gosse chose to ignore, the inspector shook his head and pushed aside the accumulation of papers on his desk. Their contents remained a mystery to Faro as they never diminished in size and their importance had never been revealed to him.

'Why am I so interested in the bookshop murder?' Gosse asked.

'It hasn't been resolved as that, sir. We have no proof as yet. All we know was that he was found dead.'

Gosse wagged a finger at him. 'Clear as the nose on your face. Bit of blood and plenty of bruises. Doesn't it immediately suggest a frail old man, useless against a strong young burglar. A struggle—'

'We don't know that for sure, sir,' Faro interrupted. 'Even coming face to face with an intruder might have been too much of a shock and caused him to have heart failure.'

Gosse snorted disbelief. 'When you've solved as many murders as I have, Faro, you'll know what to look out for. Always the motive, and this was clear as daylight robbery.'

Pausing a moment, he looked thoughtful, shook his head. 'I'm certain your lad Vince knows a great deal more than he's telling us. And I intend to find out.'

Faro said nothing. It wasn't often he shared a feeling with Gosse, who was not known for his sensitivity or intuition, but this struck a chord. He knew Vince well enough now, or thought he did, to feel there was a missing piece in the puzzle. Something Vince, not normally secretive, had overlooked or knew but wasn't going to mention. Maybe he thought it was too trivial a piece of information but, as often happened, when revealed it would turn out to be a vital ingredient.

'And now, about McLaw. Those sightings that have been reported. I've got constables following them up; God knows if they will lead us anywhere, but it's all part of the job and the sooner we track him down . . .'

And then came what Gosse considered an unexpected breakthrough. A man of McLaw's description had been seen in the High Street that Sunday, spotted by a constable on the beat, lurking in one of the closes. PC Bain had given chase, somewhat half-heartedly he had to admit, for McLaw was known to be dangerous and to be approached with caution by an unarmed constable, and Bain – apart from his truncheon – was of little use in the circumstances.

As it was raining heavily Faro had to agree with Gosse that the likelihood was that McLaw had taken shelter in the shop doorway and had forced the door open. The rest of the story was a guess: that he had gone in search of money but found only a locked cupboard, which he had forced open. Inside, the cashbox was hopeful; it felt heavy but of course was locked, so he had gone upstairs and threatened the old man. When Molesby refused to hand over the keys, he had killed him in the struggle.

Faro listened as Gosse went through it all once again, the tracks that died out or led nowhere. It was a daily routine and Faro's own thoughts were on how he was to find some means of tackling Vince on the subject. He knew that after Gosse's interrogations, it would not be easy.

If only they knew whom Molesby had been having lunch with that Sunday. This unknown person might be his killer, or indicate some lead in that direction. Did anyone know much about the old man or any secrets lurking in his past, beyond the relative who was a sailor in the mercantile marine? A can of worms, perhaps, and the only key was at St Giles' where, as a regular churchgoer, he had gone that Sunday morning as he told Vince that was his intention.

On his way home Faro strode into the cathedral. Diminished by its magnitude and awed by its magnificence, his echoing footsteps sounded like a blasphemy in the enduring peace and silence.

A tall man, dark-gowned, approached. Faro said he was making an enquiry about the late Mr Molesby.

The cleric, whose name was Burrows, shook his head: 'Ah, yes, yes, poor man. Most unfortunate.' He shook his head. 'He has been a member of the congregation for many years, as many as I have been here myself. But we never really got to know him any better than the first days.'

That wasn't very helpful. 'Did he have any special friends?'

A shy smile in answer. 'Not that I was aware of. He wasn't sociable, didn't join anything and kept himself very much to himself.'

Faro frowned. 'We understood that he was having lunch with someone, perhaps another member of the congregation. Did you happen to notice him last Sunday – the day he died?'

A helpless gesture. 'He might well have been here. As you will appreciate, there are very large numbers in the congregation at each service.'

Faro persisted. 'Will you be arranging his funeral service?'

Burrows frowned. 'I think not. Although he attended services on a regular basis, he was not a communicant – an official member of St Giles' – and therefore would not be automatically entitled to such rites.'

The sound of voices approached. 'Ah, the choir are here for their practice.' As Burrows, with a brief apology, hurried down the aisle, Faro felt that he had not been displeased by the interruption.

Later, walking on Arthur's Seat with Vince, Coll racing ahead excitedly as if he'd never seen or smelt the hill before, Faro mentioned Gosse's comments.

Vince didn't seem to hear him, he looked preoccupied. Faro had to repeat it and Vince said shortly:

'Told him all I know. Why does he keep on about it, treating me like I'm the only suspect?'

As it must have been obvious to Gosse that McLaw, on the run, had entered the bookshop and killed Molesby, Faro didn't know the answer to Vince's question, except that it gave Gosse a chance to torment his detective sergeant's stepson.

He had an idea. 'Let's go to the shop tomorrow afternoon. You can skip games.'

Vince was delighted at any excuse to escape the school's holy ritual of games, as he was too small ever to make his name on the rugby field.

'We can go over Monday morning inch by inch, from the moment you entered the shop.'

When Vince groaned, Faro said sharply: 'That's what the police have to do, Vince, over and over. And you've always said you would like to be a detective.'

That was now old news. Vince had changed his mind. Wasn't Stepfather aware that since his past friendship with the grown-up, Dr Paul Lumbleigh, and lured on by all those wonderful illustrated volumes on Mr M's bookshelves, he had now turned his ambitions towards becoming a doctor?

Faro continued enthusiastically: 'I want to do this together, just in case there was something you saw and it didn't register at the time. Something perhaps quite obvious on a second visit that you missed the first time. That often happens.'

Vince was waiting for him outside the bookshop after school that afternoon. The shop seemed very lonely now, the blinds down and a padlock on the door provided by the police to keep the property safe from intruders. Faro produced the key and on the doorstep he turned: 'Remember how you came in, go over it, step by step.'

Vince obliged. He walked in slowly, opened the window blind, looked over his shoulder and said: 'It was then I saw the disorder. I guessed there had been a break-in when I went to the cupboard where the cash box was kept. It should have been locked too but it was open, like now. I saw that the cash box was missing.' Turning, he surveyed the room. 'There were books off shelves, on the floor, the desk drawers opened, their contents scattered.'

Faro nodded. 'The main purpose of most break-ins. He was looking for money.'

And he thought how desperately McLaw must have been needing money, to buy food to keep alive – and to travel from Edinburgh, perhaps south by train, to lose himself in London.

He remembered that it had been raining all that Sunday, and had the old man been found before Monday morning, footprints would have been a useful clue.

Vince said: 'This burglar didn't know much about Mr M or antiquarian bookshops, if he thought there would be great takings to steal.' He shook his head. 'There was hardly enough each week to keep the shop open, but Mr M was like that. He loved his books and having students come in to browse.'

Faro was moving silently around the shop, frowning, inspecting everything. He signalled to Vince as he approached the wooden ladder leading to the premises above where Molesby had lived.

Vince shuddered. He clearly did not relish revisiting what the police would call the crime scene again.

Faro took his arm. 'Up you go, lad. Let's get it over with.' When Vince arrived that Monday morning, enough daylight had filtered through to reveal the old man's body lying on the floor. Looking round the tiny bedroom, Vince pointed to the shutters.

'They were closed. I opened them.' The police had left them open and now the tiny room was suffused by as much daylight as the small window offered.

Vince shivered suddenly as he looked around. The bed had been stripped and the scene seemed impersonal, very different from his horrific discovery of poor Mr M.

Faro was aware of his reluctance. The police had been thorough in their search for clues but had overlooked two picture postcards stuck in the mirror frame. They were from Germany and Russia, addressed 'Dear Uncle' and with identical messages: 'a good voyage and glad to be ashore again', signed, 'Yours affectionately Tommy'. Obviously from the sailor he had been searching the docks for, but with no other means of identification, such as a surname, they would be of little help in finding him.

Faro opened the wardrobe; Molesby had few possessions, a few shabby clothes, white shirts, some cravats; no Sunday best, worn boots. No clues there either.

He put his hand on Vince's shoulder. 'Now, every detail, lad. See it in your mind just as it was then.'

Vince didn't need to think. That grisly picture would stay with him always. 'He was lying on the floor beside the bed in a pile of bedding. Very still, a smear of blood on his head, but I knew when I knelt down beside him that he was dead – and cold.'

'Had the bed been slept in?'

The pile of sheets indicated bedding, but the thought came to Faro that Molesby could have become entangled when he fell out of the bed in the struggle with the intruder. But had he even been to bed?

'Was he in his nightshirt?' he asked. 'Did you notice when he opened the door?'

Vince shook his head. 'He only opened it a fraction but I did see that he was in his underlinen, the kind old men who have money wear.'

Faro smiled at that. Underclothes were a luxury for the

poor, a shift for modest women, men hardly bothered at all. Now a picture was forming in his own mind.

'Let's assume that Mr Molesby had been preparing to go to bed and had disturbed the burglar, shouted angrily and that was his downfall,' Faro said slowly. 'Time of death was established as late Sunday evening or the early hours of Monday morning, so that was most likely possible. The burglar returned, came up the ladder, asked for the money and was indignantly refused.' He shrugged. 'We can guess the rest.'

'Do you think he was killed over a struggle for the key he kept on his bedside table with his false teeth?'

'His teeth!' said Faro.

Vince looked grim. 'Well, he still had them in, Stepfather. I noticed that 'cos his mouth was . . . was open.'

'So he hadn't been to bed.' Faro thought for a moment. 'No fatal injury, only bruises consistent with a fall, when he cut his head.'

'Do you think that Inspector Gosse might have got it all wrong, Stepfather?' said Vince anxiously. He sounded hopeful for the first time.

Faro nodded. 'I do indeed. The inspector likes to have his so-called murder cases all cut and dried. He is often too ready to assume the worst. But I think Mr Molesby might have died of a heart attack—'

'Yes,' Vince interrupted eagerly. 'As a result of that struggle, that is possible, isn't it, for an old man? And he was a bit frail at the best of times.'

Before they went back down into the shop, Faro had a final look around the bedroom, opening the wardrobe again. Was the time of death wrong and had Molesby actually died before he had a chance to dress for St Giles' and lunch that Sunday? As they left the shop, Vince did not share Faro's sense of new purpose in persuading Gosse with his theory regarding the events leading to Molesby's death.

'Can you make him understand that it wasn't me?' he said bleakly.

'I'll do my best, Vince, to get him off your back.' Then he laughed. 'Your observations have been most helpful.'

Vince almost jumped. A look of sheer panic.

'What's wrong? Is there something troubling you?' he added, anxiously watching Vince's expression.

'Of course not, Stepfather.' He recovered quickly. 'Why should there be? I've told you all I know.' And he closed his mouth firmly on that. No more to be said.

When they reached the cottage, Lizzie said: 'Mrs Brook came and brought us some of her delicious soup. Such a nice lady, said she'd made far too much, forgets she's only cooking for one. I think she misses Mr Macfie.'

She paused. 'She seemed ill at ease, though, a bit nervous and disappointed that you weren't here.' Looking at him, she frowned. 'I got the feeling that it was you she really wanted to see, the soup was just an excuse.'

Faro shook his head, but he had guessed the real reason for her visit. He must go to Liberton and talk to Tibbie right away as he had promised.

While Lizzie and his stepfather were discussing Mrs Brook's progress and future achievements as Macfie's housekeeper, Vince went out with Coll. He looked miserable and scared.

Turning, Faro watched him go and Lizzie sighed. 'What's

up with him these days, Jeremy? He's not himself. I can't make him out. He's got me worried.'

He tried to reassure her. 'This is a difficult age for Vince.' He still remembered what it was to be almost fourteen, neither boy nor man, in Orkney, with all those violent surges of emotion. 'Maybe that's what it is all about, Lizzie.' He didn't add his own feelings of resentment that the lad had probably plenty of problems facing him without being suddenly thrust by Gosse into the world not only of grown-ups, but of possible murder.

'I've tried talking to him,' Lizzie said. 'He used to tell me everything. Every little detail of his day. But no more. It's as if he wants to keep his thoughts to himself.'

She and Faro were closer than they imagined. For Vince was worried and preoccupied and it wasn't anything to do with Inspector Gosse's interrogation about the shop break-in.

Vince had a secret.

CHAPTER EIGHT

What Faro didn't know, or anyone else at this time, was that Vince wasn't sharing his secret with anyone, least of all his parents.

All his life he had suffered from being overprotected. Of course, as he got older and guessed more about adult emotions, he gave his mother the excuse of being a sad war widow, one of many whose lives were ruined and left with young children. She had no one else but him and that was why he was so cosseted.

His infancy and childhood were a bit of a blur, punctuated only by strange scenes, sharp and vivid like pictures on a wall but isolated, tiny islands in his existence, with no idea of what had happened before or immediately after they appeared. He remembered little of his early life, except that it wasn't easy, and as he left childhood behind, he often wondered if his mother's behaviour, her sadness and reluctance to discuss the past, was not only because it wounded her to talk about his brave father being killed in India now so long ago. Was there something else, something missing? As he relived over and over the picture of that last battle his imagination had created, hearing the fatal gunshot but yearning to be told more, he had come to recognise this as a topic to be avoided for the distress, the anguished, haunted look it brought to his mother's face.

Until now he had told her everything, answered all her questions about those everyday things of his life, trivial things that seemed to be of such infinite interest to her, where had he been, who had he seen on the hill on the way there and back from school and who did he sit next to. In fact all the details of the classroom, however boring they seemed to him.

But now all that had changed dramatically since he met the gypsy Charlie and had given him his word that he would keep silent about that encounter.

Having his daily walk on the hill, with Coll as usual racing ahead, tail wagging furiously as he sniffed the ground for rabbits, out of sight Vince had heard a yelp of pain from the dog and prayed that he hadn't been caught in a trap. He ran in the direction of the sound and there was Coll standing near a boulder, quivering, looking scared.

He wasn't hurt; his nose had led him not to a rabbit, but to a man lying concealed by a boulder. And this man had thought he was being attacked and had hit him.

The man looked up wearily as Vince approached and sighed, 'You're just a lad, thank goodness. Sorry I slapped your dog, didn't mean to hurt him. I was afraid when he rushed over that he was going to bite me.' As he spoke he was rubbing his ankle. And Vince noticed a large bruise on his forehead.

'What happened? Did you trip up?'

'No, dammit, my horse did – and threw me.'

Vince didn't know what to say, but under his stepfather's guidance he was fast learning the technique of powers of observation and deduction. The man, he guessed, was young, despite his beard, wild hair and ill-fitting clothes: a fine black jacket, too tight to button up properly and revealing a glimpse of a dirty-looking shirt, too short in the sleeves and trousers that only reached his ankles, as if he had outgrown them. These were hand-me-downs like those for a youngster whose parents were too poor to buy him new ones. Yet the clothes were of good quality, Vince could recognise that, the kind well-off men, proud citizens of Edinburgh like Superintendent Macfie wore.

Listening to the man describing how he had been thrown off his horse, Vince realised Stepfather would have been proud of him. Judging by the man's appearance, he decided he had most probably come from the gypsies' camp on the far side of Arthur's Seat. They had moved in recently, preparing for the winter months, scavenging for food and hoping to survive by moving closer to civilisation, with its rich pickings from clothes drying on lines to opportunities provided by open windows.

More tinkers than real gypsies, their presence was generally unpopular with everyone, but the police, after the usual warning about trespassing, preferred to ignore them as long as no incidents were reported of thieving or assault. At least on that side of the hill they were well out of sight of the more heavily populated areas of the city. It would have been different, an outcry, if they had ventured into the Queen's Park and the precincts of the royal residence at Holyroodhouse. That certainly would not have been tolerated. They would have had to move on, by force if necessary.

If the wind was in the right direction, sometimes voices and smoke from the campfires drifted over as far as the Faros' cottage. In the evening there was often singing too, a strange foreign, yet exciting sound, Vince remembered, as he asked politely what he could do to help.

The man laughed, looking him over, and Vince guessed at his thoughts. Just a boy, what could he do?

'I doubt whether you could get my horse back. I reckon he'll be miles away by now.' He paused: 'How old are you?'

Vince drew himself up. 'Fourteen,' he lied boldly.

The man smiled. Those curls, not very tall, the boy looked more like twelve than fourteen.

'Where were you going?' Vince asked. A shrug was the answer. 'You're a gypsy,' he added, trying not to make it sound like an accusation. 'Did you steal the horse?'

The man's eyebrows raised, he grinned. 'Of course not. Just borrowed it for a while.' A quizzical look. 'How did you guess I was a gypsy?'

Vince said: 'You don't sound like our local people. I mean, your voice is quite different.'

'Is that so, now?' The man bit his lip, watching him closely for a moment's careful consideration. Then with a shrug, he said, 'As a matter of fact, I was heading for the Borders, to the Faws camp at Kirk Yetholm. I don't suppose you've heard of it. They would protect me, I am one of them, you know. That is my right, my inheritance.'

And Vince was delighted. He had guessed right as the gypsy, still rubbing his ankle, which was obviously very painful, sighed deeply. 'I cannot go anywhere with this, can I now? I need a stick to walk, and a place to rest up, keep out of sight for a couple of days.' He paused. 'Get some food and my strength back,' he added pointedly. 'Do you live nearby?'

Vince nodded, but said nothing. Telling his mother was out of the question. She had a weakness for waifs and strays of the animal kind, never turned one away, but would make a terrible fuss about him talking to strangers. And this one didn't speak Scots like ordinary Edinburgh folk. That would be because the gypsies had their own foreign tongue.

He did some rapid thinking. Stepfather was a calming influence on Ma, he might understand, but he was a policeman, the natural enemy of the gypsies and it sounded, between the lines as it were, that this man was running away from something or someone he had offended.

Perhaps he was a sneak-thief, and that was how he had come by those strange, ill-fitting clothes that looked well tailored and expensive, not the kind a gypsy would wear.

'That jacket doesn't fit you very well,' he said politely. 'How did you get it, and those trousers too?'

The man laughed sharply. 'You are observant, aren't you?' He shrugged and Vince persisted.

'They look like a gentleman's clothes. Have you stolen them?' he asked sternly.

The man's eyebrows rose again. 'You're very direct, young fella. Of course I didn't. What makes you think that?'

'They don't fit you. But they're very smart—' He stopped himself in time, having almost added 'for a gypsy'.

Again the man laughed. 'You flatter me. They belonged to an old chap who came for shelter to us at the camp and died. Had a terrible cough. They'd have sold them so I just borrowed them, when no one was looking,' he added apologetically, straightening his shoulders. 'For my journey, you see, I have to look presentable.'

Vince regarded him thoughtfully. 'Have you done something wrong?' he asked, hoping not to sound accusing. He was rewarded with a cold stare.

'And what kind of wrong had you in mind?' he asked, carefully choosing the words.

Vince shrugged. 'Oh, I don't know.'

A sigh. 'Very well, I will tell you, seeing that you've taken such an interest and want to help me. The truth, lad,' he added slowly, as if measuring every word, 'but you must promise not to tell anyone. Just between you and me. Promise, now!' he added sternly.

Vince nodded.

'That's not enough. Say it. I promise—'

'I . . . p-promise.' Vince had an uneasy feeling that what he was doing wasn't right as the gypsy went on:

'They, back there –' he jabbed a finger in the direction of the camp '– they wanted me to marry this . . . this old ugly woman. I didn't want to. I refused. But she's the chief's daughter and things got a bit rough. She wanted me, so I had to make a run for it.'

Vince vaguely understood the problem. This was one of the challenges of the adult world. Unhappy marriages, whispers overheard in their conversations, often a lot of significant nods and an unwanted baby involved. He felt suddenly flattered to have been trusted with this information.

A short silence followed, then the man said: 'All I need is a place where I can rest for a couple of days, perhaps a bit of bread, and some meat. Is there somewhere round here?'

Around them the distant sound of hammering, the skeleton shapes of houses still to be built. The almost demolished Lumbleigh House gave Vince an idea.

He pointed to it, and explained briefly: 'You see all the building going on. That house was once owned by a rich man, part of a big estate, and there are still stables over there. You could hide there.'

The gypsy nodded eagerly. 'Good. But I do need something to eat.'

'I'll bring you something.'

'Do you live nearby?' Vince was asked again. 'Will that not be difficult?'

Vince thought of his mother and his heart failed him. 'See down there.' He pointed vaguely towards the cottage, smoke issuing from its chimney.

'I live with my parents. But my mother is often out or too busy to notice things.'

The man looked pleased. 'Your father?'

'Oh, he's out working all day.' Vince decided he'd be tactful and not mention that his stepfather was a policeman.

The sun had almost set. It would be dark soon. The old stables were a good idea. A convenient place to hide and not too far from the cottage. 'If you wait a while till it's dark, you should be able to get across there without being seen. After we've had supper, I'll bring you some food. You can have Coll's stick to lean on. Here,' he added, handing it over. 'I always keep a stick when we're out here. You never know when you might need it on the hill. There are a lot of secret caves, you know, and a lot of wild creatures still.' He always hoped as well as feared that he might meet a wolf, although he was assured the last of them had gone some years ago.

The gypsy smiled. 'And you won't tell your parents? You promised, remember.'

'I remember.'

'Good.' He held out his hand and Vince helped him to his feet. With a groan he leant on the stick. 'Thank you for that, lad. My name's Charlie, by the way.'

'I'm Vince.' Shaking Charlie's hand, it wasn't rough like a workman's. He leant down and ruffled Vince's hair. 'Good lad, Vince.' He added thoughtfully, 'You remind me of someone I used to know long ago. All those golden curls wasted on a lad.'

Vince winced. Those golden curls were the bane of his life, the subject of some teasing among his schoolmates, until they learnt that he had strong fists and was good at using them. That, as well as the fact that he was small for his age. No matter how his mother tried to console him, he knew he would never be tall, as his soldier father had been, or over six foot like Stepfather, who he thought was the best-looking man he had ever seen, even more handsome than his late father had been, by all accounts from his mother. He regretted he had never seen a photograph of him; maybe they were not so fashionable when he went to war, but it would have been such a treasure to keep all his life. To say to people: 'This is my soldier father.'

At supper that evening, Lizzie was pleasantly surprised at Vince asking for second helpings. She always worried that he didn't eat enough and tonight he even jumped up to clear the table and said he'd wash the dishes. Ma could put her feet up for a change and he would take Coll for a last evening walk, usually Stepfather's task.

Hearing him in the kitchen, calling to Coll, Lizzie shouted. 'Be careful in the dark, Vince.'

'I won't be long, Ma.' As the door closed, Lizzie turned to Faro and said: 'Well, what do you think of that?'

'A pleasant change,' was the reply.

'And so thoughtful, Jeremy. Did you see what he ate, too?'

Faro smiled. 'It was a very nice roast chicken, dear.'

Lizzie smiled. 'Yes, but he ate as much as you tonight.' Sighing, she shook her head. 'Anyway, it's a great relief. Looks as if all our fears were nothing and all will be well with him from now on.'

Faro touched her hand. 'I told you it was probably just his age.'

She smiled. 'And you were right, as always, dear.'

Before they retired, Lizzie remembered the three blankets she had put on to the line outside for airing. There were only two. She looked around. Had the missing one fallen from its pegs? No, it had definitely disappeared.

'Someone's stolen one of our blankets,' she told Faro who was preparing for bed. 'It'll be those gypsies again,' she added indignantly. 'It's time your lot did something about them, thieving like that. Some of the women were around the other day telling fortunes and selling clothes pegs.'

And working out the lie of the land, thought Faro, while assuring her there wasn't much the police could do unless they were caught red-handed.

If, however, that night they had had access to a crystal ball from one of those fortune-tellers, they would have seen a very dark picture ahead.

Their troubles, and in particular, Lizzie's had just begun.

CHAPTER NINE

When Faro reached the Central Office next morning, it was to find Gosse and everyone around him in a high state of excitement. There had been an assault and robbery in Fleshmarket Close in the early hours. The victim, an elderly man named Price, had been brought to the infirmary. Fortunately his injuries were not fatal and, furious, he was only too eager to tell the police all about the attack and Gosse was only too delighted to hear that the assailant answered to the missing McLaw's description.

Price's yells for help had alerted the beat policeman, PC Bain, who had given chase, again somewhat half-heartedly, he had to admit, as a quick glimpse of the running man fitted the description of the killer McLaw, and like the first time, Bain was unarmed apart from his whistle and his truncheon – not much use in apprehending a dangerous criminal.

Nevertheless he had set off in pursuit, but being portly and middle-aged was just in time to see the suspect leaping aboard the Glasgow train as it gathered steam and moved out.

'We've telegraphed Glasgow station and they will hold him there. We'll get him this time and I am going personally to see he doesn't escape us again,' said Gosse triumphantly.

Faro nodded with the uneasy certainty that once more Gosse was counting his pre-hatched chickens. The wily McLaw had disappeared before and the chances were that he would do so again. They would be too late. If they missed him in Glasgow he would be heading for the Highlands, and once protected by the familiar tracks he knew so well in those wild mountains and glens, they would have even less chance of tracking him down.

'You go to the infirmary, Faro, get a statement from Mr Price – he was badly shaken had some cuts and bruises – see if he has recovered enough to sign a statement.' Gosse sighed happily. 'All cut and dried, Faro, we have definitely got him this time.'

One of the constables came in with the information that the police waiting at Glasgow station were holding the passenger answering McLaw's description.

'They're quite sure it is him?' asked Gosse.

'Yes, sir. They searched him, and what is more he still has the wallet and stolen money on him.'

Bain was lingering, awaiting instructions. He started on a long-winded apology for his fruitless chase but Gosse cut him short:

'Let's not waste any more time. You come with us. We'll need you to identify him.' And to Faro: 'You go and get that statement. Be here with it when we get back.'

At the infirmary, Faro was met by consternation. Mr Price was no longer there. He had insisted that he was well enough to go home and would not take no for an answer.

Said he was an old soldier and that these cuts and bruises were nothing to what he had suffered serving Her Majesty in his young day, etc. etc.

The nurse shook her head. 'We couldn't do anything, sir. We could hardly tie him up to make him wait for the police to come and interview him.'

Faro sighed, got his address and realised he must go to Kirk Liberton. A fortuitous coincidence; since he was in the area he would also take the chance of saving a second journey, killing the proverbial two birds with one stone and fulfilling his promise to Mrs Brook by calling at Celia Simms' address. From all accounts, the maid Tibbie would still be there and talking to her might throw some light on the other mystery that bothered him, Agatha's empty coffin.

As he climbed the hill to Liberton, Faro stopped occasionally to admire the fine vista of Edinburgh, from Arthur's Seat to the castle. His destination was one of the attractive old villages which had been incorporated into the city. An ancient settlement up a steep hill accessible from the old drover's road to Dalkeith, it was dominated by a handsome church with origins dating back to a ninth-century Celtic church and a later chapel granted by David I in the Great Charter of Holyrood signed in 1143.

Price's house was typical of the old-style Scottish mansion, with less frivolity and pseudo battlements than were now fashionable in the city. A uniformed maid opened the door, followed by a sharp-faced, elderly woman who he gathered was Mrs Price.

Introduction made and object stated – a business matter – thankful that he was not in uniform, Faro was ushered into a small room, a book-lined study where

Price sat in a chair by the window, his head bandaged. He turned round; a red face and heavy white moustache gave him the air of a military man.

'Someone to see you,' was his wife's comment as she lingered anxiously, regarded by her husband whose brusque gesture clearly indicated that her presence was not required.

Price indicated the chair opposite and Faro sat down, took out his notebook. He had a feeling this was not going to be an easy interview as Price blustered in answer to his first question: Why had he left the infirmary without further examination?

'A lot of nonsense, of course it was a shock. I was taken quite unawares. I was taking the quick route down to the station by Fleshmarket Close. It was still dark and I had been visiting – friends on Castle Hill. A convivial evening, wining and dining, no hiring cabs in sight. Realised I might get one at the station to bring me home. It was then this young man sprang out at me, knocked me down and took my wallet and my money. I yelled for help, although that seemed unlikely, and I gave chase. But I'm not very fleet these days, I tripped – and that is how I got all this.' He stopped and pointed to his bandaged head.

As Faro handed him the statement with murmured sympathy, he was wondering why Price had seemed so ill at ease with his wife's presence, which seemed to be caused not through pain but whatever else was troubling him. Their conversation had been carried on not much above a whisper, with Price darting sharp looks towards the door, as if he feared his wife might return and intervene.

'Of course I'll sign it,' he said, going over to his desk and, seizing a pen, he scribbled a signature. Waiting for the ink to dry, he handed it back. 'There you are,' he sounded relieved. 'And I'll thank you to recover my ten pounds, a large sum to lose, you will agree.'

Pocketing Price's statement and after a final question regarding his attacker, there seemed little more helpful information forthcoming. In retrospect, the long haul Gosse had sent him on all the way to Liberton was yet another job that could have been completed by a constable, except that it went along with the inspector's delight in bequeathing his sergeant tasks that were beneath him, a satisfying method of keeping him in his place. Especially now, when Gosse was basking in the glory of achievement, returning from Glasgow and locking McLaw in the condemned cell to await the hangman's rope.

About to leave Mr Price, Faro remarked, 'I see you had only a vague description of your attacker.'

'That was all I got. The light was poor, but as I've stated already, he was tall, youngish and bearded, wearing a long overcoat and keeping the lower part of his face hidden by a muffler.'

It all fitted McLaw perfectly. Heading for the railway station, it suggested that he had been lying in wait, hoping that someone would come down the steep stairs so that he could get money for his fare. Why was Price so evasive about his own movements at that hour of the morning?

Faro said tactfully, 'It was rather late to be walking down the steep steps of Fleshmarket Close in the early hours. As you know, it has a bad reputation at the best of times. Didn't you consider that it might be dangerous, going down there in the dark alone?'

Price received this question with a resentful look, but

obviously felt that more had to be said to justify his actions.

'As I told you, I was taking the short cut to the station, hoping to pick up a hiring cab. I am a retired lawyer,' he said. 'Visiting friends at the club and we had rather a lot to drink.'

Faro smiled. 'Happens to us all at some time. Could the club not have got you a hiring cab?'

'Not at four in the morning.' Price cleared his throat before adding: 'I trust you will be treating this as confidential. I do not wish it to go any further, or that any of my . . . er, friends might be involved. That would be quite deplorable and my wife would be very upset at such publicity, should it find its way into the newspapers.'

'I am sure that will not be necessary, since there was no one except yourself involved.'

Price gave an audible sigh of relief. So that's what had been troubling him, and suddenly Faro had a very clear picture of the reason for his reticence. This respectably married, retired gentleman had not been drinking with his old chums but had in fact been to one of the high-class brothels, sometimes disguised as gentlemen's clubs, which were rife in the Lawnmarket district. That also accounted for the lateness of the hour and the fact that he had decided against getting one of the hiring cabs in that area.

Thanking Price, who seemed anxious to close the door on him as speedily as possible, especially as Mrs Price, no doubt overcome by curiosity, might make an appearance in the hall, Faro said:

'I am to call at a house called The Elms. Can you direct me?'

'The Simms' place? Just across the road and round the corner.' Price paused to sigh, perhaps awaiting further information for Faro's visit. 'We were all very sad to hear of Miss Celia's tragic death.'

'Did you know the lady?'

Price chuckled, in an almost light-hearted way, for the first time. 'Strange you should ask that. I courted her for years, that was before I met my wife,' he added hastily, 'but she wouldn't have me. According to rumour, the only man she ever wanted went off with her sister and she never forgave either of them. Apparently that was enough to finish her with men, decided we were all alike so she shut herself up in that house, her family home.' He shook his head. 'Some of us tried to get her back into the social round, but no, she just got odder and odder as the years went by. Just herself and that lame lass, an orphan she more or less adopted from the poorhouse, the two of them rattling about in that great house with its wilderness of a garden. The neighbours complained about weeds and overgrowing trees spreading. We're very proud of our gardens. She couldn't manage it alone, so there's a man in from time to time managing to keep the weeds at bay and the garden looking tidy.'

Pausing, he regarded Faro curiously. 'Tibbie Shiels, the maid – she hasn't done something wrong, has she?'

'Not as far as I know, sir. I'm merely enquiring for the housekeeper of a friend of mine. She thought Tibbie might be needing a new home and she needs a new maid.'

As the words fell out so slickly, Faro decided he was getting quite good at the glib lies, which, when required, now came to him quite spontaneously.

Price said: 'Excellent idea. The lass hasn't anyone now, and Miss Celia dying unexpectedly like that – I doubt whether she had made a will. Wouldn't have a thing to do with lawyers, although my old firm had handled all the Simms' family affairs for generations.'

Faro decided it might be useful to have the lawyers' name, which was willingly provided with assurances regarding their competence and reliability.

Thanking him, he went down the street, turned the corner as directed and was outside the Simms' residence. A squat, ivy-covered, ugly house, antique only in the number of years since it was built. Rusting gates and an overgrown garden added a look of sorrowful neglect, which fitted the pattern of the woman who had lived there, an old, unhappy recluse.

Approaching the front door, he thought what a wasted life. Here she had lived for the past twenty years, her days eaten away with bitterness and resentment, keeping up the fuel of hatred against her sister. Fate had gone against Agatha; left her widowed, childless and destitute, and finally forced into spending her remaining years in the poorhouse. By forgiving her, Celia could have buried the past and the two of them could have lived in this huge house together, consoling each other that it was the man who courted one sister and married the other who was the real villain of their wasted years. And perhaps, Faro thought sadly, the tragedy of Celia's own shocking death would never have happened.

A sad story indeed.

CHAPTER TEN

As he waited on the doorstep, the bell echoed old and rusty through the house. There was no answer so he rang again and waited. Again, nothing as the sound faded into the emptiness beyond.

There was no one at home. Sighing, he realised he would have to make the journey again, so he scribbled a note that he was a friend of Mrs Brook who was anxious for news of her. Would she please call at Sheridan Place at the earliest.

It was all he could do and as he was walking back to the gate, a young man pushing a wheelbarrow appeared round the side of the house. Muddy boots and grimy hands declared him as the gardener.

'So it was you making that awful racket, ringing the bell. There's no one at home,' he added huffily, stating the obvious.

'I wished to see Tibbie. When will she be returning?'

The man shook his head. 'Dunno. You're too late.'

'She is still living here?'

The man shrugged. 'Dunno. She was. But just yesterday she went off with a man in a carriage.'

'Did you know him?'

The man stared at him as if this was a ridiculous question. 'Of course not. Never seen him before. Not from these parts. A stranger, but it was a mighty smart carriage,' he added encouragingly. 'And he was a gentleman.'

'Did she know him?' Faro persisted.

'How would I know that? I hardly know her. Just did this job as a favour to the old lady.' Frowning, he added as an afterthought: 'Mind you, Tibbie didn't seem all that keen on getting into the carriage. He was arguing with her.' He shrugged. 'Seemed a bit upset.'

The gardener didn't strike him as particularly observant, and Faro did not care for the sound of that. 'You mean, she was going against her will. Did she have any luggage?'

'Dunno about that, didn't see none. But he looked a fine, respectable young gentleman,' he added reassuringly. A shake of the head, a disapproving: 'Too young and grand to be her sweetheart, if she ever had one, that is. And even if she was struggling a bit, I reckoned it was none of my business. Besides, Tibbie's a bit deaf, mebbe that was why he was having to shout at her.'

Faro left him with a feeling of unease. The picture conjured up was a sinister one. If Celia had been run over and killed deliberately and Tibbie had seen the runaway carriage, then she would be in danger. And so might Mrs Brook, in whom she had confided.

The fine day had faded and there was a chill wind blowing across the landscape, which looked considerably less attractive under heavy grey clouds, bringing with them a threat of rain. By the time he reached home, tired and footsore, he decided to delay calling on Mrs Brook, hoping that his fears were wrong and Tibbie would have been in touch with her.

As he opened his garden gate, thankful the hammering was over for the day, he decided worrying must be infectious, or did it come with marriage and a family, even a happy one?

Lizzie's welcome smile and a hug always gladdened his heart. Vince was out with Coll. Was he hungry? When he said that he hadn't eaten since breakfast, Lizzie was shocked at such appalling information.

'Of course you can't wait for supper, dear. Here you are,' she added, placing a piece of leftover pie on a plate.

Vince came in with Coll and was tempted to share it. That didn't affect his appetite as Lizzie, with a mother's gratification, watched him having a hearty meal with them later. Or so it seemed, although it was for a very good reason that they knew nothing about. He was now eating for two, himself and a hungry gypsy confined to the disused stable with an injured ankle.

At least it was a comfortable lodging, Vince thought, the old loose boxes still filled with straw were reasonably warm, especially with the blanket he had whipped from the clothes line and had to listen to his mother outraged that this was a theft by one of the those gypsies. At least she was wrong about that and he wondered anxiously how long it would be before Charlie was fit to go on his way. And of more pressing concern, just how long he could get away with feeding him and concealing his presence from his mother and stepfather?

He had looked in at the stable on his way to school, hoping that the gypsy he had befriended would have gone. But there he was, lying asleep under the stolen blanket with the empty plate, which had contained Vince's second helping of last night's supper. He hoped he could sneak it back into the kitchen and that, given that he had done the washing up, his mother hadn't noticed it was missing.

Charlie stirred sleepily.

'Hope you were warm enough,' Vince said.

'Thanks, yes. The blanket helped a bit.'

'How's your ankle?' Vince asked eagerly.

Charlie stood up, staggered a few steps and winced. He groaned. 'Still too sore to do anything like walking.' He grimaced, then forced a smile. 'I'm always in danger if they come after me, you know.' Sighing, he bent and rubbed his ankle doubtfully. 'Hope it won't take long to mend.'

Vince hoped so too. He was also in danger.

CHAPTER ELEVEN

In the Central Office, Gosse greeted Faro in an unusual good humour, rubbing his hands with glee.

'Got him this time, Faro, and caught off that train with his victim's money on him. Not even sense enough to get rid of the wallet by throwing it out of the window.'

He laughed. 'McLaw must be slipping, not the wily bird he once was. He's slipping, losing his nerve.' And rubbing his hands together, 'Aye, all the better for us. They're holding him at Glasgow. I'm going through to collect him.'

Faro was a little surprised until Gosse added: 'Not trusting that to any of their constables. Want to make absolutely sure this time that I put the cuffs on him, see him safely to he gallows and deliver him in person to the hangman,' he added grimly.

Taking down his greatcoat, he said: 'I'm off to catch the train now. No more delays. I'll take Bain with me. You go down to Alwick, take the train and sort out that insurance business for the hotel fire. The insurance folk aren't satisfied, they're suspicious and want us to investigate.' He pointed to the paper on the desk: 'Seems they're claiming vast sums for valuable pictures and jewellery destroyed.'

Faro was quite relieved that he was not to accompany the inspector, who huffed and puffed each day about his busy life, and although some minor officers like himself could have made the Glasgow trip and collected McLaw, Gosse enjoyed sending him on errands such as this insurance investigation. It made sure he was kept well in the background with no more chances of promotion, always hoping that he might make some gross error and be demoted back to the beat.

The Pleasance, just minutes away from the cottage, was the terminus of a local train, the Edinburgh and Dalkeith Railway, built in 1831. Familiarly known as the Innocent Railway, this was not due to the legend that no one was ever killed while it was being built, but because it was originally horse-drawn in an age where steam engines were still considered dangerous. Originally laid down for the purpose of conveying coal from pits in Dalkeith into the capital, to the surprise of the promoters the public rapidly took to this convenient and novel way of travelling, and, particularly with the lure of the Musselburgh Races, it became as lucrative and important as freight to the railways, with open carriages, wagons and converted stagecoaches supplementing the rolling stock.

Surveying the map, the Alwick Hotel was at Dalhousie, one of the halting stations on the line, and Faro decided that if he made good time with the insurance claim enquiry then Gosse was doing him a personal favour. He could continue the journey on a later train and visit the poorhouse at

Belmuir, a couple of miles beyond Dalhousie and another halt just short of the terminus at Fisherrow. Although not particularly hopeful, he might find some answers to the mystery of Agatha Simms's empty coffin.

Faro loved trains, any kind of train, and it was a pleasant, relaxing experience to escape for a few hours, away from his normal daily routine and into the surrounding countryside without the smoking chimneys of Edinburgh's 'auld Reekie' clouding the horizon and a seamless landscape of hills, undulating fields and sky.

He sat back in one of the wooden seats and sighed with relief as, leaving the Pleasance, they went through the long tunnel at the base of Arthur's Seat, a tunnel which was already the bane of the railwaymens' lives since local residents had decided that it was a suitable dumping ground for all manner of rubbish, including the occasional broken chair or old mattress.

Emerging into daylight again, Faro decided to make the most of travelling on this tranquil, sunny day along the coastline of East Lothian with its fine views across the Firth to the coast of Fife. As they steamed through tiny villages, a happy reminder of the railway's origins, where else would one find a railway board at all stations forbidding the drivers to stop by the way to feed their horses?

Enjoying the journey and in no particular hurry, he reached Dalhousie, the hotel with its scarred windows clearly visible as he left the station. He had to stoop to enter the unprepossessing original entrance still with its lingering smoke fumes. Kept waiting while a sullen barman went in search of Mr Evans, he studied his surroundings. Once this had been a coaching inn, a stop for travellers on the drove road south; a sprawling, ancient building, more for convenience than comfort it had been updated some twenty years ago by the present owner, the main reason for this achievement inspired by the hope of attracting racegoers from Musselburgh wishing to extend their visit and spend their winnings in a fine, modern country hotel.

Such was the hint of the ragged poster in the public bar, which had miraculously escaped the fire, confined to the main house. Distant voices, footsteps and the barman returned alone, shrugged and said: 'Manager says you're to wait, he has things to sort out.'

Faro decided that a little conversation to fill the interlude might be useful and illuminating. 'You were here on the night of the fire?'

'I was not. It was early morning, I was asleep in my bed, the public bar closed.' The barman's mouth also closed firmly. With an unkempt appearance, sadly in need of a shave and a bath, he was no good advertisement for the poster either, thought Faro.

'Have you been here long?' he asked, addressing the man's back while he thoughtfully regarded, as if counting, the bottles shelved behind the counter.

'Too long. I'm leaving the day,' was the brisk reply as he indicated a large sack, presumably luggage, propped up against the wall.

'No more customers to attend?'

The barman gave him a withering glance. 'Not even if there was one, I'm still going. Never been paid, that's why.'

'The fire, of course, I understand there might be a problem.'

'Not the fire, even before, mean as hell, the old devil.'

And warming to the theme, 'Never had any money, been run at a loss for months, owes everyone for miles around. In fact, the fire was the best thing that could have happened to him.' A shake of the head. 'Aye, it was that.'

The best thing as described was somehow sinister, it implied arson, and Faro was appreciating this information as Mr Evans came in, or rather stumbled in, clutching an empty glass and bringing with him the strong reek of whisky.

'What is it you want?' he demanded.

Slowly, clearly, Faro explained the reason for his visit, the insurance claim and so forth while Mr Evans listened, nodding from time to time impatiently and darting vicious glances in the direction of the sullen barman who was viewing with interest from behind the counter this interchange between his late employer and the new arrival.

Without the politeness of offering Faro refreshment, Evans tapped the empty glass, yelling: 'More!'

'Help yourself,' was the reply as the barman brushed him aside, picked up the sack and departed.

'Ungrateful bugger!' was hurled after him. 'Glad to be rid of him, for a start.' And staring balefully at Faro he demanded suspiciously, 'And what, may I ask, is your interest in this fire which ruined me? From the insurance again, are you?'

'No, sir. I'm a detective. The insurance wish for some—'

Evans interrupted by thumping the table. 'Bringing in the police, are they? I'll not have that—'

'You will need to attend to their requests, sir,' Faro reminded him firmly, 'if you wish to receive the compensation you have applied for, which they consider rather difficult to justify.'

'Difficult to justify, is that it?' Scowling, Evans dragged out a sheaf of papers from his pocket and thrust them at Faro. 'We'll see about that.'

The next half-hour was very tedious as Evans shouted and blustered while Faro tried to make him understand that this claim was not only insubstantial, but if Evans insisted, he might find himself not only not receiving one penny but also standing in the dock facing a charge of arson.

Having made his point, at that Faro took his leave, watched by a somewhat subdued and nervous Evans whose wife, a dishevelled blonde bearing a bottle of whisky, put in a late appearance. Evans could expect no sympathy from her. She was shouting abuse at him, an expert in foul language, and Faro could still hear every word as he thankfully made his way back across the road.

Consulting his map, following the general direction of the railway line, a two-mile walk would take him to his next call, hopefully less strident, at the poorhouse at Belmuir.

CHAPTER TWELVE

Faro was faced by an unexpected dilemma as the poorhouse loomed on the horizon. He had not given any thought as to how to make an entrance, or invent a reason for his visit, realising that he could hardly roll up without some valid excuse. Even in plain clothes, a policeman making enquiries about an empty coffin, or rather one filled with stones, if Tibbie's second-hand description was correct, would cause a flutter of unease at least, and perhaps even panic among the residents.

Having followed the path by the railway line, it emerged by the rear of the building where he watched idly as several men carried out large boxes, their contents marked, 'garden produce – fragile', presumably to load on to the train to Edinburgh.

Having been out since early morning and it was now late afternoon, his feet were sore and he was in need of some refreshment since none had been offered him on his two duty calls. He sighed, regarding the approaching train steaming towards the halt and had a sudden, almost irresistible longing to be boarding it and going home.

He had not yet seen the front of the building, but the back suggested that it was large and probably of the same ugly institutional design that marked its kind. He was now regretting his promise to Mrs Brook, made on an impulse to be kind because she was so distraught with her incredible tale of the two estranged sisters and the sinister burial. As for the missing Tibbie, he should have contacted her before making this journey, as it seemed highly unlikely that the poorhouse would have any useful information in their records of the orphan girl who had left them long ago.

He knew he had been unwise to so rashly get himself involved, when there were more urgent events needing his attention. At least by the time he returned, Gosse would be back from Glasgow, triumphant, with McLaw. Faro could picture him, sitting at his desk, basking in the glory as if the recapture had been all his own work. After the many sightings leading nowhere, this would be a relief for them all, one to score off the daily routine list.

He was hungry and glimpses through the trees of a stately home on the skyline suggested a large estate on which the poorhouse building had been erected, while smoke from surrounding chimneys unseen hinted at some form of habitation. He would take his chances on a village and the existence of a tavern.

He was in luck for Belmuir resembled a feudal village with a cluster of houses overlooked by a castle forming a neat square round a green, while the presence of an inn sign cheered him as the most likely place to gather useful information and a tactful approach for his enquiries.

The Coach and Horses was a vast improvement on the Alwick Hotel and he took a seat at a clean, well-scrubbed table with an appetising smell of cooking lingering in the air.

The man who came forward, smartly dressed with a white towel over his arm, suggested this was the landlord. With a welcoming smile and an amiable greeting, he asked Faro for his order. A pie and a pint of ale would do nicely.

He departed through the closed door of the kitchen and a few moments later a serving-man about his own age approached, and as he silently went about setting the table to Faro's requirements, his anxious, preoccupied look had nothing to do with any pressure of other customers waiting to be served and Faro decided they must have some other cause.

'This is a fine place. Been here long?'

'I live here.' The answer was tinged with scorn, and Faro, naturally curious about why a handsome, well set-up young man was trapped in an isolated country tavern, although a second glance readily identified him as the landlord's son, decided to ask some more questions.

'A very agreeable place to live. I envy you, given I come from the depths of the city.'

With a shrug and no further comment, Faro was left to enjoy his excellent pie, his window seat providing a fine view of the mansion brooding on the hill. He exchanged a polite nod with the only other customer, an old man with a long white beard sitting at the bar who had watched him come in. Landlords and barmen at a quiet time of the day, or customers with a free drink, tend to be gossipy, particularly when in an area where not very much usually happens and there is a local murder still making news.

Faro was hopeful as the landlord, with a more affable manner than the serving-man, hovered nearby and, realising Faro was a stranger to these parts, was politely curious, so Faro invented a story about living in Edinburgh and wanting to bring his wife and family to such a delightful place in the summer.

'There's not much in the way of accommodation hereabout, we don't cater for visitors, but you might find something up there,' said the landlord, pointing towards the hilltop. 'Things aren't what they were before the old gentleman passed away, and these days the new laird might be glad to help you.' The frown that accompanied this latter statement indicated that there was not a lot of money at the big house.

The solitary customer, a regular judging by his hearty greeting with the landlord, joined them. He was also curious about this stranger and having overheard their conversation, he nodded to Faro.

'Excuse my interruption, sir. We let rooms if you'd be interested,' he added eagerly.

Faro interpreted the shake of the landlord's head, that only he could see, as a warning. 'Comfortable room and good plain food,' said the old man.

Faro's offer of a pint of ale was gladly accepted, received and paid for. The landlord, feeling his services were no longer needed, took his leave and the old man who introduced himself as Ben Hogg sat down and prepared to talk at some length about the excellence of the accommodation on offer.

While he was drawing breath to drain his pint, Faro seized the opportunity to get a word in. 'Is it a safe enough place?'

A frown. 'Why do you ask that, sir?'

'Well, my wife, she's a bit nervous. You know, after all that business we read in the newspapers.'

Ben laughed. 'Oh, you mean the McLaw lass. She deserved all she got. He shouldn't have killed her but we were all a bit sorry for him. What a life he had; she was well known not only in Belmuir but to everything in trousers that set foot in the place. Poor bugger, he didn't seem to notice, either.'

Seeing that the old man was inclined to be talkative, this offered an unexpected opportunity to explore the dead woman's background.

'You knew McLaw?'

Ben nodded. 'Aye, everyone knew him. Came down from the Highlands looking for a job and got it with us in the gardens up at the poorhouse over yonder. Hard worker, right enough.' He shook his head. 'Didn't seem an ounce of violence in him. Nice, gentle lad, loved flowers. But you never can tell, can you?' Pausing, his nod indicated the landlord, 'Joe Robson, here, the lassie's stepfather, looked after Annie and her sister Nora – she made a good, respectable marriage.' He sighed. 'Before McLaw came along we all thought Annie would marry Frank.'

At Faro's puzzled look, he said: 'Frank – he's the barman here, Robson's only son. Even as bit bairns they were always together.'

This was something of a revelation, and hoping there was more useful information coming, Faro explained that he had walked by the railway line and arrived at the back entrance of the poorhouse. For good measure and encouragement, he added that he had heard good reports of it in Edinburgh too.

Ben nodded. 'A good place, aye, my widowed daughter works there. Its run by the Belmuirs and its not one of those awful places like the city ones, which are more like prisons for the poor souls.' He stopped and nodded. 'Aye, right enough, a good God-fearing place with a chapel on Sundays. My lass says the Belmuirs watch over them all, never known to turn anyone away.'

Leaving the old man with the hint that he would consider his offer of accommodation, Ben nodded eagerly: 'Aye, tell your wife she can expect all the best of everything with us. Clean, comfortable bed, excellent food and plenty of it. And my wife waits on our guests personally, even does laundry, if necessary.'

Faro bought him another pint of ale and with a promise to consider Mr Hogg's offer, going over to the counter to pay the landlord he said: 'This is a very attractive place you have here, set around the green. More like a feudal village in the south of England.'

Robson's eyebrows raised at that. 'You've been down to England?' he said in an awed tone, making it sound like a far-distant planet.

When Faro said yes, he shook his head and sighed. 'I've never been anywhere, not even in Scotland. Been to Edinburgh a few times and didn't like it much.' He returned to polishing glasses. 'I'm quite content. I was born here, on the estate, and I expect I'll die here too unless I'm called on to fight in any of them foreign wars our lairds used to get involved in.' He shrugged. 'Have a lot to be grateful for. Belmuir has always been good to his tenants and set a fine example to us all. Provided the poorhouse over yonder. Gave up a bit of their land and helped finance it.'

Faro thought of the great, ugly building and decided they could have spent more on a better architect as the landlord continued: 'Not like the ones in the big cities I've read about. Ours is a service to the community, not only to the poor and destitute but for the elderly who are sick and live alone, and there's a special ward for TB sufferers, isolated from the rest of them in case of infection.'

Listening to him gave Faro an idea. He would call on the poorhouse and invent an aged, frail relative. In this case, his mother, Mary Faro, who would never forgive him for that word 'elderly', priding herself on her excellent health and being very secretive about revealing her age. Faro reckoned she must be late fifties at least, possibly sixties, but for this purpose, he told the landlord that she had been very ill (lie) and lived alone far from here (true). He added that they were at their wits' end what to do about her.

'Away on one of those islands in the north, we can't visit her and she can't stay with us, our cottage is too small and we're expecting a new addition to the family soon,' he added, making it sound as if they were already living ten to a room. 'Besides, Ma is used to space, but she is getting frail and needs some nursing care now.'

'And you can be sure she'll get it,' was the reply. 'She'll enjoy her last days in peace and quiet and you can see her too. This local train from Edinburgh is a godsend for visitors.' He smiled. 'You'll have peace of mind, knowing your old mother is in good hands, receiving the best possible care. They watch over the sick and don't work even the fit ones to death, either, like some of those other places; the fit ones work in the gardens. You maybe ken this already, but Belmuir is famous for their kitchen garden produce, sent regularly by train to markets in Edinburgh,' he added proudly.

Leaving the inn, Faro took the short cut across the estate grounds to the poorhouse that the old man had indicated. Pretty woods and a winding path through thick shrubbery that suddenly erupted as two labradors darted towards him. He had a care about big strange dogs, a fear common to all policemen, and they were sniffing around him eagerly, probably alerted to the smell of Coll. Trying in vain to push them away, he looked round helplessly. Where was their owner?

A whistle and from the distant undergrowth a woman emerged and gave Faro the fright of his life.

In that first glimpse he thought he was back in Kirkwall, seeing Inga again.

Inga St Ola.

CHAPTER THIRTEEN

Inga St Ola. No, that could not be possible. Inga was in Orkney.

As the woman came closer he realised he had been deceived. Or was he never to escape his lost love, was she to be present in every woman, except his dear Lizzie? This woman was the same height as Inga, the same long dark hair and slim figure. Even her walk. But there it ended. As she came closer, those were not Inga's eyes in a face, which was older and had been beautiful when young but age was taking its toll, the cheekbones sharper, the full lips thinner.

Speechless, he stared at her and she took his startled look for fear.

'Your dogs, ma'am?'

'Don't see anyone else around, do you?' she said mockingly. 'And they won't bite strangers, not unless I tell them to,' she added mischievously, as the dogs ran back to her side and sat down obediently, regarding him eagerly, tails wagging in a frenzy of friendliness as if they would like to make further acquaintance.

At that moment, the undergrowth erupted a second time and a young man rushed on to the scene, flourishing a rifle. Even at a distance he looked angry. The woman laughed. 'He won't shoot you, either, although he's a crack shot. Missed his target, however, and the rabbits we're overrun with will live to enjoy our vegetables for another day,' she added with a touch of malice.

The man reached their side, stared down his nose at Faro. Faro guessed from their likeness that they were brother and sister as she smiled scornfully and said: 'Rotten luck again, Hector.' The looks they exchanged suggested hidden depths and, even before a stranger, hinted that these siblings might not be on the best of terms.

And turning to Faro, the woman who looked like an older Inga asked coldly, 'May I ask what you think you are doing here? Might I remind you that this is private property?'

Faro began to explain about the poorhouse, found he was stammering, something he hadn't done since childhood. This wasn't Inga's voice either. This was upper-class Edinburgh, the voice of aristocratic Scotland used to commanding servants. And all the time she was looking him over, narrow-eyed.

Although neither would ever know it, in that moment they had something in common, for he reminded her of someone she had known long ago, the love of her life, but a poor, insignificant artist, with no breeding. She couldn't have him and her family had sent him packing and sent her off to salve her broken heart with an old aunt, married to a count in Bergen. When she returned home he had sought her again and lost his life in a shooting accident, so it was said.

But this man, this stranger, could have been the one she had lost but could never forget. Tall, fair-haired, above-average good looks, high cheekbones, a full mouth and slightly hooded deep-blue eyes. A good body too, she was sure, and a face like a Viking warrior, from what she recalled of museum visits in Norway all that time ago.

She sighed, pushed the memory aside and tried to concentrate. He was talking about the poorhouse.

'Perhaps you would be good enough to tell me who I ought to see?' He had asked a question and was waiting for her answer.

Allowed to wear plain clothes, it often suited him when meeting the public or making enquiries not to reveal his identity as Detective Sergeant Faro, and he cut a dashing figure in his dark greatcoat, which was long and suited his tall figure. While considering it wise not to reveal his identity, he had recovered his voice again. And she liked that voice too, a fine, deep timbre, a hint of an accent that wasn't ordinary working-class Edinburgh. 'The person in charge is not available at present,' she said.

Hector had approached, coming from the direction of the poorhouse, the manager who was never there. She looked hard at him, but giving Faro a sneering glance that suggested he was of less value than the rabbits, Hector turned on his heel and walked quickly away.

She said: 'You may ask me about the information you require.'

'And who might you be, ma'am?' There was just a hint of amusement in his voice and she bridled at that. It indicated, as usual, that men thought women were incompetent at managing anything other than the domestic scene.

She drew herself up to her full height, tall for a woman and impossible to look down on a man who was two inches over six feet tall.

'I am Belmuir.'

Faro frowned. 'You are a relative of the laird?' Then who was Hector?

Her back stiffened. 'I am the laird. Lady Belmuir to you.'

Faro was taken aback, not used to dealing with lady gentry. It was a new experience, and remembering his manners, he made acknowledgement in the short bow to his betters that politeness demanded.

A gesture with her hand. 'If you will accompany me, I will take down the details and pass them on.'

He made to follow her but she wasn't walking towards the poorhouse. He was following her through a gate into a well-stocked and very large, walled kitchen garden where groups of people who were working between the rows of vegetables raised heads, then stood up and touched caps or curtseyed to their laird.

A quick inclination of her head, a smile and she walked rapidly towards another door leading into a formal rose garden. Two men pushing wheelbarrows touched caps, and said: 'Good morning, m'lady.'

'Good morning. And how are the new plants?'

'Fairly well, m'lady, if the snow keeps off.'

'Then let us keep hoping.' Turning, she walked briskly up steps bordering a handsome stone staircase guarded by two heraldic lions and leading up to an ancient, studded door.

So this was home. Faro looked round briefly at the

magnificent view and in the far distance the ruins of an old abbey, which he suspected had provided many of the stones of this new mansion two hundred years ago.

Opening the door that creaked with age, she looked back at Faro with no more interest than at the two labradors. 'This way!'

They were in a panelled hall, with the sun throwing rich patterns through stained glass windows across a vast staircase winding upwards. A door opened and led to an interminable narrow stone corridor with appetising smells denoting kitchens.

She pushed open another door and a flustered, red-faced cook curtseyed 'm'lady'. The dogs bounded to her side.

'Feed these two. They've had their walk for today. And bring tea.' Then to Faro, 'Sit down,' she said, pointing to the well-scrubbed kitchen table. As he took a seat she went to a drawer, rummaged about and took out a book and writing implements under the cook's watchful eye.

'Where's the tea? Look sharp, now.'

The cook said nervously, 'Them's housekeeper's books, m'lady.'

'So what, I only want a page. See.' As she tore it out the cook quavered and rolled her eyes heavenward.

'Get the tea, now,' said Belmuir emphasising each word. And to Faro: 'Well, what are you waiting for? I haven't all day. Your name?'

He told her and she repeated: 'Jeremy Faro. And what is it you want?'

So he told her the lie, the story about his mother.

She listened, frowned, asked a few questions, and laying aside the pen, said: 'Very well. We will see if we can accommodate her. A note from her doctor would be of some assistance.' And standing up, a gesture of the hand again and he was dismissed, the interview over.

Another word. 'You would need to walk back to Fisherrow, but the train halts at Belmuir. This is one of their days for taking market produce into Edinburgh.' She turned and looked at the huge clock with its merciless tick dominating one wall. 'You have five minutes before it leaves. Go back by the short cut.'

'Thank you, ma'am.'

He wasn't going to call her 'm'lady'. He was no servant; a polite bow, no more, and she watched him walk away through the door. She liked that walk too. She had noted his address was near Solomon's Tower. Almost a ruin, the ancient pele tower, so old its history was lost, the very stones hinted that it had arisen out of the extinct volcano that was Arthur's Seat. That was an illusion, of course, but the past was important to her and she was a patron of a society to preserve ancient monuments, now at the mercy of the developers who wanted to pull down the tower and make room for their plans of opening up the area with more of their vile terraces. She had signed a petition against it, using what influence the Belmuirs, her ancient name, would have.

She felt sudden excitement at this desire to see Mr Jeremy Faro again. His image that so reminded her of the once beloved ghost from her past had reawakened a memory to haunt her. The society's meeting next week would provide the perfect excuse, a reason to call at his cottage, find out more about him. She had a pleasing fantasy that he was unmarried and therefore not inaccessible.

* * *

Faro took the short cut through the rose garden and the two gardeners looked at him curiously. They looked healthy, well cared for. Small wonder, Belmuir sounded like an admirable laird overseeing a desirable poorhouse far superior for most of its inmates than the homes they had come from.

Had McLaw also worked with either of those two gardeners? He had not time or excuse today for conversation with them, but he wondered if they too, while accepting that McLaw was guilty, were also sympathetic, knowing an intolerable life with a cheating wife who was caught in the act and therefore deserved what was coming to her.

He reached the halt just in time, the train was gathering steam, preparing for its return journey to Edinburgh. As it moved, a woman was approaching the fence from where he had seen the market produce waiting to be loaded.

She was lame, looked distressed, and must have signalled the train to stop. Then he saw she was being pursued: a man rushed forward, seized her bodily and dragged her away. She was obviously calling for help, against the sound of the train engine.

Faro was helpless to intervene, and as the train began to gather speed, he said to one of the railwaymen sitting opposite, quite unconcerned, 'Didn't you see that? They could have stopped the train for her.'

'Can't do that, sir.'

'The woman was lame and she was trying—'

The railwayman grinned and yelled above the noisy rattle of the engine. 'Come on, sir. One of their loonies at it again.'

'What do you mean?'

The man sighed. 'Trying to get away, of course. Have to be watched, they're at it all the time.'

There was no going back now, and he could hardly leap off the train and rush to her assistance. Too late for that. And loonies trying to escape presented a darker side, a grimmer tale than that so widely spread of a splendid poorhouse with perfect living conditions.

Faro had another reason for disquiet, the lame woman in the scene he had just witnessed was perhaps not one of the loonies. Lame, pale and thin, she fitted Mrs Brook's description of the missing Tibbie.

CHAPTER FOURTEEN

Returning to Edinburgh, Faro left the train and walked over to Sheridan Place.

Mrs Brook looked relieved to see him but her eager smile faded when he shook his head and told her that Tibbie was not at the Simms's house in Liberton. Trying to reassure her by mentioning that she had been seen by one of the neighbours getting into a gentleman's carriage, this information alarmed Mrs Brook. Having omitted witnessing the scene from the train that hinted to a fierce argument, for her his report neither implied a highly improbable romance nor security and she said: 'I fear she has been kidnapped.'

'What makes you think that?' he asked, although the same thought had entered his own mind.

'Well, sir, it's like this. What other reason would this gentleman have? Tibbie knew no one, she was a recluse like Miss Celia and she knew her place in society. She was from a different class, so what would a gentleman with a carriage want with a lame servant lass who was no longer young?'

Faro guessed that she was well ahead of him in interpreting what had befallen Tibbie as dangerous and frightening. After all, she was a witness to Celia's accident. She had reached the Mound just after her mistress had been knocked down and had seen the carriage responsible bounding down the hill, apparently out of control. Celia had been dead on arrival at the hospital, but it would have been sensible to expect that the carriage owner, if this was a dreadful accident he had been unable to prevent, would have at least made himself or herself known by an enquiry about the woman who had been injured.

However he looked at it, Faro's suspicions were growing steadily stronger that this incident was linked with the mysterious disappearance of Agatha's dead body and the empty coffin.

Leaving Mrs Brook, he sighed. He had failed in his promise. She had been hoping for consolation and was feeling let down, expecting too much of him, believing that as a friend of Chief Superintendent Macfie he shared a similar aptitude for solving mysteries.

Faro now had an added concern for her welfare. He could not warn her without arousing her fears, but if there was some sinister purpose behind the disappearance of Tibbie, then she might also, by association, find herself in deadly danger.

Heading homeward past the thunder of hammers and flying dust and grime as another skeleton of scaffolding headed skyward, he acknowledged a cheery shout from the workmen. After all, they were not to blame for the disfigurement of what had once been a peaceful country scene. They were not responsible for the miscalculations of the developers and architects who employed and paid them. They were merely family men like himself.

With some regret he realised that another visit to the poorhouse was inevitable; his excuse, accomodation for his frail old mother. Could he also solve the sinister riddle of Agatha Simms' empty coffin and Tibbie's disappearance? Had she been taken to the poorhouse, kidnapped from Liberton by the fine gentleman with his carriage, and kept a prisoner and was she trying desperately to escape?

At least McLaw's final recapture meant that futile search was over and, as always, he was glad another working day with all its trials was over. Time to draw breaths of fresh air and, longing for the peace beneath the smoke arising from the cottage chimney, he thought with delight how lucky he was to be a happily married man with smiling faces awaiting him. Already he was looking forward to spending the evening with Lizzie, busily knitting for the baby or quite absorbed in a romantic novel.

Faro regarded her fondly. She felt cheated and quite cross, throwing the book aside, if the author failed to provide a happy ending. Real life, she knew from her own bitter experience, was not like that, but one expected better treatment in fiction.

'That's not fair,' she would say and the author, more often than not a woman, would be firmly crossed off her list of future books from the library.

He never discussed his crime cases with her and she shuddered away from details about any local crimes, or killers like McLaw, but as she was preparing supper, knowing how he loved trains, she asked if his journey had been successful. He realised then that she might be interested in Belmuir House since it had all the right ingredients for one of her romances, including a lady laird.

Omitting any details of his activities or the reason for his visit to the poorhouse, he described his encounter with Lady Belmuir and her dogs and his impressions of the stately home with its lovely gardens and the pretty village.

When she said: 'How lovely, and such a nice train ride too, right to the gates,' he suffered a pang of guilt at her wistful expression. Although she never complained, he realised she didn't have much of a social life, taking care of him and Vince. Sometimes he took her to a concert, but he was aware that she didn't enjoy opera or classical music as much as he did. Beethoven and Bach were lost on her; what she really loved was an evening at the variety theatre, with its comics and sentimental songs. She loved dancing too, but a little of that went a long way with a policeman who suffered sore feet from excessive walking every day. Their reading, when he had time for such relaxation, was poles apart and poor Lizzie, he thought guiltily, had few treats beyond the activities afforded by the local church, like the women's guild. And when the baby arrived she would be even more restricted.

What was it that had brought on this line of thought? Was it the meeting with Lady Belmuir who had aroused memories of Inga and a bond that was infinite but indefinable? Unrelated to transient material things like literature or music, it was rooted somewhere deep within them, in the history of Orkney, this island of myth and legend, wild seas, tall cliffs, whirling seabirds, and high winds, a vivid breathing landscape where they once roamed hand in hand, bound together in a physical attraction that neither could deny.

He made a sudden decision, and putting an arm around Lizzie, he kissed her gently and said: 'On my next day off, we'll have a train ride. I'll take you to Belmuir and we'll have lunch at the Coach and Horses. Would you like that?'

She clasped her hands. 'Oh, Jeremy, that would be wonderful. Maybe we could see those lovely gardens too.' And hugging him: 'You are such a dear, you are so good to me.'

That made him feel guiltier than ever, and taking her for granted was seriously neglecting his home life. He made a silent resolution to do better. After all, being a detective sergeant wasn't the most important thing in his world. Lizzie and a family came first, otherwise he was in danger of becoming like Inspector Gosse.

Vince came in from school but over supper he didn't share his mother's excitement about Belmuir House or even ask wistfully, as he did on the rare occasions when they discussed some planned excursion, could he go with them. During these past few days he had seemed preoccupied, frowning over his Latin homework, which, apart from hearing his recitation of the irregular verbs, was an area of his education his stepfather couldn't help him with. Foreign and ancient languages hadn't been on his Orkney school curriculum.

Faro observed that whatever was bothering Vince did not affect his appetite. After a hearty supper, he once again sprang from the table, gathered the plates and offered to wash the dishes and take Coll out for his evening walk.

Faro had given up protesting that Vince enjoyed that particular task, as the boy insisted: 'I want to do it, Stepfather. You and Ma need a bit of peace, a quiet moment after working all day.'

Their eyebrows raised at that, both somewhat surprised by this new Vince.

'He has always been a good lad, but he is so extra considerate these days,' sighed Lizzie, patting her belly where the baby was now making his or her presence seen and felt.

'He's growing up,' smiled Faro, 'almost a man, dear.'

Lizzie shook her head. 'I know, but I like my little lad. I'll miss him,' she said wistfully and frowned. 'If I didn't know better, I'd think he had a sweetheart, some local lass he was secretly meeting out on the hill.'

Faro laughed. 'He's still a bit young for courting.'

Her words, however, struck a chord. There was something odd in Vince's behaviour. Normally he told Lizzie everything and this new secretive quality didn't fit his personality, or his relationship with Faro either. This healthy, oversized appetite was strange too.

'He eats more than you, Jeremy,' Lizzie said in surprise.

Faro sighed. He had plenty on his plate, of the non-digestive kind, to concern him without worrying about Vince's appetite or his mysterious behaviour. Perhaps it was an interest in some local schoolgirl, as Lizzie suggested. After all, he had fallen deeply in love with Inga St Ola when he was fifteen, although it was two years before she, some five years older, recognised and briefly returned his passion.

'Definitely a lass, don't you think?' said Lizzie firmly.

But she was wrong. It was no lass, but the gypsy Charlie

who occupied a major part of Vince's thoughts, the object not of affection but of constant anxiety.

How much longer could he deceive his parents, smuggling out food that never seemed enough for the hungry young man in the stables?

'Is that all?' was his constant moan. 'Couldn't you bring a bit more? I'm starving.' Vince felt little sympathy as he too was starving, saving half his meal for Charlie.

'How's your ankle? Is it any better today?' A question always met with the same reply.

'Not much.' Charlie sighed. He could now stand with the stick and hobble about, but he too was fed up with living in this cold, disused stable with the wind blowing in through cracks everywhere.

He had made a decision. He must move on and for that he had to have the boy's help. What he needed more than food was money, enough for his journey and to survive.

There must be money in the cottage. He knew that. The boy was educated, and his parents didn't seem poor. The father was working – Vince had been vague about where, he hadn't said more than an office. Probably a clerk and that sounded like good money. He'd only glimpsed the mother from a safe distance, youngish, small and a bit plump, with a shawl over her head.

Still, it didn't seem right to steal from them even presuming he could get away with it. He had a slight attack of conscience, although he knew that after all his experiences he could no longer afford finer feelings. But stealing would be letting down this nice young lad and getting him into an awful lot of trouble. After all, Vince had saved him, taken care of him; but the main thing was that he had to get away as soon as possible.

Vince was greatly relieved that evening to hear that Charlie must move on and to be free of his main concern of how much longer he could conceal his gypsy's presence from his parents.

'I need money,' said Charlie firmly. 'I can't walk properly yet, but I can get on a train. Are there trains to this Kirk Yetholm place?'

Vince liked trains, studying timetables and planning all manner of imaginary journeys. He knew all the direct routes north and south, and from his geography map was aware that Charlie's destination was in Northumberland. 'The nearest station is in Newcastle.'

'That is excellent. I expect there will be some means of getting to Kelso by coach.' So saying, he looked hard at Vince. 'But I must have money.'

Vince realised he would do anything now to get Charlie on his way. But as for money, his weekly pocket money of sixpence would never do. However, he had been saving for Ma's birthday and even something for the baby too. Two pounds was a fortune, a lifetime's savings. He was reluctant to let it go, even to get Charlie away, but he left the stable that evening promising he would try and get a few pounds from somewhere.

Next day, coming home from school, he took a route by the High Street. Perhaps there might be some coins from the broken cash box lying about, overlooked in the dark outside lavatory, dropped when the wanted man McLaw, according to the police, made his escape.

To Vince's surprise the shop door was open, the window blinds raised and when he stepped over the threshold he saw that Mr M's bookshop was open again for business, what little there was of it.

The only person at the counter was a rather pretty girl who smiled at him, and a young man, fresh-faced and eager and introducing himself as Tommy Wilder, came forward and greeted him affably.

'I'm a relative of the late owner, a second cousin, really, but I always called Mr Molesby uncle.' He laughed as they shook hands and Vince knew that this must be the sailor who had sent those postcards from abroad, stuck on the bedroom mirror.

'I used to look in and see him for a while whenever my ship docked in Leith, but that wasn't very often, I'm afraid.' He shrugged. 'I live in Dundee and I've given up the sea. This summer was my last trip.' And stretching out his hand to the girl, she put down the book she was looking at and came to his side. With an arm about her, he said: 'We wanted to get married, you see, and Lily wouldn't have a sailor for a husband – not with all those years wasted and empty while I was away on two-year voyages.'

Lily squeezed his hand and gave him an adoring look. Vince was very impressed. She was an extremely pretty girl with long auburn hair.

They smiled at him, then suddenly the mood changed. Tommy looked solemn. 'I was very cut up about Uncle's death. I only heard about it from an Edinburgh pal,' he added ashamedly and Vince saw the black band around his sleeve. 'I've just arranged for his funeral. He would want to be buried in Greyfriars with his Molesby ancestors, who were from these parts.'

The girl smiled at him sadly and Vince was suddenly

bereft of words. Since Mr Molesby's death had been recorded as a heart attack, there would be no problem from the police of his release to relatives for burial, but Vince wondered how much Tommy knew of the details, as he said apologetically: 'I hadn't been over to visit Edinburgh for the last few months. I'm afraid I've sadly neglected Uncle; had I known about his poor health I'd have made every effort to see him and see that he looked after himself.' He shook his head. 'It's a long haul from Broughty Ferry and I've been trying to get work. My da's a fisherman, but I didn't want that either.'

Sighing, he looked at the crowded shelves, the books tumbling over each other and added wistfully, 'I've always loved books, especially the old ones, and history in particular. I'll miss old Uncle Jim.' He shook his head. 'What an awful thing to have happened when he was all alone here. I had to come and arrange the funeral and sell the bookshop. But when I saw it again and how Lily just loved it, we both knew this was what we wanted.'

He regarded Vince thoughtfully. 'I gather he disturbed a burglar, so I was told, had a heart attack. Is that so? It was an accident?'

Vince thought of all Gosse's horrible interrogations but said: 'I think so.'

Tommy nodded. 'His heart was bad, I seem to recall that runs in the family. Perhaps he had some warning, knew he was in danger but chose to ignore it. He was that kind of old gentleman. Last time I saw him he said he had always wanted me, his only kin, to have the bookshop, but in those days I was so keen on the sea, I couldn't think what it would be like to be shut up all day. But now . . .'

He paused to tighten his arm around Lily. 'Now that I'm to be a married man,' he added proudly, 'I cannot bear to think of us being parted for two days never mind two years at a time.'

'Did your uncle leave a will?'

'Oh yes, I had the lawyers' name and I've been to see them. It's all there in black and white, the bookshop to be mine. I think I'll grow to like Edinburgh.'

'You will, Tom,' whispered Lily. 'We both love it already.'

He smiled down at her. 'Well, I hope so.'

Believing like everyone else that Mr M had no family and hearing that he had left the bookshop to Tommy Wilder was news to Vince and gave him sudden hope.

Perhaps Tommy would give him a weekend job like Mr M had, the chance to earn a few extra shillings. If he gave Charlie all his money, maybe he could save up enough to buy Ma a present after all.

'I worked for your uncle at weekends,' he began, and he looked round the shelves. 'I was going to catalogue the books for him.'

Tommy whistled. 'I say, that is a good idea.' And with a glance around, 'They are in an awful muddle, right enough.'

Vince cleared his throat and said boldly. 'I was wondering if I could do the same for you, sir, come in on Saturdays and a bit of Sundays for the cataloguing?' he added desperately.

Tommy looked dubious, he frowned and Vince guessed that he was asking a lot. However, Lily squeezed Tommy's hand. She had taken a liking to this good-looking young schoolboy.

Now Tommy smiled at her. 'I'm sure Uncle would have wanted you to continue. When I last saw him he said he was getting too old for running the shop but if he could find a nice, bright lad, say, from the Royal High, his old school, who wanted to make something of himself and loved books and was to give him a hand at weekends, that would be a great help. He made it sound like a very busy shop.'

Pausing, he smiled at Vince approvingly. 'I see by your uniform that it could have been you he had in mind. What an odd coincidence, he must have seen into the future,' he added. And with that he opened a drawer and took out some coins. 'Here, take this – in advance. And start on Saturday.' He grinned. 'I think we'll get along well and you must feel free to borrow any you like, as long as you return them. I'll trust you.' He laughed. 'What's your name?'

As they shook hands, Vince felt very proud at that moment. Great to be trusted by another grown-up the same way he had been trusted by the gypsy Charlie. It was great to be in the shop again, he loved the smell of it, of old books, the solemn leather line-up of works on law and medicine and philosophy all tightly packed together and overflowing the shelves.

For the first time he noticed something that hadn't been there before. On the wall behind the counter there was a picture of a younger Mr M smiling, shaking hands with an important-looking man.

Tommy saw him looking at it and said, 'That's Uncle on what he called the best day of his whole life. It was taken with Sir Walter Scott at Abbotsford – he was one of his best customers. I found it in a drawer and I wanted everyone to see it, it deserved a place of honour, although Uncle was too shy and too modest to hang it in the shop.

Good for business, too,' he added shrewdly. 'I hope a lot of our customers will be delighted to see it and be impressed by the connection with our most famous author.'

Vince thought his stepfather for one would be interested as Sir Walter was his favourite after William Shakespeare. He went closer for a better look. A good likeness of Mr M, still slim and with all his hair, a nice-looking, middle-aged man in his best Sunday clothes.

As he left the shop with the new owner and his pretty wife-to-be, he hoped he too would meet some girl as attractive as that in a few years' time. What a lucky man Tommy was. And he thought about the younger Mr M. There was something familiar about that photograph hanging on the wall, something lodged in the back of his mind that refused to come forward. It nagged him like the fragment of a forgotten dream all the way home.

What on earth could it be?

CHAPTER FIFTEEN

Before he went to bed that evening, Vince slipped out to the stable as usual and handed over the coins to Charlie.

'It is all I have so far, I'm sorry.'

Charlie weighed them in his hand as if testing that they were genuine. He sighed. 'You're a good lad, Vince, but this isn't nearly enough.' He shook his head. 'I can't get very far on this, I'm afraid.'

Vince awoke in the middle of that night. He had had a dream, or rather a nightmare. He sat up in bed. It was the photo of Mr M in the bookshop. The clothes he was wearing, they were the same as Charlie's. Much too tight and made for a smaller man. Smart clothes he claimed had belonged to an elderly man who had died in the gypsy camp that he had 'borrowed' to run away to the Borders from that forced marriage.

Vince now had a sickening feeling that the dead elderly man version was correct, only not in the gypsy camp but in the bookshop. He gulped, remembering that Mr M had been found dead in his underwear. What was bothering him was that when he and Stepfather had looked in the wardrobe, there was only his rather shabby, everyday clothes and not the best suit he would certainly have worn to go to church at St Giles' on Sunday.

He was in a furore and felt cold all over. Had Charlie been his killer? A thief and a liar? If this was so, he might try to rob the cottage and then Ma would be in danger.

He thought desperately. Charlie needed money. Well, he should have it, the sooner the better, and Vince was prepared to hand over the money he had been saving for Ma's birthday present to get him on his way, as far away from Edinburgh as possible.

He would have to confide his awful dilemma to Stepfather, but that would involve the police. He shook his head. No, better not, he had made a promise to Charlie and that at least he must keep.

Faro went off to work across the hill that morning, accompanied by warm sunshine and birdsong. There was a lot of life going on in the heather, as if the small animals hadn't recognised that summer was over and were still lazily enjoying each day.

In reasonably good spirits to face the daily routine now that McLaw had been recaptured, he wondered what would be next on Inspector Gosse's urgent list and whether it would allow him to give consideration to his own problem of how he was to fulfil his promise to Mrs Brook and put her mind at rest by finding Tibbie.

However, a surprise was in store, a frenzy of activity. Instead of constables yawning and pretending to work while

122

reading the local newspapers, the station was in an uproar.

Expecting to see a triumphant Gosse basking in the glow of McLaw safely returned and grimly awaiting the gallows, an infuriated Gosse rushed towards him.

'You're late, Faro – again.'

Ignoring that, Faro said: 'Glad to see you've returned, sir, after your successful journey.'

'Successful!' screeched Gosse. 'No, it damned well wasn't successful.' His face was growing redder and redder as he thumped his fists on the desk. 'Oh, yes, I got my man – that I did. Except that it wasn't McLaw. This was the attacker, right enough. The money and the wallet still on him, no doubt about that, didn't even deny it. But he was not McLaw!' he yelled. 'That whole bloody train journey to Glasgow and back was a complete waste of my time and my money, having to stay overnight. Any of the lads could have done it in a day.'

Faro listened in silence, indeed he could not have got a word in had he tried. At last, when Gosse paused for breath, he asked quietly, 'This is indeed a surprise, sir. What happens now?'

'The search begins again, that's what. Oh no, McLaw is not getting away with it. We'll find him, even if I have every constable searching every corner of the area for twenty-four hours a day.'

That, thought Faro, was a vast undertaking and a complete waste of time, given that if he was wise, and that he did not doubt, McLaw would have left the scene of his lucky escape from the overturned carriage and by now had probably put a hundred miles between himself and his pursuers.

'He'll not get away from me this time,' shouted Gosse, and observing the consternation on the constables' faces, Faro knew that the same thought was going through their minds. Just another waste of time. But obsessed with the fear of failing to recapture McLaw, his humiliation – and that was one thing his pride would not suffer – Gosse could no longer see straight or recognise the impossibility of what was involved in the task he was suggesting. Listening to him, Faro knew that the inspector had lost all sense of proportion.

He regarded him anxiously. Gosse was going mad, and in his role as senior officer, Faro tried to direct anxious constables into some kind of routine, for the inspector had disappeared, presumably taking a rest before outlining the details of the new search. Considering the list of urgent enquiries and allotting tasks to each constable, Faro listened to their murmurs of rebellion. What sort of fruitless activity was this, as they remembered combing every inch of Arthur's Seat and the surrounding areas the first time in miserable weather? Were they all expected to do that again with the same hopeless result?

'Sir,' they appealed to Faro. 'Can't you reason with him? It's useless.' And emphasising what he and they already knew only too well, 'McLaw will be miles away by now.'

By the end of the day, checking in the returning constables and their reports, and after seeing that all was in order, since Gosse had not put in a reappearance, Faro was glad to be going home.

Walking through the Pleasance, his mind now focused on domestic matters, particularly his stepson's odd behaviour. Those extra helpings, that missing blanket from the clothes line, his willingness to clear dishes away and walk Coll each evening.

Vince, he decided firmly, was hiding someone. But where? There was one way to find out. Following him that evening at a safe distance, he watched him go into the stables after a moment's hesitation and a quick look round first. As it was too late to confront whoever he was helping without causing consternation, given that Vince's involvement would upset Lizzie, he kept well out of sight. Waiting until after his stepson returned and the cottage slept, he went across to the stable, entered noiselessly and the sound of deep breathing led him to one of the stalls, where he looked down on a youngish man, his bearded face barely visible beneath Lizzie's stolen blanket.

So this was Vince's secret; Faro had a strange feeling of unease. Vince, in common with his mother, took people on face value and believed their stories. In this case he might well have been quite unknowingly giving shelter to a criminal.

Hoping that he was wrong and that this was just some beggar man who had taken advantage of his stepson's kind heart, he returned to the cottage. Confrontation must wait until morning.

He slept little that night, thinking about the man asleep in the stables and the consequences if he had a criminal record. His thoughts were like a rat trapped in a cage – round and round they went and the circumstances of such an idea were appalling.

Gosse would have a field day if this unknown man had a police record and his hated detective sergeant's stepson had been assisting a criminal.

At last he fell into an uneasy sleep, plagued with nightmares, to awaken at dawn to Lizzie tapping his shoulder. She had a shawl over her nightrobe and whispered, 'Wake up, Jeremy. There's been an accident on the railway line, a man trapped. The constable's waiting for you downstairs.'

Pulling on his clothes, Jeremy found the beat policeman PC Oldfield waiting. 'Sorry to disturb you, sir, but we need some help to get the man out from under the carriage and your cottage was nearest.'

It was a long, difficult job and by the time they got the railwayman free, unconscious and bleeding from a shattered leg, and into a carriage heading for the infirmary, Faro had forgotten all about the man hiding in the stables.

That would have to wait till he got home, life and death were the important issues of the day.

Vince had also endured school with considerably less enthusiasm than usual, anxious to get home to see that all was well: that Charlie, to whom he had given all his precious savings, would be away by now and that that he would find the stable empty.

Charlie had other ideas, however. He was sure that there must be money in the cottage. Vince's father went out every day to work, described vaguely as working in an office. That suggested he was probably a railway clerk with a weekly salary. He would watch for Vince's mother going out with her shopping bag and then take the opportunity to lift any spare cash, or failing that, jewellery lying about that he could turn into money.

She did not leave that morning. He watched anxiously.

Was she ever going out that day? Finally, just after noon, he saw her distant figure taking to the road and made his way hastily across to the cottage. He realised that time was not on his side; if he delayed much longer, then Vince would be home from school and finding his friend Charlie raiding the cottage would not reveal him in a good light. But it had to be faced.

There were unforeseen problems on the horizon.

The first was that Lizzie had only gone a short distance when she realised she had forgotten an urgent letter that Faro had given her to post. She must get it, and with a sigh she turned her steps towards home again.

The second was that Vince, anxious to confirm Charlie's departure, had managed to skip games. Complaining of a sore throat, he had been excused and was also hurrying homeward.

As for Charlie, delighted to find the cottage with an unlocked door, he had not been met by the suspicious snarling dog he had feared, instead an eager-to-be-friendly, tail-wagging Coll had welcomed him. Setting to work, ransacking ornaments and drawers for money or some jewellery, he was caught unawares. Behind him the door opened and there was Vince. The boy stared at him accusingly, unbelieving of the scene before him.

'How could you, Charlie? Stealing from those who have taken care of you. I thought we were friends.' He pointed to the door 'Get out – now, before my stepfather gets here and I tell him. He's a policeman, and if he finds you here, you'll go to prison for this.'

At that moment the door opened. Ma had returned.

She stared at the two of them, bewildered. Vince went to her side and started to explain. But she pushed him aside, rushed towards Charlie.

127

Was she going to attack him? But no, Vince could hardly believe his eyes. They were laughing, in each other's arms, hugging, greeting each other in a strange language he did not understand, with only the occasional anxious glance in his direction.

Having reached his own conclusions regarding the refugee in the stables, Faro's speedy and unexpected return shattered this scene of joyful reunion.

Vince, Lizzie and, yes, McLaw – it was he, undoubtedly – turned to face him. All looked terrified.

He rushed over, seized McLaw. 'You are under arrest.' Regardless of the fact that the man was unarmed, Faro took out the handcuffs he always carried in the deep pockets of his greatcoat and snapped them on with the thought: what a triumph over Gosse. His detective sergeant bringing in this most wanted man and stealing all his glory. He could hardly wait to see his face.

'Now, you will accompany me back to the cells,' he said sternly, looking at Vince and Lizzie, the latter shivering, staring at him, and McLaw with terrified, tearful eyes. Seizing Charlie, shaking him roughly, he added, 'And if you have harmed either of these two—'

'No, no,' said Lizzie.

'You are all right, and you, Vince? He hasn't touched you?'

Vince nodded, utterly bewildered and unable to work out the scene he had just witnessed: his mother and Charlie, the thief who he thought had been his friend and had betrayed his trust. The two of them, whispering together in that foreign language and glancing in his direction as if he might overhear.

'Very well, then.' said Faro. 'Take care of your mother, Vince. I will be back as soon as I have delivered this wretch to the proper authorities.'

Going to the door, Lizzie rushed between them and stood with her back against it. Faro stared at her. Was she afraid that he could not get McLaw to the cells, that this man, a killer, might harm him in doing his duty?

'It is all right, my dear.'

She seized his arm. 'No, it is not all right, Jeremy. You can't take him – not now,' and glancing at the handcuffed man, she whispered, 'Not ever.'

'What on earth are you talking about?' Faro asked gently. 'I am not in any danger, I can look after myself.'

'Jeremy, Jeremy,' she regarded him with tear-filled eyes, clutching his arm. 'You don't understand. You cannot arrest him.'

This was taking human kindness and compassion too far, even for his gentle Lizzie, who clung to him so fiercely and said slowly, 'He is my brother.'

CHAPTER SIXTEEN

Faro felt as if someone had thumped him hard in the chest, taken his breath away, as his sense of triumph faded away. He could only stare incredulously at McLaw and then at Lizzie, as the full horror of the situation began to seep through his mind. For one moment only, he thought he was having an absurd nightmare. Yes, that was it. He blinked furiously, the method he had used all his life to bring himself awake from bad dreams. But no, they were still there, three terrified faces staring up at him.

Still keeping the handcuffs on McLaw, he indicated the table with a shaky hand. This dreadful scene with all its terrible implications clamouring already in his brain . . . it was as if they had climbed a vast mountain and all of them were breathless, exhausted and needed to sit down and gather strength to continue, to face reality.

'Will someone please explain,' he said weakly. And while Lizzie and Vince opened their mouths, and, unable to find words, closed them again, he turned to the criminal who was now his brother-in-law.

'You are McLaw, the wanted man—'

'I am, sir, but I am not guilty,' said McLaw firmly. 'That is why I tried to escape. I haven't ever killed anyone. I was wrongly convicted of Annie's murder – no one would believe me, but I am innocent.'

With a gesture Faro cut him short, saying coldly: 'I have read all the accounts of your trial. You were proved guilty. That is all I need to know.'

'I did not do it,' McLaw insisted, 'whatever the judge and jury decided – I was being sentenced to death for a crime someone else committed—'

Faro held up his hand, shook his head. 'Justice has been done and I accept the law's decision.' He had heard it all before. All murderers said that, denied everything as sentence of death was pronounced.

His head swivelled round to Vince and Lizzie. 'What I want to know is how my wife and my stepson are involved in breaking the law, sheltering a wanted man,' he said coldly, and pointing a finger at Vince, he added sternly, 'I guessed from your odd behaviour that you were hiding something – or someone. Knowing you shared your mother's weakness for waifs and strays, I thought you'd found a poor tramp and were befriending him.' He shook his head. 'Right at the beginning, the blanket off the line supposedly stolen by gypsies should have given me a clue . . .' Pausing, he regarded McLaw contemptuously. 'If my mind hadn't been fully engaged with all of Edinburgh's police force on searching for this scoundrel . . .'

'Let me explain, Stepfather,' Vince cut in.

'Please do, I am listening,' Faro said grimly.

And so Faro and Lizzie heard a brief account of his meeting with McLaw on the hill outside, discovered by Coll, and his tale of fleeing from a gypsy marriage, overthrown from his horse, his sprained ankle.

'I made a promise not to tell anyone, Stepfather. I thought it was just for a day or two, but he told me he needed money for his journey to the Borders.' Shaking his head, he cast a reproachful look at McLaw.

'Last night I handed him all my savings to help him on his way.' A helpless look at his mother and stepfather. 'I believed he was speaking the truth, never doubted that until . . . until I went to the bookshop again and saw the photo Tommy, Mr M's cousin, had hung up.' He gulped. 'I saw that the clothes Mr M were wearing were identical to those ones which fitted Charlie so badly. They were far too small, and he claimed they had belonged to an old man who died at the gypsy camp.'

Vince drew a deep breath and looked angrily at McLaw.

'I did some calculations, Stepfather, and if they were correct, then I realised this man I had befriended was Mr M's killer—'

'Who is this Mr M?' McLaw interrupted indignantly. 'I've never heard of him and I certainly did not kill him, either—'

'Be quiet!' said Faro, tightening his grip. 'Proceed, Vince.'

'That was all I knew, Stepfather. I got off school early and was coming home because I was afraid Ma might be in danger – I didn't guess he was McLaw, the man all the police were searching for—'

'Or that you could go to prison for protecting a wanted

man and assisting his escape,' Faro reminded him harshly. Thank God he had been in time, but for the curious and dreadful fact that this man claimed to be his wife's brother, he might have come home to find them both dead.

Lizzie was whispering to McLaw and Faro said sternly: 'In English, if you please, so that we can understand. Neither of us speaks Gaelic.' And to Lizzie, 'A language you seemed to have conveniently forgotten, like so many other details of your early life,' he added reproachfully.

Lizzie reached across to take his hand. 'Teàrlach – Charlie – is my younger brother, there is only a year between us. We were always close but we haven't met since I left home' – she darted an anxious glance in Vince's direction and added the quick lie – 'to marry your father.'

'Poor Ma, you were disinherited for that. Marrying a brave soldier, they should have been proud of you,' said Vince.

Faro closed his eyes. He hadn't seen yet another complication – that somewhere now, very close by, lurked the truth that Vince must be told. But Charlie knew and behind Vince's back Lizzie gave her brother an imploring glance, a warning.

Faro had heard enough. He stood up, dragging McLaw towards the door. 'You come with me.'

'No!' cried Lizzie. 'I beg you, Jeremy. They will hang him.'

'In due course, no doubt,' was the heartless response.

Lizzie stared at him in horror. 'You cannot mean that, Jeremy. You cannot see my brother hang.'

Faro looked at her coldly, an expression she had never seen in his eyes before. She had a momentary horrid glimpse of that other Faro. The gentle, caring man who was her husband and who she loved with all her heart had been taken over by another image, the cruel Viking warrior who had stormed and conquered Orkney long ago, a transformation she had never expected or would have believed could exist until this moment.

'Please, Jeremy,' she whispered. 'I beg you, please.'

He shook his head. 'You are forgetting, Lizzie, what I am, what I do, what I believe. That justice must be served, my duty is to protect the people of this city.'

'Even if it means sacrificing your own family, apparently,' she said bitterly.

He shuddered at the implication, but went on. 'That, too, is a sad but inescapable fact.' And to McLaw, 'You will be chained up in the stable where you have had so much hospitality until we sort out some family matters. Then your fate will be decided.'

He detected a gleam of hope and said to Lizzie, 'I must do what is right. If you killed a man, Lizzie, or Vince here, it would make no difference.' But even as he said the words, he knew it would, his heart would be broken, his life over. All he would want was to die, to end it all.

Vince gave him a bewildered look. He too was taken aback by this new, less likeable version of his gentle stepfather. He put his arm around his tearful, inconsolable mother as Faro left them, marching McLaw across to the stable still protesting his innocence, shouting, 'Let me explain, I beg you, please listen.'

Ignoring him, inside the stable there were still chains in the loose boxes. Undoing one of McLaw's handcuffs, Faro clipped it on, tested its security and left without another word, ignoring his pleas to be heard.

Hurrying back to the cottage, he felt defeated, crushed under the inescapable burden of this disaster that had overtaken his marriage, so happy until a few hours ago. Now everything in a few brief words had changed for ever. Arthur's Seat looked threatening, its landscape changed, no longer benign, no longer a friendly place for his daily walks with Vince and Lizzie. Worst of all, his wife, too, had undergone a change of character, new and alien.

Lizzie had come into his life fully formed, a gentle, pretty Highland lass with a cloud of yellow hair, when they first met. He knew now that he was living with a stranger, that he had married her knowing nothing of her life before the tragedy that had let heartless parents bar the door for ever on a disgraced daughter and the unwanted baby who had become such a blessing and was promising to be a fine, upright young man.

Perhaps it was a sense of delicacy that had not allowed him to ever mention the past, knowing only that she had been fifteen years old, a servant in their laird's great house, raped by an aristocratic guest at the shooting party, resulting in Vince. Who these parents were, who had so speedily abandoned her, he had no idea, and there had been no mention of any siblings. He knew only vaguely that her father was a lay preacher as well as working for the local laird.

It wasn't much to go on, but utterly convinced of her integrity and overwhelmed by compassion, he was happy to forget her tragic life before they met. He did not want to spoil that feeling of love, tarnish it with the memory of the cruelty that had however brought some good into her life and his. The unwanted child she had given the name Vincent Beaumarcher Laurie.

Back in the cottage they were skating across normality. Lizzie had dried her tears, put on an apron and made tea. Asking if either of them were hungry, she received brusque negatives. How could anyone eat at such a moment? But sitting around the table, Vince and Lizzie looked across at him with imploring eyes. Eyes that were curiously echoed by Coll who, as if aware of some threat to his beloved young master, was sitting close to his side while Puskin, quite unmoved by these human trials, snored gently by the fire.

Accepting a cup of tea, Faro sighed. They were waiting and he had to make a start somewhere, easier without McLaw's presence.

'I thought your name was Laurie,' he said to Lizzie. She was near enough to touch but he avoided taking her hand. Laurie was the name she had married him under.

'It is my mother's name.' And he remembered bitterly now, vague problems over birth and death certificates, glossed over and explained away, Lizzie saying that they did not abide by such nonsense in the Highlands and unfortunately (as it transpired, conveniently for her, if it was true) that all such papers had perished in a fire in their croft. No one had ever bothered about such things, anyway, she said, it was not until she came to live in a big city that they were considered of any consequence.

Faro regarded her in silence and then asked: 'Did you never connect our search for . . . McLaw –' he could hardly bear to say the words '– with your brother?'

'No more than if he had been called McDonald. It is the name of the clan to which we belong. And his name is Teàrlach – Charles in the Gaelic – not John.' She sighed miserably. And Faro realised how little interest she ever showed in his daily activities, her roots in a simpler crofting society owing allegiance still to a feudal laird. After her own bitter experience, she wanted to hear no more about violence, wicked men and murderers about to be hung. She wasn't interested in the newspapers he brought home and preferred the refuge of romantic novels with their happy endings to the harsh, grim cruelty of reality.

Suddenly Vince and Lizzie were both speaking together, asking, pleading what was to be done.

Faro could not answer their questions but one thing was abundantly clear. He could not deliver McLaw into the hands of Inspector Gosse without implicating his wife and stepson. And those implications were horrendous. He closed his eyes, he could see Gosse's scarlet face, his delight that at last he had something that would bring down his hated sergeant – and for Faro's family's mistake, Gosse would enjoy every moment of his triumph.

Sick at heart, Faro knew there was no way out, that the instant he handed McLaw over, his career with the Edinburgh City Police was at an end. In his thirties, he would be an outcast, a disgrace, all the hopes and dreams on which his life was founded from his earliest days would be at an end.

That was bad, but there was worse to come. He looked across at Lizzie and knew that his marriage too had failed, ended the moment of this dreadful revelation, and however he tried in the future, if he turned McLaw in, Lizzie would never forgive him. The memory of her brother's betrayal by her husband would for ever stand between them.

Having loved Jeremy Faro with such a passion, Lizzie

would try to cobble together their ruined marriage, but every day he would see that haunted look in her eyes, hear her sigh. And how would they both survive that other day when great crowds stood at the tolbooth to watch the man who was her brother hang by the neck until he was dead? By then, the news would have spread far beyond Edinburgh that while the police had been searching every inch of the countryside, wasting time and money, the wife of one of their own detectives, a highly respected officer, and his stepson had been hiding the wanted man.

Faro groaned. At best they might not be prosecuted, just sent to jail to spend an unspecified time at Her Majesty's pleasure, but he could envisage a long and tedious set of circumstances while they and he tried to accept and prove Lizzie Faro's incredible story that she had no idea that the murderer McLaw and her brother were one and the same man. Heads would be shaken, scornful laughter: a detective's wife! What incredible nonsense. Who would ever believe such a story? Did they never talk together? Did she never read the papers?

He looked at Vince. What about his stepson, so young and so promising with all the world before him? What about his new dream, to go to the university and become a doctor? For his part in hiding a wanted man, he too would be disgraced, doubtless expelled from the Royal High School and, on the verge of manhood, already marked down with a police record, his future scarred by the scandal involving his parents.

One thing had become perfectly clear. The only thread of hope lay in DS Jeremy Faro breaking the law.

He must get McLaw away from Edinburgh before the

truth became known, see him safely on the way to freedom and to hell with justice! In this case, not only himself but also his family had too much to lose.

He rose from the table, took a deep breath. He would start immediately, find a way of smuggling McLaw out of the stable, across Arthur's Seat and getting him on to a stagecoach. He would need some form of disguise. And how could he do that?

There was an obvious answer. It could be accomplished easily in his role as a policeman, of course, by taking a handcuffed criminal down the borders into England. Then another little demon raised its head: *You could get out of the carriage, kill him yourself and bury him out on the moors. Then you would all be free . . .*

Except of my conscience. I would live with that for the rest of my life, the inescapable fact that I had killed my wife's brother.

Faro sighed deeply as the terrible flaws in his plan became evident. But there was no time to lose. By tomorrow, twenty-four hours' time, by some means they would be rid of McLaw and be able to breathe again.

'Stop your chatter,' he said to Vince and Lizzie who were continuing to bombard him with questions. 'I'm thinking. I have an idea, an idea that might save your wretched brother, Lizzie. And more importantly our own skins, for if ever this came to light we would all be ruined, there is not the slightest doubt about that. You might ever spend the rest of your life behind bars,' he ended ruthlessly, looking at her.

Lizzie ignored that. A wan smile and she reached across and touched his cold hand. 'Thank you, Jeremy. Oh, thank you.'

He turned sharply away from her. 'I hope you realise this is not for McLaw – your brother,' he added bitterly. 'I would cheerfully see him hanged, as the law demands. This is for you and Vince.' He moved quickly away from the table. At the door he turned and said: 'I will be back in a moment. Lizzie, I need a razor and a pair of scissors, if you please. And search round my wardrobe for suitable clothes.'

Lizzie stared at him in astonishment and he repeated: 'He will need clothes, he can't travel in an old man's clothes several sizes too small for him.'

Lizzie frowned. 'But yours will be too big.'

'Better that way. Get out your sewing box and shorten the trousers.'

In the stables, McLaw had slumped down against the stall. He looked up despairingly at Faro's approach.

'Up! Come along!' Faro yanked him to his feet.

McLaw looked scared. 'Where are you taking me?'

'To the cottage – where else?'

'Why won't you believe me—'

'Please – not all that again.' Still holding him firmly, praying that they were not seen by anyone strolling about, such as the beat constable, Faro pushed him towards the cottage. Throwing open the door, he pointed to the table.

'Sit down! We have work to do. Water and a basin, Lizzie.' She brought it to the table and he picked up the scissors and nodded. 'Cut off all his hair, close as you can.'

They stared at him. 'What are you waiting for? We have to transform McLaw, the man they are all out looking for. So for a start, cut off his hair and hand me my razor.'

Later, by candlelight, beardless, the wild hair gone, he

looked very different from Charlie's gypsy. A new man was emerging, a good-looking young man in his twenties and, as Faro observed with a sinking heart, his strong likeness to Lizzie was very evident, his hair – that with a good wash would be yellow and curly – like Lizzie's.

He frowned. 'Take more off that hair, Lizzie – here, give me the scissors.' A few clips and Faro took up the razor. 'We need to shave his head. This is more effective, let's get rid of those curls.'

Finally, without handing Charlie the mirror, the three of them regarded the result. He certainly didn't look as if he was capable of killing anyone, just a frightened lad.

'That's the best we can do. At least he doesn't look like the drawing of McLaw the artist did at the trial. That's one mercy. I would have been happier if we could have dyed that hair, but with a close crop, he should get away with it. And a bath in the washhouse would not go wrong. Now the clothes. Follow me.'

Charlie went with him into the bedroom and removed the late Mr M's jacket and trousers. 'Put on these.' Faro handed him his second-best trousers, a good shirt and a reefer jacket. Lizzie knocked on the door.

Frowning he said, 'They're a little on the large side.' Charlie was less than six foot, but they would have to do.

Lizzie said: 'I'll turn up the trousers, that will help.'

The day was almost over. Lizzie and Vince, a silent observer of this transformation, sighed with relief that Faro knew was far too early. There was still a long way to go before they were out of this particular dark wood.

'I have to go in tomorrow, make some excuses to Gosse, and then as soon as it is dark we will leave.' And turning to

Charlie, he said sternly, 'Setting you on the road to freedom is against every vow I have ever made as a policeman. So make no mistake, this is for your . . . sister and the lad here. Even if you claim to be innocent of the murder of your wife, you are still guilty of Mr Molesby's demise.'

Charlie shook his head. 'The bookshop man. Vince told me about it. It was raining. The door was open and I took shelter. I was soaked through and I'd torn off the sleeve of my coat climbing a fence. I saw this coat and trousers over a chair – and I put them on. It was like a godsend. I was never anywhere but in the shop.' He shook his head. 'I guessed that he was in bed and asleep. If he was dead, then it had nothing to do with me. I have never killed anyone.'

Vince and Lizzie regarded Faro hopefully. He said coldly, 'If what you are saying is the truth, you are still a guilty man, you will go to prison for burglary – and be lucky if you are only transported.'

Charlie said, 'Mr Faro, I cannot thank you enough for all you are doing for me. I can never pay you back.'

'Indeed you can. By going away and never letting the police or us ever clap eyes on you again. That is all we ask of you,' he added heavily, and to Lizzie, 'Lie low, keep him out of sight and if you have any callers' – he pointed ceiling-wise to the trapdoor to the attic – 'put him up there and hide the ladder away.'

A prey to new and terrible anxieties, Faro made his way out of the cottage he loved so well, no longer a happy and contented family man, no longer counting these blessings, which had turned overnight to curses, with a happy marriage doomed to disaster and a young stepson's

142

future in hazard. And for the first time he realised he had not even given a single thought to that other burden fast approaching: Lizzie's long-awaited baby.

Praying that all this would not cause another miscarriage, he thought of Charlie's words as they went to their beds. As well as piling on words of gratitude, he had said: 'There is another solution to all this, sir.'

'Is there, indeed?' had been Faro's caustic response. 'Then I would like to hear it.' Charlie nodded slowly. 'There is a solution that would free all of us.'

'And what might that be?'

'Prove my innocence. Find the man who killed my Annie. Bring him to justice.'

CHAPTER SEVENTEEN

No one slept much that night, they felt as if a bombshell had burst on their cottage and blown the fabric of their lives apart.

Faro got up at dawn and walked out on to the hill, so lovely in its awakening, as if the whole world around him sleepily opened its eyes and yawned its way into another day. These were private moments he had learnt to treasure, moments of healing as if the great pagan gods who had once ruled the land were also awakening. Sometimes these ancient gods were easier to believe in, he felt ashamed to admit, than the Christian God.

Lizzie would have smilingly made excuses for him, saying that his old Viking ancestors as well as that selkie grandmother Sibella Scarth, with her strange legend, her webbed fingers and feet, had left their spell on him.

Do pagan gods provide guardian angels or guides, he wondered, or was that his mix-up of theological matters? If so, he desperately needed one just now.

God's will, the ministers would cry. On his rare visits to church Faro listened, but because of the nature of his life – the violence, the cruelty even the law exercised and excused, seeing a man hung by the neck until he was dead, still according to the Biblical ruling of an eye for an eye, and a life for a life – such actions were hard to reconcile with the god of love that Jesus Christ had promised in his Orkney Sunday school.

Dear God, help us.

He stood very still, looking towards the east, waiting as the first gleam of sunrise crept over the hill. So had many thousands of men from the earliest times of human habitation stood here on Arthur's Seat, watched and waited as he did, for the blessing of a new day, a new life. He remembered his joyous gratitude so many times for the blessing of Lizzie, and those other cruel mornings when, during the night, she had awoken in blood and tears to the heartbreak of loss that a hoped-for son or daughter for her beloved Faro would now never be born.

As the sun rose into its full glory he wondered, should he throw himself down on his knees and pray? He was going to need all the help he could get for what lay in store that day, for the task that went against his integrity, his fight for justice, smuggling a killer out of the hands of the law. But it had to be done, he told himself, he must put aside the rules that had governed his life, to save his marriage and to save Lizzie the heartbreak of seeing her brother hanged.

As for Vince, still innocent Vince, Faro knew that, somewhere close by, the truth of his nativity lurked uneasily. He guessed that Lizzie had saved the situation by talking in Gaelic with her brother, but when it was spelt out in the language they all understood, what then? Listening in horror and hearing that there never had been a brave soldier father, would Vince ever forgive his beloved mother for building his frail existence on a lie? A lie that had saved him. Would he understand or care that if she had abandoned him he would be now living in the poorhouse, one of countless unwanted children, with no future into adult life after harsh child labour?

Such was Faro's miserable torment as he walked up the High Street that morning. He needed time, time most of all, some excuse to have a few days' leave from the Central Office to smuggle Charlie out of Edinburgh, see him over the Border. Senior officers were privileged to have a week off each year given that they worked every day, and even the public holidays should an emergency arise – they had to be ready for action, day or night.

Would Gosse agree without making excuses that he was needed at this time? If only Macfie had not been away, he could have confided in him. Yet that must remain a secret. Macfie must never know, never be told since he would never consent to Jeremy Faro breaking the law, becoming an accessory to plotting the escape of a wanted man.

As he opened the office door to be assailed by its familiar daily smells, indefinable apart from tobacco smoke, aware that he had left behind a dangerous situation smouldering at the cottage, he braced himself against the inevitable: that every minute Charlie remained under the cottage roof put them all in danger.

In the office Gosse sprang from his desk, scattering papers in all directions.

'So you're here at last,' was his greeting, although the

church clocks had just struck eight. Gosse's colour was higher than ever, denoting a state of great excitement.

'I'm going to catch him, if it's the last thing I do.' He pointed to the desk, a rough poster of a bearded man and a description: 'John McLaw, wanted for two murders, who has escaped from the gallows. A reward of £50 for information leading to his recapture,' he read. 'Well, what do you think of that?' Gosse asked proudly.

Faro's eyes widened. 'Fifty pounds is a lot of money. Will the authorities provide?'

'Damn the authorities,' snapped Gosse. 'A fine mess they've made of it, so far.' Thumping the desk, he stared across at Faro, his eyes gleaming. 'This is my money, from my life's savings, and I'm willing to see it go. Aye, just for the joy of watching that bugger swinging at the end of a rope.'

And at that moment, Faro felt pity for Gosse, a man so obsessed that he could make such a sacrifice just to watch a man die. He thought with sudden compassion that maybe Gosse had little else to lose. His wife, supposedly looking after some sick relative for a short visit, hadn't been seen for more than a year. Gosse had shaken his head, hinted that, yes, she had been home briefly, but had to go back again to look after this sick relative who had no one else. But no one believed him; the truth was that Gosse's marriage had long been in ruins, there were not even children to cobble it together again. Now, for all intents and purposes, Gosse behaved as a single man, insinuating himself into the company of unmarried policemen, sharing their evenings of wine, women and song, believing that he charmed all the ladies of the town, despite his unattractive appearance, allied with an even more unattractive leering, which made younger constables wince.

147

He was flourishing the poster. 'I have given orders that this is to be distributed immediately everywhere, on every post in Edinburgh, with copies sent to every village in the Lothians. And the search is to begin again, right now.' He added, thumping the table again, 'Every constable to be out there, combing the district.'

Faro looked at him. He did not dare to speak his thoughts, that this was a waste of police time and in Gosse's case a waste of money. The constables would rebel, murmuring among themselves. As for the poster, a bearded man with a lot of unruly hair was hardly a distinguished or memorable appearance and soon every village would be able to produce a McLaw, know of someone answering to the description, or make a hopeful guess. With the lure of all that money, a fortune for the many, Faro guessed there would be queues of eager informants from far and near at the Central Office every morning.

He groaned inwardly at the hopeless waste of it all. At least as a senior officer, a detective sergeant, he would not be expected to join the constables combing the heath of Arthur's Seat – so dangerously near the cottage – searching for a long-vanished man. With a suppressed shudder, he drew himself up and asked the routine morning question.

'What are my duties for the day, sir?'

'I want you here,' he said, thumping the desk, 'here helping with enquiries, taking details as they come in, and then you are to follow them through, go out to every person in the neighbourhood or in the Lothians who has made a sighting, take constables with you and search every house, every barn, comb every blade of grass; as they say, leave no stone unturned.'

It was a humiliating task for his rank and both he and Gosse knew that, but Faro realised that it also opened a tiny door, a blessing in disguise, for it freed his movements from under Gosse's eye. He might invent a few sightings down the coast, of folks claiming the reward, inform Gosse that he was away to inspect them and make his own arrangements. A day or two was all he needed. And he was getting very good at lying.

The day seemed endless and he returned home with a heavy heart, which did not get any lighter when he opened the door. One look at Lizzie's face, her hand on her stomach, told of imminent disaster. His immediate thought was about the baby.

'Are you all right?' he said anxiously.

She smiled bitterly, shook her head. 'Of course, Jeremy. I'm fine – but it was awful. Mrs Brook called – there was someone following her, a man.'

'Who was he?' Surely it was too early for the wanted-man poster.

Lizzie shook her head. 'No one, just one of the builders needing water. Their supply had been cut off temporarily.'

Mrs Faro had become popular with the labourers, not only as a pretty woman, but a generous one, too. Often, if they called on her with some excuse, she would give them a batch of scones or some bread and cheese or, as in this case, also water from the rain barrel outside the cottage while their own supply was being repaired. The lads had soon realised they were on to a good thing and took it in turns to call at the cottage.

Lizzie was saying: 'Mrs Brook had a message for you. As soon as he saw the man, Teàrlach grabbed the ladder and climbed up into the attic, as you told him to.'

'The message?' he interrupted, hanging his coat behind the door, precipitated once again into the mystery of Agatha Simms's empty coffin and her sister's accident with a runaway carriage on the Mound, which sounded uncommonly like murder. Sighing, he was reminded of the promise he had made, an obligation he could well do without at the present moment.

Lizzie went on: 'Someone called Tibbie is coming to visit Mrs Brook and she wishes you to call at Sheridan Place and meet this lady the day after tomorrow between 10 and 11 in the morning.'

Faro breathed a sigh of relief. At least Tibbie was alive and might provide some useful information.

There was a groan from the fireside, the man in the armchair stirred and Faro realised that Charlie was resting his foot on a stool.

'I see you are taking your ease,' Faro said bitterly. 'Well, get all the rest you can. I hope to have you on your way tomorrow.'

Lizzie stared at him wide-eyed. 'He can't go anywhere tomorrow, Jeremy.' She pointed to his bandaged leg.

'I fell,' Charlie supplied.

'When Mrs Brook left, I was holding the ladder for him to come down,' Lizzie added with a look of anguish. 'But he missed his footing—'

'With my bad ankle – now the other one is damaged,' Charlie groaned.

Lizzie shook her head. 'I've done the best I can but he won't be able to walk for a day or two.'

Faro looked angrily at this criminal who was also his most

unwanted brother-in-law. As if there were not complications enough even for a man fit on both legs; but there was no way he could possibly transport Charlie out of Edinburgh, a wanted man with posters everywhere, now hobbling painfully on two sticks and who, despite Lizzie's nursing, needed attention from a doctor, if not the infirmary.

Vince came in, home from school, and the tale of woe was related to him, his anxious glances in his stepfather's direction said that he knew what was at stake. He regarded Charlie scornfully, without a scrap of sympathy for this new relative fate had thrust upon him. The pretend gypsy, a criminal on the run, who had told him a pack of lies and extracted a promise to hide him for a day or two and not tell his parents.

If only he had told them, he thought with infinite regret, if only he could turn the clock back, aware that by sheltering a wanted man he had put his mother's future in jeopardy. She might go to prison. He closed his eyes, trying to shut out that terrible vision, almost as terrible to contemplate was his stepfather's disgrace and the end of his life as a detective.

'There are posters everywhere on Calton Hill, outside the school and on lamp posts in Princes Street, all the way home,' he said. 'It's as well you shaved off his beard and his hair.'

Lizzie had done her best, but Faro and Vince tackled supper with less enthusiasm than it merited. Lizzie gazed fondly and anxiously at her brother, sighing and patting his arm, gentle actions that Faro resented bitterly, since he was the cause of their present calamity. She took away his unfinished plate and said anxiously:

'You're quite well, are you, Jeremy?'

151

He tried a consoling smile. 'Just not hungry, that's all.' He pointed to Vince. 'Someone else seems to have lost his appetite, no longer eating for two,' he said bitterly. 'That will be less of a strain on Lizzie's cooking our daily meals, to say nothing of the extra marketing and the expense involved,' he added with a scowl at Charlie, who seemed unperturbed by the shaky state of his future as well as the disaster he had brought on his sister and her family, showing a hearty appetite to make up for those meagre snacks during his sojourn in the stables.

In a desperate effort to get back on the rails of normality, trying not to think about the delays caused by Charlie's further accident, Faro helped Vince with his homework, while Lizzie resumed her knitting and paid all her attention to her brother as they caught up on events in their missing years. The pair, now so obviously brother and sister, were almost like twins in appearance, carrying on an animated conversation in Gaelic, making Faro realise even more forcibly than ever that this woman, sitting there smiling, carrying his child, was a stranger to him.

Occasionally they glanced in his direction without bothering to translate, lost in the past and presumably happier days of growing up together, with the reminiscences Faro could not hope and did not even wish to share.

Once Charlie, as if aware of his discomfiture and anxious to make amends, looked across at Faro and Vince. 'When I first met the lad there, I knew he reminded me of someone, the curly hair, something about his features.' And to Lizzie, 'I never saw you, only in the distance with a head shawl, but now I see he's your image.'

As Charlie could not climb the ladder, Vince would sleep

in the attic and Charlie would occupy the box bed in the kitchen, a safe refuge as its shutters, with a heart carved out in each (not merely a sentimental touch but also a means of ventilation) could be closed.

On his way along the Pleasance next morning, the postman, who always had a friendly greeting, met Faro. He flourished a letter. 'Glad to meet you. Here, take this. Save me a walk up to the cottage.'

Thanking him, Faro glanced at the writing. It was from his mother. He opened it and with feelings of foreboding, read her cheerful news. She would be arriving on Friday off the Orkney boat and expected him to meet her at Leith.

Four days' time. In the recent catastrophic events he had forgotten or merely pushed her imminent visit to the back of his mind – and his calendar. This was terrible, nothing short of another disaster.

How on earth could he deal with her insatiable curiosity, questions he and Lizzie had dreaded about Vince's supposedly dead hero father that now seemed a fraction less vital in the face of the present catastrophe? How were they to conceal Charlie's presence from her daily visits, or the fact that they were sheltering a murderer wanted by the police? He could see her smiling face, just dropping in on Lizzie to get to know her nice daughter-in-law better and to give her a hand in her delicate condition.

CHAPTER EIGHTEEN

Returning to the cottage, he handed Lizzie the letter. How would she take the news of her mother-in-law's arrival in four days' time? Expecting her to be horrified and upset, she merely smiled and said that she would be delighted to see her again, adding apologetically:

'Sorry we can't have her to stay with us, Jeremy, but she will be happy and well cared for at Sheridan Place. And I expect she will want to spend a lot of time here, as much as she can, I am sure.'

Faro looked at her. Had she not realised the complications of Charlie's presence, the situations that might arise, the explanations that would need to be made? How was Lizzie going to explain all that as merely a normal family visit from her brother?

That would never do for Mary Faro. She would ferry all manner of questions. When had they last met, had it been a long time between visits? Were there other siblings? And then she would want all the details of their

154

childhood home before Lizzie had left to get married.

He groaned. Marriage would extend the inquisition further, details about the soldier hero, Vince's father. How was Lizzie going to get over that hurdle with Vince listening to every word?

But worst of all was Charlie's identity. Mary was more interested in the details of her son Jeremy's career than his wife. Proud of him, by the time she had seen all those posters on the way from the port at Leith, she would be ready to bombard him with questions about this terrible criminal who had escaped and what were the police doing to catch such a man whose existence was putting all of Edinburgh in peril of their lives. She had sharp eyes. Would she see beyond the poster and recognise the man who was living under her son's roof?

With another interminable day on the horizon, Detective Sergeant Faro expecting a trail of informers at the police station, there were in fact only three. A man who pestered them regularly on all kinds of issues regarding matters he believed they were neglecting, now claimed to have seen McLaw lurking in his backyard, searching through his dustbin. So could he have the fifty pounds please?

Two frightened women followed him. One, from Fountainbridge, identified McLaw as this beggar who came to the door, asking her for money. She said he had threatened her and, terrified, she had slammed the door and had rushed to tell the police as fast as her legs could carry her. The other woman, from Granton, claimed that she had been staying with her daughter and last night they had seen McLaw sleeping huddled in one of the closes off the High Street. Yes, yes, these were definite McLaw sightings and all three ended with the same demand. Could they now have the reward money?

Faro sighed. It could have been worse. However, he did not doubt that there would be more tomorrow, followed by a tide of claimants. The news of that fifty pounds just hadn't had time to sink into the wilder reaches of the Lothians where there might be one to suit his purpose of an excuse to get McLaw on a train. He was grimly determined that, sprained ankles or no, Charlie had to go using a stick, and he was indifferent to the train's destination as long as it carried him as far away as possible from Edinburgh.

Sleepless nights were becoming commonplace and as he looked down at Lizzie, nestling close to his side, smiling gently as she slept, perhaps with happy dreams about that baby, he wondered if he would ever sleep without nightmares again.

At breakfast next morning, he told Lizzie he would be calling at Sheridan Place.

'Oh, in that case, you might take back this bowl she left with me.' Obviously curious about this Tibbie he was to meet through Superintendent Macfie's housekeeper, she added: 'Remember to tell her that your mother will be here on Friday. I hope that will give her enough time for her to prepare.'

Faro was reassuring. 'I'll give her your message, Lizzie. My visit is in connection with a missing person's case,' he said, and no more than that.

Mrs Brook had struck him as being the sort of person who could cope with any situation and her role in his mother's visit seemed negligible. At least he did not have to be ever vigilant each moment she was in the cottage that terrible revelations about the past – and present – might be revealed.

And then there was Charlie. They hadn't had time to give that due consideration, that keeping him out of sight and sound of his mother's informal daily visits would be impossible. No, somehow his presence had to be explained or his continual absence might arouse suspicions.

He walked past the scaffolding and the houses that were steadily arising to transform the old drove road and across through the pillars of Blacket Place. At least that area retained a quiet serenity reminiscent of an earlier world, when Edinburgh, as part of the Age of Enlightenment, took the cultured world by storm and Sir Walter Scott helped to move on the pace of history by engineering a visit from the monarch himself, King George IV. Faro always regretted that he had missed that event, still spoken of by his elders either in admiration or whispered derision, depending on their political outlook.

As he approached the gate of Sheridan Place, his footsteps rustled along pavements scattered with the first splashes of scarlet and yellow. Some of the abundant trees had already begun the yearly shedding of their heavy loads.

Ringing the bell, he took a deep breath. In a few moments he would be meeting Tibbie, Celia's maid, one of the missing pieces in the giant puzzle, like some maze in which he found himself searching for the right path.

Mrs Brook opened the door. Before she spoke a word in answer to his greeting, he knew by her expression that all was not well as he had hoped.

'Oh, come in, Mr Faro. I must apologise for taking

you into the kitchen.' As he followed her down the hall, there were stacks of boxes waiting to be opened and he remembered in sudden panic that the furniture had been scheduled to arrive while Macfie was still abroad. What if there was no guest bedroom available as yet, nor even a bed? That induced visions of going into the city and booking his mother into a hotel – and her rebellion at that. He could almost hear her voice: 'Why on earth can't I stay with you, Jeremy? Surely you can make room for me and save all this extra expense.'

Following her into the kitchen, well appointed and spacious, it was larger than their living room in the cottage. Mrs Brook went over to the window and stood clenching and unclenching her hands nervously.

'As you can see, sir, Tibbie hasn't arrived. She should have been here last night. I just don't understand it.'

Neither did he, if the information Mrs Brook had received was correct. The right day, for instance. But Tibbie's absence struck an ominous note of certainty that the woman had not willingly let Mrs Brook down and that something unexpected and probably quite dire had prevented her arrival.

Mrs Brook looked scared. 'There was no note from her. Nothing. She was coming from the house in Liberton. I don't know what to do.' She paused. 'Do you think I should go in search of her – would that help? Perhaps she is ill, alone in the house.'

Faro shook his head. He could not tell her that a visit to the Simms's house would be a waste of time and that wherever that note had come from, Tibbie had not written it in Liberton, remembering his reception at the empty house where a neighbour had seen her go off in a fine carriage with a gentleman.

He decided to keep that information to himself, information that would only terrorise Mrs Brook into the same sinister interpretations as his own.

He said as consolingly as possible, 'She may come yet. There is possibly some quite simple explanation for the delay. Try not to worry yourself, Mrs Brook.' And with relief he changed the subject. 'My mother is arriving on Friday, earlier than we expected,' he said apologetically. 'Of course, I realise that the house is not yet ready for visitors and perhaps it would be inconvenient for you to have her at this time, as the superintendent suggested,' he added, so that she might not feel guilty turning Mary Faro away.

'Oh, of course, of course, Mrs Faro is most welcome.' Mrs Brook managed to smile and for the moment push aside her anxiety about the non-appearance of Tibbie. 'The furniture has indeed arrived and has been installed, although as you no doubt noticed in the hallway, a lot of the effects remain to be unpacked. But I will have a room ready for your mother, Mr Faro, and a very comfortable one. Rest assured of that. A fire will be lit and the bed thoroughly aired.'

She regarded him, smiling. 'I shall have everything in readiness and I am so looking forward to having her here. It will be such a privilege to have your mother to look after, quite takes me back to my early days as a lady's maid,' she added.

Feeling considerably relieved that the problem he had imagined did not exist, indeed he took a moment to chide himself on getting rather overanxious these days, a frame of mind that was new to him. Perhaps its origins could be associated with the matrimonial state, one of the drawbacks of being a married man with a wife expecting their first baby.

That would be enough for most men, he thought grimly, without a wanted murderer living under his roof who also happened to be his brother-in-law. He wished again that he had someone in whom he could confide and that Macfie was home again, to offer advice. With all the superintendent's years of experience, surely he might see the way out of a situation that was beyond his own powers of finding any solution other than handing McLaw over to justice and thereby devastating the future of Lizzie, Vince and himself. Thanking Mrs Brook, he left, with thoughts of some amusement about how Mary Faro would be taken aback and even a little dismayed at being treated like a great lady, used as she was all these years to taking care of herself, as well as playing lady bountiful to the needy community in Kirkwall. However, kept blissfully unaware of the unseen dangers being concealed from her each day inside the cottage walls, the experience of being waited upon by the efficient Mrs Brook would be a change, and an undeniably pleasant one, in the elegant surroundings of Sheridan Place.

CHAPTER NINETEEN

'You don't believe him, do you, Jeremy?' Lizzie whispered as they prepared for bed that night, now the only time they had alone together since Charlie was always with them, a hovering uneasy presence, trapped in the house and ready to leap up and to stumble into the box bed at the slightest noise or hint of strangers.

It was not going to get any better, Faro decided, worse when his mother arrived, spending a lot of each day with Lizzie, waiting eagerly for his return from work and Vince home from school, envisaging a jolly family supper together, which she would doubtless help Lizzie prepare, making the most of a chance to boast her own excellent culinary skills.

Worst of all from Faro's point of view was the serious damage Charlie's presence was having on their marriage. In a few days this new and unwanted brother-in-law had managed to destroy their blissful existence, turn his contentment and hopes into suspicion, resentment and

161

deadly fears for the future. Maybe Lizzie was unaware, in the novelty of finding her brother long lost to her, of a dangerous chasm looming in her marriage. For Faro, it might already be too late and too difficult to regain the happiness he felt was crumbling away as he watched her spending so much time with Charlie. It seemed that her brother had suddenly become the centrepiece of her existence as they increasingly retreated into their native Gaelic, regaining those early years lost when Lizzie was fifteen and they were wrenched apart.

'You don't believe that he is innocent,' Lizzie's voice was sad as she climbed into bed. A sigh from Jeremy, whose expression she could not see in the darkness, and she added reproachfully, 'I hoped once you had met that you of all people would realise a terrible mistake had been made. That my Teàrlach – Charles – could not possibly be a murderer.'

'I have only the summary of the trial,' was the cold reply. 'That was the evidence against him and what the jury and the law decided.'

'The law! It is not always right, it can make mistakes too. You have said so yourself on many occasions.' She sat up. 'You have seen him, talked to him. You have seen many evil men in your time. Does he remotely resemble one of them? Answer me truthfully now.'

That was a difficult question, especially from a woman. No girl was willing to accept that her lover was a killer. No mother could ever believe she had produced a monster, or sister that she shared the blood of a killer.

As he could not bear to put that into words for Lizzie, he said gently, 'My dear, such men look like everyone

162

else, folk we pass by in the street and wouldn't give a second glance. They don't wear the brand of Cain—'

'You have looked into his eyes, tell me honestly, are they the eyes of a killer?' she interrupted shortly. That was true. His eyes were like hers. Hazel eyes, wide-spaced and appealing, almost too much so for a male countenance, he thought. His hair, which appeared as a rough, dark, unkempt mass on the wanted poster had revealed fair curls once identical to her own before they were carefully shaven off.

'Do I look like a killer, or does Vince?' she went on.

He took her hand, kissed it and drew her into his arms. Stifling a sob, she lay against his chest. 'Oh, my darling girl,' he sighed, 'what am I to do – what are we to do? My mother will soon be here. Don't you see the danger that puts us in? How are we going to explain his presence?'

She laughed. 'Dear Jeremy, that is easy. We have thought it out. An answer so simple I am surprised it hasn't occurred to you, especially as in a way it is true. My brother is visiting me from the Highlands, of course. On a short visit. Surely that is enough?'

'That he never goes out of doors—'

'He has an injured ankle.'

'He is young and strong, many men overcome such minor injuries by walking with a stick.'

· She ignored that and he added, 'I am warning you, my mother has a very curious nature. She will soon be asking what is wrong with him. Is he ill? Why is he always watching from the windows and rushing to hide when strangers approach the cottage?'

Lizzie was silent, thinking. Then she whispered: 'What are we going to do?'

'There is only one answer. And I have thought of that. I have got to get him away from here – somehow – and as soon as possible.'

'Jeremy, this is my brother,' she wailed. 'I don't want to lose him.'

'You have to lose him. Surely you realise he can't stay here indefinitely? Every moment of his presence puts us all in danger, even you, his beloved sister, who he would never want to cause any harm to.' He paused. 'Surely you have thought of the dreadful consequences? If Gosse found out, you would go to prison, Lizzie,' he reminded her again, and he added slowly, 'and I would lose my job, probably join you there. What about Vince? What future would there be for him? And this wee baby we're bringing into the world. What about him?'

'Her,' she said firmly, touching her stomach. 'I'm sure she's a girl.'

He shook his head in the darkness. He wished that was all their concern – whether it was a boy or a girl she carried.

In the silence that followed, he thought she slept, then a whisper.

'Jeremy. Are you awake?' He moved and she said, 'Teàrlach is innocent. I am certain of that, and you are the only one who can help to clear his name.'

The idea was ridiculous. Although Faro had read all those notes of the trial, he could not expect Lizzie to ever believe that her beloved brother was guilty.

'Please at least talk to him,' she whispered. 'At least let him tell you what really happened, then I think you will change your mind.'

He sighed. It was a forlorn hope indeed, but he said: 'If you wish.'

'I do wish, with all my heart.' A short silence, then a whisper: 'Do you still love me, Jeremy?'

'Of course I do, my dear. What a question.'

'Then, please, do this for me, for us all. For Teàrlach and Vince and our wee girl, waiting to come into the world. Find who killed poor Annie. I know she cheated on him, but she didn't deserve that.'

In the Central Office, Faro had another day dealing with a new set of people from the environs of Edinburgh, all prepared to swear that, yes, it was definitely McLaw they had seen and could they have that fifty pounds please. There were none as yet from further afield with plausible reports that he could give Gosse as a reason for going out to interview them and putting into action his own plan of setting Gosse's most wanted man on a train to freedom and, God willing, out of their lives for ever.

He returned weary at the end of the day and could only shake his head at their anxious looks and frantic queries about what was to be done. Lizzie reported one scary moment that day when the beat constable had called. At the sight of the helmeted uniform, Charlie had been terrified and leapt into the box bed.

PC Oldfield had known Faro a long while and he thoroughly approved of his pretty young wife, who was calling the dog, Coll, inside as it was raining heavily. Water was dripping off his helmet and after a friendly greeting she realised she could hardly rush in and close the door without offering him shelter and a cup of tea. In anguish, she sat at the table feeding him scones and trying to keep up a cheerful conversation about the building activities while keeping an anxious eye on the box bed. What if Charlie coughed or sneezed and Oldfield heard?

Would the rain never cease? It did at last and no one had ever been as thankful as Lizzie, whose prayer had been answered as she watched him head off towards the Pleasance.

She had Faro's sympathy for that anxious half-hour and he fully understood the terror she had endured. Safe today, but for how much longer would their luck hold? Mary Faro would be with them tomorrow.

There was a moon that night and Charlie was desperate to breathe some fresh air and exercise his ankle. He had to go out. He said he would take his stick and stay close to the cottage.

Faro followed him and they walked together in silence.

'I am not ungrateful for your company,' Charlie said. 'I realise this is not for pleasure but just that you do not wish to let me out of your sight, although it seems unlikely that I could run away. I am still rather lame, as you can see, and you would most certainly catch up with me if I even attempted to do so.'

Faro ignored that and as they returned he indicated the garden wall. They sat down together with Arthur's Seat gleaming ghost-like before them.

Charlie was nervous and ill at ease in this formidable brother-in-law's presence, surprised and suspicious about this desire for his company.

Faro lit a pipe and offered him a smoke, which he declined. 'Never got that habit, I'm afraid. Tried it once and couldn't see the point of it.'

After some preliminaries regarding the state of his ankle, Faro asked:

'About your trial. Why did you never make an effort to establish the identity of your wife's lover?'

Charlie shrugged and Faro went on: 'You know that was one of the main factors that went against you with the jury. The question was asked repeatedly but you had no answers beyond "not guilty" and they concluded the reason was that you struck the fatal blow yourself.'

Charlie said slowly, 'I was innocent. What was more important than finding the guilty man was proving my innocence.'

'You hardly went about it in an efficient way; the jury found it easy to read what seemed like indifference as guilt.'

'I am innocent, ' Charlie said firmly, adding 'sir', having not yet the inclination or the feeling that it was right and proper to establish the relationship of kinship with the policeman whose job it was to hunt him down and see him hang.

'Very well, first of all prove it to me.'

'And how, pray, am I to do that?'

Faro sighed. 'I was away from Edinburgh and missed most of the trial but I have read the records of it, all the evidence. I want you to go through what happened on that fatal evening, step by step.'

Charlie sighed and thought for a moment. 'I had been out, drinking, I'm afraid – and rather too much, as usual. If I could avoid it, until I ran out of money, I rarely came home sober.'

'Where did you do your drinking?'

'At the local, of course. The Coach and Horses. The

167

landlord is – was – Annie's stepfather. When it closed I was thrown out, as usual. Always last to leave and reluctant to stagger home – our croft was on the edge of the Belmuirs' estate, the old woodcutter's cottage, and I did a bit of gardening for them and at the poorhouse.'

'What was your main employment at that time?'

The moon had disappeared behind a cloud and in the darkness Charlie shrugged. 'Odds and ends, I had no proper job. Got what I could find, labouring on the railway line, gardening, like I said – that was about it.'

'How did you manage to survive?'

'Annie helped. She did her bit, as a kitchen maid and from other sources that I did not go into.' He paused, his voice bitter.

'You mean she was living as a prostitute.'

Faro felt rather than saw him wince. 'If you call it by that fancy name. She had one or two rich men, or so I gathered, willing to pay well for her favours.'

'So this lover could have been any one of them.'

Charlie shrugged. 'And for obvious reasons, he wasn't going to come forward with his name. If Annie even knew it. They came for an hour or so, paid her for her service and away again. This was a one-woman business,' he added grimly, 'and she was good at it. Besides, it saved them the trip into Edinburgh. I doubt if she even knew their names – friends of friends, that sort of thing.'

This was bad news. Small wonder Charlie had realised the hopeless task of trying to identify the man who was her client that night.

'Then if he was one of many, and her activities were presumably well known locally, why kill her?'

168

Charlie did not answer and Faro went on: 'Let me put to you possible reasons. Was this someone you both knew? Perhaps he hadn't visited before, this was the first time, a new experience. What if he was a popular local man, highly thought of in the community, with a reputation of respectability, like a doctor or a minister?' Pausing for a moment, he continued thoughtfully: 'Timid and scared that you would recognise him and give him the good hiding he deserved – or worse, tell his wife. So in a panic that all would come out and be revealed, he lost his nerve, got in first, and according to your story knocked you out.' He let that sink in. 'Tell me, what can you recall? Anything about him.'

At his side Charlie rubbed his head, as if he still remembered the blow. 'He wasn't anyone I recognised but then it was dark and I was very drunk. There was no candlelight either. I doubt he was a timid man. He was taller, stronger than me, your height, and he just leapt at me. I knew he was naked – you know the feeling of someone naked – the smell of sex. When he hit me, I heard Annie yell at him but he never said a word, just a big fist coming at my face, knocking me down. I heard Annie scream again as I hit the ground.'

He paused. 'I don't know how long I lay there unconscious. It had been quite some blow, and when I opened my eyes I felt a bump on my head that was going to turn into a mighty bruise. Some time must have passed, I had come in after midnight and now it was getting light, dawn was breaking. I felt chilled to the bone. I got to my feet and I smelt blood.' Again he paused, said slowly: 'And there was Annie, lying on the floor beside me. I was

169

confused. I thought she must be asleep but why was she not in bed?' He took a deep breath.

'Then I saw the knife, sticking in her chest. I dragged it out, perhaps she was only hurt. But no, she was dead and already cold. I didn't know what to do. I ran into the kitchen. There was a trail of blood from the bedroom, I slipped once or twice and almost fell. I poured water over my head, tried to think straight about this man who had killed her.'

He shook his head. 'But I was sober now and I knew even as I rushed out to find someone to help, which was too late, and to tell the local constable, that I would get the blame. Everyone who knew Annie's reputation would put together the obvious story. I had come home very drunk, found her with a man, discovered I was living with a whore and had enough of it, lost my temper and killed her. In everyone's opinion it was as simple as that.'

He sighed again, closing his eyes, shutting out that terrible scene. 'I went to Annie's stepdad. He said nothing, handed me a drink, and told me to stay where I was. I thought he had some plan to help me, but he came back grim-faced with the local constable who took one look at me covered in blood. Next thing I knew I was in handcuffs in the local lock-up waiting for the first train to be taken into Edinburgh.'

Faro waited until he regained his breath and then asked. 'The knife?'

'Carving knife, from the kitchen.' The man must have run into the kitchen, seized the knife and returned with it, but Faro still did not understand why he had bothered to kill a well-known local prostitute. There had to be

170

something other than his reputation at stake, such as a very jealous wife.

'I need to ask you this,' Faro said delicately. 'Was there any possibility that she was carrying . . . disease? Syphilis, for instance,' he added, imagining the consternation of wives with roving husbands if she was spreading that about the village.

'I doubt that. Never wanted children – she used to laugh and say all men were careless but she had ways and means of avoiding pregnancy. Very meticulous about washing herself down there after I'd been with her, much more than most respectable women, I imagine, since she had too much to lose – her nice steady income.'

If this was true, then it sounded as if her killer had some urgent personal reason for wanting to get rid of Charlie and used this as a great opportunity.

'Was it someone you knew? Someone you might have made an enemy of?'

Charlie laughed. 'I had no enemies that I knew of. They were all my mates, drinking companions, and I had never tried to seduce their wives or sweethearts, if that is what you are hinting. They all knew about Annie and imagined I had plenty of that at home with an oversexed wife to want any on the side,' he added grimly. 'And I'm ashamed to say they knew that I wasn't objecting to her helping to keep a roof over our heads and a wastrel husband in drink. That was her hold over me.'

Faro was visualising the scene. A sordid murder case. The kind that the police knew only too well, with a few subtle differences. The married pair were well aware of each other's shortcomings. As Charlie condoned his wife as a prostitute, there was no necessity to kill her. She was, in fact, the goose laying the golden egg, keeping him in drink and an easy-living style between occasional jobs. That was what held the marriage together.

What about the other people, the shadowy ones offstage? Apart from the killer, her stepdad and his mates, who knew all about Annie?

'Did she have any family?'

'A married sister, a nurse at the poorhouse. Nora is very respectable, a pillar of the church and the women's guild, bitterly ashamed of Annie's behaviour letting down the family, in common parlance she refused to let her darken their door.'

Faro made a mental note. This was one to interview. Nora might be the kind who absorbed local gossip and enjoyed relating it to her friends.

'Did she get on well with her stepfather?'

'Well enough. He had an older son from his first marriage.'

Faro remembered the young man he had talked to at the inn. A handsome stepson. That was an interesting possibility. As if Charlie read his mind, he laughed. 'I know what you're thinking. But Frank has an invalid wife, they've been married for years and he's devoted to her.'

Devoted or no, that was another interesting possibility. Another reason for not being found out. Faro frowned, his mind was racing back over Charlie's details of the scene of the crime. The picture that Charlie's return to consciousness had evoked. All those bloodstains between the kitchen and the bedroom. None of these details had been recorded in the police report – merely that she had been found in the bedroom, lying on the floor with a knife in her chest.

Now a very different pattern was emerging. After her client had knocked Charlie out, Faro imagined him hastily dressing and pushing Annie aside, hurrying through to the kitchen, presumably on his way out of the house. Had Annie, enraged, followed him, perhaps in his eagerness to escape, he was forgetting to pay her, something like that? She had tried to stop him leaving, even going as far as seizing the carving knife and threatening him. A struggle, but a big, strong man, according to Charlie's description of him, he had turned it on her. Perhaps he had never meant to kill her but there she was, lying with a knife in her chest. He panicked, had to think of something fast and he had the answer, dragged her back into the bedroom and put her down beside Charlie. The perfect and obvious answer that the police would accept. Her husband had come home, found her with a man and killed her.

Charlie was watching him. It was growing cold, a fine drizzle like a requiem to his wretched unhappy tale was drifting down from the top of the hill. At last he said:

'You're very silent, sir. Do you believe me now – that what I have told you is the God's honest truth?'

Faro sighed. 'None of these details were reported in the summing up of the evidence.'

'Would it have changed the verdict, do you think?' Charlie asked eagerly.

'It might well have done so.' He had no intention of telling Charlie what he thought might have happened, but this murder was a sordid domestic case with elements all too familiar in police records. 'Get it over with and have a hanging,' avoiding unnecessary delays by suppressing prisoners' statements, was Gosse's motto.

What calamity of destiny had brought Charlie to Edinburgh?

'What brought you here?'

Charlie laughed. 'I can hear it in your voice – anywhere but here. Sorry about that, sir.'

'What did you leave – what about your parents?'

Charlie seemed surprised. 'Ealasaid has not told you?'

'Not a word, nothing about her past – before . . . before Vince.'

'Poor Ealasaid. They were so cruel to her.' Pausing for a moment as if remembering that terrible revelation, he went on. 'We had a relentless, God-fearing father and he died of apoplexy the year after . . . after that. He was preaching at the time and everyone reckoned he had gone straight to heaven. Mother always regretted Ealasaid being sent away, but there was nothing she could do to persuade Father that it was wrong, that what had happened was not their daughter's fault, that the guilt lay at the laird's door. Anyway, she had never been very strong – she took consumption, and after she died three years ago, among her things I found a letter to me from Ealasaid. It said that she was now in Edinburgh and would I get in touch with her.' He sighed. 'Ealasaid tells me there were other letters to me, scores of them, through the years but they had been destroyed by father.

'It made my decision; suddenly I had to get away, I was weary, had enough of struggling to make a living on that croft for my mother and I. Always fascinated

174

by railways and trains, I wanted to be part of that new world, so I made up my mind: better to be a labourer than a poor farmer scratching a living. I had to find Ealasaid and suddenly that was important, like the fulfillment of a dream. I can spare you the details of how I got to Fisherrow, met and married Annie. The lusts of the flesh, drinking and gambling had been born in me, I'm afraid, waiting to make sure of my downfall. I had never been in love before, hardly knew any lasses and Annie seemed like the love of my life I had been waiting for. No one ever told me, just smirked behind my back, about the devil she was. Well, more drinking to forget, lost my job. You know the rest.'

He sighed and said sadly, 'So now, too late, I've found Ealasaid who could have redeemed me. Even as a child, she was always a good influence.'

The door of the cottage opened, a light shone across the yard and Lizzie called, 'Come in, you two. You'll catch your deaths sitting out there in the cold.'

Since death had been the subject of their conversation both men managed a weary smile.

'Coming, Lizzie.'

'Thank you, sir, for believing in me.'

'I wouldn't go quite that far yet. We have to prove it to the police. And stop calling me sir, will you?' he added wearily. 'My name in the family is Jeremy.'

Following him indoors, Faro recognised that in this intimate conversation, Charlie had revealed much about himself. In fact, he had got to know more about his brother-in-law in half an hour than he had learnt about his wife since their first meeting and all their time together as husband and wife. He had not even known that Lizzie's name was not Elizabeth but Ealasaid, until Charlie informed him.

But now, in addition to those other problems, there was a new and vital one with no time for delay. If what he had heard this evening was right in every detail – and his gut feeling was that this was the true story of Annie's murder – with so much flimsy evidence, how could he possibly prove Charlie's innocence and set all of them free?

CHAPTER TWENTY

'What on earth have you two been on about, out there in the cold?' Lizzie asked.

Charlie laughed and said something in Gaelic. Lizzie's eyes widened, her eyes filled with tears as she rushed across and put her arms around Jeremy, hugging him. 'There, I told you, now you see he is innocent.'

That, Faro decided, was taking it a bit far as she added, 'You are a clever detective, now all you have to do is to prove it.' Again that assumption, as if it would be an easy matter before Faro had even begun to outline the difficulties. He would need to go right back to the beginning, before Annie's murder. He thought of all those clients anxious to remain anonymous, one of whom was her killer, and that made a search for the legendary clue in a haystack simple by comparison.

He would start with her sister Nora, a nurse at the poorhouse, which might lead to some of the gardeners and railwaymen, possible mates of Charlie's. A very slight thread, like Ariadne's through the Minotaur's maze, but perhaps a nod in the right direction of also establishing what had happened to Agatha Simms's remains, which now seemed somewhat irrelevant in the search for Annie McLaw's killer. Or was he back at the very beginning and this a tiny knot to unravel another murder – if murder it was – that of Tibbie's mistress Celia?

And to cap it all, where was Tibbie and why had she failed to meet up with Mrs Brook? Was Tibbie connected with the poorhouse? Was she the lame woman, the one he had seen being forcibly restrained from boarding the train from Musselburgh – the one described by the railwayman as 'one of their loonies'?

Such were his gloomy thoughts amid the air of family celebration around him. Vince still regarded Charlie with a modicum of suspicion, angry that he had been fooled into believing that story about the gypsy camp and Charlie's escape from a forced wedding, but most of all Charlie making him promise to remain silent was hardest to forgive, especially when it also put his mother and his stepfather in danger from the law for sheltering a killer.

But Lizzie was jubilant and oblivious; as far as she was concerned, they were in the clear and her clever Jeremy had listened to Teàrlach and understood. He would put this particular Humpty Dumpty together again, find Annie's killer and proof of his innocence would bring about a 'happy-ever-after' end like the romantic novels she relished.

Faro, watching her, tried but failed to echo the laughter, the relief. Poor Lizzie, did she not realise even after her own tragic story that life was not like that and reality provided for most people, not happy endings, but compromise, taking and accepting what the dice, fate or God, whichever you believed, had directed your way?

All he had when he started off next morning back to the Central Office was the terror of a wanted man hiding from the law, concealed under the roof of his cottage, a brother-in-law he now felt might be telling the truth, or was he just being hopeful that he could prove his story?

Remembering other crimes that he had solved, crimes that in retrospect seemed easy because he had only himself to put in danger, sometimes emerging with a narrow escape from death and a bullet or knife wound as a permanent souvenir, he sighed deeply. He had been a single man then, not married with a wife and stepson in jeopardy, aware that they were breaking the law and, if they were found out, would go to jail. And his disgrace would follow, the end of his career with the Edinburgh City Police.

He thought with uncharacteristic envy and lack of compassion how easy and simple it would have been had McLaw, guilty as charged, been taken to prison and in due course hung by the neck. As for Lizzie, she hardly ever looked at the newspapers, relying on Faro to read her any news of interest, avoiding horrible crimes. She skirted round such matters even if her husband had been eager to discuss the details, the solving of which added up to their daily bread. It was as if their mention might cling and somehow sully the atmosphere of their dear little cottage. But what if she had known that John McLaw was in fact Teàrlach, the beloved brother she had not seen for fifteen years?

As he was walking up the High Street a hansom carriage with its coat of arms passed him and stopped a few yards ahead. The passenger opened the window, glanced briefly in his direction and then moved on.

He had a glimpse beneath the large hat of long dark hair, the woman who at first glance so resembled Inga St Ola. Would that sight never cease to send his heart racing, even after so many more urgent matters that needed his attention? The woman was readily identifiable as Lady Belmuir, doubtless on one of her shopping visits to the city.

As he entered the office, Gosse was sitting at his desk behind a mound of papers, plus a weighty addition of what were now daily reports of sightings of McLaw and claims to that reward. He pushed some over to Faro.

'See what you make of this lot. I'd appreciate your comments.'

Faro picked them up, some were ill-written, hardly legible. Today he had twelve in his hand, from near and far, from the city limits to Peebles, but all began the same: 'I have seen this wanted man in our village/ street/church/inn/garden and I am claiming the reward of fifty pounds.'

'When you've read these – they're the most legible – there's another ten.' Gosse groaned. 'It's like a flood every day now. You can't do them all and we haven't enough constables for the local ones. Most are rubbish, anyway.'

Was the inspector beginning to regret that poster, which had instigated such a flood? Faro refrained from gently reminding him that he should have recognised that this would be the inevitable result. Surely he knew enough of the greed of mortal men and women to realise that the enticement of an indifferent illustration of a wanted man, rough-looking with a beard, and the promise of fifty pounds on delivering him to the local police would produce an avalanche of claims.

'Where would you like me to start today, sir?' Faro had noticed one from Dalkeith, the end of the local railway between Edinburgh and Fisherrow. He handed it to Gosse. It was better written and would provide the excuse he needed to drop off the train at the poorhouse and talk to Annie's sister, Nora, as well as making some enquiries about the missing Tibbie.

Gosse glanced briefly at the letter and skimming through the claims, said, 'You might as well take these other two and do Fisherrow on the way back. You can take the train but you'll need to do it on your own. I cannot spare any of the lads, they had better concentrate on those close by,' he added with some relish, doubtless anticipating the inconvenience and humiliation that would cause his sergeant, little guessing that, this time, he had behaved exactly as Faro wished.

About to part company, they were interrupted by a constable at the office door. 'Sir, there is a lady here wishing to speak to DS Faro urgently.'

Faro looked up. Was this Mrs Brook here to report Tibbie as a missing person? Gosse nodded tight-lipped, and gave him an angry look. He had a different interpretation, about to give Faro a right telling-off if this was his wife here again keeping him from his duties.

But it was neither Mrs Brook nor Mrs Faro.

'Lady Belmuir, sir,' announced the constable as he was pushed aside to admit a vision, emerging in a cloud of perfume, beneath a large hat and a velvet cloak.

Gosse leapt to his feet, bowed extravagantly. 'Your Ladyship—'

He got no further. The laird of Belmuir turned her back on him and swept round to face Faro whose acknowledging bow was less extravagant than that of his superior who was looking open-mouthed, clearly taken aback by this aristocratic visitor from the ranks of the gentry.

She pointed to Faro. 'It's you I wish to see.'

Gosse, speechless, stared from one to the other. How were these two acquainted and how dare she ignore him, addressing his sergeant as if they were alone together and Inspector Gosse did not exist?

'Mr Faro,' she was saying, 'I am here to report a robbery from my town house, in Moray Place.'

Tall for a woman, they were almost eye to eye, both a good six inches taller than Gosse, who was not impressed and interrupted:

'If you please, Your Ladyship, this is my province, not my sergeant's.' That was a lie, to start with. It was usual to report such incidents to the constable seated behind the main desk inside the main entrance.

Gosse had recovered from the imagined insult, pulled himself to his full height and, bowing, smiled: 'I am Detective Inspector Gosse, and I will immediately attend to Your Ladyship's report of this incident.'

'Report,' snapped that lady. 'It's more than that. I am Belmuir and a valuable painting has been stolen, a priceless Leonardo, been in the family for countless years.'

Gosse, whose neck was rising rather red above his collar, was sweating slightly as, with another bow, he motioned a seat to Belmuir. She stared at it contemptuously, preferring to remain standing where she could overshadow this menial.

He cleared his throat, another bow. 'Detective Sergeant Faro will take the details, Your Ladyship.' Ignoring him, she swivelled round to face Faro, who took out a notebook, preparing to take down the details of when and how, etc.

'Proceed, Faro, what are you waiting for?' Gosse snapped, and with another bow, 'This will not, I hope, delay Your Ladyship,' he added with a gulp, for this was gentry in his office, almost royalty and an exquisite lady to boot. Here was a chance to prove his efficiency and, more than that, exert all his charisma on the female sex. What a chance! Imagination flashed a momentary glimpse of the future, of sitting at the dinner table by the side of this graceful, gorgeous creature. What woman could ever resist him, he decided, as he said:

'I will be honoured, Your Ladyship, to take on this case for you and handle it personally.'

'Honour be damned,' she snapped, eyeing him coldly. 'Find the thief, that is what I want. Put him in jail and get me back my picture, if he hasn't disposed of it already.'

Gosse bowed again, even closer to the ground this time.

'Come on, man, look smart. And be quick about it.'

Temporarily ignored and regarding the scene through narrowed eyes, Faro was aware of surreptitious glances in his direction that said this was not the outcome Belmuir had wanted.

He felt almost sorry for Gosse, put at such a disadvantage, the detective inspector called 'man' and ordered about like a lower servant at the castle. He sighed; yes, having witnessed this humiliation before a member of

183

the aristocracy, Gosse would doubtless make him pay in due course. It was beginning now.

'Well, Faro, what are you waiting for? You have work to do,' Gosse said in poor imitation of Her Ladyship's voice of authority.

'Your Ladyship.' Faro inclined his head, not as a servant, a gentleman's mere inclination of the head. And clutching the batch of letters, he left them, aware that Belmuir would eat Gosse alive, and as he walked down the corridor, he would have liked to have been invisible, following them down to Moray Place, feeling almost sympathy for Gosse's grovelling attempts to ingratiate himself by doing a mere constable's work of recording details of a robbery.

Despite taking to his heels down the High Street, by the time he reached the Pleasance, it was too late and he had missed the train to Dalkeith. The afternoon one would delay him and was considerably less convenient for his plan. He had better spare Lizzie's tendency to worry that he might not be home until very late and tell her not to keep supper for him. He had not yet succeeded in assuring her that such delays were not because some disaster had overtaken him and only hoped and trusted that her excessive apprehension would end with the arrival of the new baby; that the anxieties of motherhood would overcome those of a husband facing a policeman's normal daily hazards.

Frustrated by his attempts to begin enquiries, he decided to call on Mrs Brook and see if there was any news of Tibbie.

There was none. Mrs Brook's anxious face as she opened the door told him all he needed to know. She asked if she could report Tibbie as a missing person. Shaking her head dolefully, she whispered: 'I am sore afraid something has befallen her.'

Those were Faro's thoughts too. But after all, she knew nothing of Tibbie, they had only met once and the police might just push it aside as unimportant. Also, this anxious woman was not a relative. There was no family connection that she knew of and this Tibbie might have just forgotten, or for some other reason decided not to visit the housekeeper at Sheridan Place. Perhaps she had given a message to a young lad in the street, saying this was an urgent note to deliver – but as often happened, the would-be messenger, eagerly pocketing the penny, had cheerfully gone on his way.

All Faro could do was to advise her to leave it for a day or two and when he came back from his enquiries, where he hoped to see the inside of the poorhouse, there might be some news.

Mrs Brook reminded him that all was now in readiness for his mother's visit. She repeated anxiously that she hoped Mrs Faro would find the room comfortable and the bed well aired.

At the cottage Lizzie said anxiously: 'Try not to be too delayed, Jeremy. Remember when your mother arrives, Charlie doesn't need to hide. He is my brother from the Highlands. We haven't met for some time, and he was heading south to work on the Borders. Unfortunately he sprained his ankle.'

She had it all prepared. She had already altered Jeremy's second-best trousers and shortened the sleeves of the jacket to make him look respectable. Faro mentally crossed his fingers and hoped it would work. He had to leave it to

Lizzie to keep his mother's well-known curiosity at bay and he was thankful that at least the brother and sister could retreat into Gaelic, a foreign language she wouldn't understand, if imminent danger threatened.

However, it was with a heavy heart and a sense of foreboding that he went down to the Pleasance to find that the train was delayed. There had been a fallen tree on the line and there would be nothing until tomorrow. The whole service was disrupted.

CHAPTER TWENTY-ONE

It was very fortunate that Faro was still at home next morning, as with breakfast over, he was preparing to go to take the early train to Fisherrow when the sound of a carriage arriving and approaching footsteps had Charlie leaping back into the box bed and closing the shutters.

'Who on earth—'

Faro opened the door and Mary Faro flung herself into his arms. Hugs and kisses exchanged with Lizzie, she said crossly:

'I thought you were coming to meet me, Jeremy. I had to take a hiring cab,' she said, following him into the kitchen. 'Why weren't you at Leith when the ship docked?'

'Mother – wait a moment. When you said eight o'clock, I presumed you meant evening.'

'Of course I didn't,' she snapped. 'I stayed on the ship overnight.'

Faro sighed. 'You might have made that clear.'

'Never occurred to me, thought you'd remember that

187

after all your trips home.' Discarding her cloak, she set down her luggage. 'Anyway, I'm here now.' No longer interested in reproaching Jeremy, her fond smiles were for Lizzie. 'How are you, my dear?' And with a downward glance. 'All well with the wee one?'

'Yes, I'm very well,' and patting her increasingly rounded stomach, Lizzie whispered: 'And so is she.'

Her mother-in-law asked the obvious question. 'How do you know?' She was hoping for a grandson.

Lizzie merely shook her head and smiled. 'Have some breakfast. You must be hungry.'

'I ate early, on the ship while it was unloading. But I'd love a cup of tea.' And sitting down at the table, Mary looked from one to the other. 'You both looked very startled when I came in. Is there something wrong?' she added anxiously.

Faro avoided Lizzie's eyes and patted his mother's hand. 'Of course not. It's good to have you – any time.'

Always sensitive to atmospheres, Mary frowned. 'What about this place where I'm supposed to be staying. Is it going to be all right?'

Faro explained that it was a very nice house just a short distance away. The home of his great friend Superintendent Macfie who she would remember had looked after Vince while he and Lizzie had been in Orkney with her on their honeymoon. The gentleman was abroad at present but his housekeeper would look after her.

Far from the complaints he had expected, she sounded impressed and grateful. 'Will you take me, Jeremy? I could have gone straight there in the cab, but thought it was better to have an introduction.' She looked around appraisingly. 'This is such a pretty little house.' And pointing triumphantly to the box bed. 'I could have slept in there, you know—'

'Not nearly comfortable enough,' Faro said quickly.

Further explanation was mercifully cut short as the trapdoor to the attic opened and Vince emerged. Coming down the ladder, he looked anxious too, and then saw it was a lady sitting at the table, not the police here to apprehend the man who was his Uncle Charlie concealed in the box bed.

Mary held out her hand, smiling. 'So this is Vince. I'm your grandma, glad to meet you. And what a fine young lad you are.'

He went to her side and kissed the proffered cheek with just a mite of embarrassment, while over her head he exchanged an anguished glance with Lizzie and Faro.

'You're sleeping up there? It can't be very comfortable.'

Vince would have heartily agreed, seeing there was hardly room to stand upright, but Faro's glance at Lizzie, his slight nod, indicated that this was the time for explanations.

Lizzie said hastily, 'We have a visitor just now, Mother. My brother Charlie is with us. He looked in unexpectedly on his way down from the Highlands, to a job with the railways in Carlisle. Went for a walk on the hill out yonder and unfortunately sprained his ankle—'

'Where is he?' Mary asked sharply.

Lizzie pointed to the box bed and whispered. 'He's occupying it at present. Couldn't climb the ladder, which is why Vince had to go up to the attic. He's still asleep,' she added, a finger to her lips.

Faro groaned inwardly. What a situation. The best he

189

could do was to remove his mother as soon as possible, let Lizzie sort it out with Charlie and together cobble a convincing story. One that would have to be very good indeed, since Mary was a very sharp lady; in fact, he rather suspected that he had inherited his abilities as a detective, his intuition regarding clues, directly from her.

As they headed towards Sheridan Place, Mary walked blithely at his side, chattering all the while about how lovely Lizzie was and how lucky he had been to find such an excellent wife after all her misgivings that he was to die a bachelor after all, and she would never see a grandchild. Vince, too, came in for high praise, a delightful boy, so handsome. Faro hoped she wasn't going to ask about his hero father but she skipped on, and a keen gardener, was making helpful suggestions about what they might plant.

His responses were automatic, a nod, and a yes or no, with only vague ideas of what she was talking about, his mind heavily engaged on other vital matters like how he was to get Charlie out of Edinburgh, while his mother cheerfully reorganised the cottage with firm recommendations on 'what I would do if I were you', such as building extensions to make best use of all existing space.

Did he think Lizzie would approve? Domestic improvements were well past his concern in a shaky future, as Mary stopped in her tracks to view the scaffolding and the busy workmen with a disapproving eye, particularly the crumbling stones that were all that remained of Lumbleigh House.

'Why doesn't someone stop them? A horrid terrace of four-storeyed houses, just a blot on the horizon.' She shuddered and shook her head. 'I can tell you our Kirkwall authorities would never have allowed such desecration, spoiling the landscape.'

Faro let her go on unchallenged, useless to try to intervene and explain that the slums of the High Street and the elegant New Town mansions were no longer adequate to house Edinburgh's constantly growing population, and the city boundaries had to be extended out of necessity into the countryside beyond the south side.

There was one nasty moment when Mary spotted the wanted poster attached to the lamp post newly erected on what would be the new Dalkeith Road.

She paused to look at it and exclaimed in horror. 'This dreadful man is still roaming about? How awful.' She shuddered. 'And there's Lizzie alone all day at the cottage. I hope you are safe enough with a killer on the loose. We don't want to be murdered in our beds.'

Thinking of the irony of it all, with the murderer hiding asleep just yards away in the box bed, he made reassuring murmurs about the cottage being watched over, having police protection.

Mary frowned. 'I hope you'll catch him soon.'

'We're on to it, Ma. Don't you worry,' he said, escorting her across the road where she waxed lyrical over the charm of a lodge with gates that could be locked each evening. The garden of Macfie's new home also met with approval, while Faro eyed the closed door with considerable anxiety.

It was opened by Mrs Brook who managed to conceal her surprise at this unexpected arrival with a welcoming smile for Mary Faro. Behind the back of the newcomer she ushered inside, a shake of the head confirmed Faro's fears about the missing Tibbie, as he listened to the footsteps of the two women ascending the stairs to the waiting guest room.

Mrs Brook left the visitor to unpack, saying she would be making a cup of tea. Downstairs, Faro was looking out of the window and she whispered: 'Not a word from Tibbie. Something must have happened to her. What can you do about that, sir?' she added anxiously. He shook his head. The answer was, not a lot.

Observing Mrs Brook's distress, he said: 'You can go into the police office and tell them you were expecting a friend who has not arrived and you think something has happened to her. They will listen and want her address and personal details, description and so forth, but it is a slow business, I'm afraid.'

'Especially as I know nothing about her except her surname,' sighed Mrs Brook and as she walked through to the kitchen to make the promised tea, Mary Faro reappeared, beaming with delight over the lovely guest room.

'I know I'll be very comfortable here, Jeremy.'

That was a relief. He smiled, glad of the excuse to depart. 'Excellent, Ma, but I have to go now.'

'What about tea, surely you can stay for a little while?' she said, reluctant as ever to let him go. 'After all, I haven't seen you for months,' she added reproachfully.

He sighed. 'I have to work, dear. I am not on holiday,' he reminded her. 'And we will be seeing plenty of each other while you are here.' However, the lure of Mrs Brook's tea and one of her delicious scones was irresistible, while Mary chose to ignore the housekeeper's apology for still unpacked storage containers, saying that the house was just perfect and thanking her for doing so much.

She put down the empty cup. 'If you really have to go, Jeremy dear, I think I will rest in my lovely room for a while.' And with a yawn, 'I did not sleep a great deal on the Orkney boat last night, a very uneasy crossing. I'm sure Lizzie will understand and excuse me. I'll see all of you at supper.'

Far from minding, he felt that Lizzie, and especially Charlie, would be greatly relieved, acutely conscious of the terrible anxiety induced by Mary's presence. Faro was also relieved by the absence of any posters in the Blacket Place area to suggest that Lizzie's brother on a visit from the Highlands was none other than the murderer wanted by the police, with a substantial reward for his capture.

Time was not on their side. He had to get Charlie away as soon as he could walk – or preferably run. But how? As he was walking across the Pleasance towards the railway terminus, two constables who he knew but didn't immediately recognise saluted him. And that gave him an idea, how uniform and helmet were a disguise in themselves. He was jubilant; he would obtain these from the police store on some pretext, and as a detective sergeant travelling with a constable, Charlie would be safe. No one would give them a second glance. It would be easy, he decided, as he bought a ticket and took a seat on the train, heading for the first of his interviews with the claimants of the reward, already sure that it was a waste of time.

Suddenly his plan made him smile: the irony of getting Charlie McLaw away from under Gosse's nose disguised as a constable. As well as irony there was the ever-present haunting thought of discovery, which would mean the end of his career and possible imprisonment or transportation, and what would become of Lizzie and their baby, and young Vince?

The train window was jammed open and he couldn't close it as they sped through the long dark tunnel at the outset of the journey. Absorbed by the darkness, the stifling atmosphere smelt vile from more than the normal steam from the engine, and in the flickering light from the candle sconces, which offered poor illumination, he noticed the number of sacks alongside the rail and decided that a lot of local folk, perhaps also the builders on the nearby road, were guilty of finding it a useful disposal place for rubbish.

Once out of the tunnel his fears were momentarily soothed by the gentle countryside moving past the windows, the peaceful sights of what had now taken on the atmosphere of a world lost to him, remote from the hazards of a harrowing present. For a while, he let the soothing motion overcome his anxiety, absorbed again by his love of trains. How lucky to live in this modern age; what a difference the railways had made to the lives of ordinary folk as he thought of the alternatives, the stagecoaches infrequent and highly uncomfortable with their wooden seats. Only the rich could afford the luxury of a well-padded carriage and a coachman.

The other alternatives were horseback or to go by foot and Faro was never completely comfortable with the first of these means of travel. Like most of the police, from constables to detectives, once out of the city with its horse-drawn omnibuses he had to walk, mile upon mile every day.

Faro consulted his notes for the addresses, one in Fisherrow and one in Musselburgh itself. This was a perfect opportunity to call at the poorhouse and make enquiries about the missing Tibbie, who he felt certain had a connection there, with his gut feeling that she was the lame woman he had seen trying to board the train, and as an excuse for the visit, he would produce once more the ailing, frail mother.

As the train steamed past the grounds, there was no activity. This was not one of their days for ferrying the market produce to the city. Onward to the furthest of his two calls.

He was pleasantly surprised when he stepped off the train.

The Romans settled Musselburgh, just five miles from Edinburgh, in the first century AD following their invasion of Scotland, and built a defensive fort, long vanished, a little inland from the mouth of the River Esk.

The bridge he walked across that sunny morning was a descendant of the original the Romans had built over the river downstream from the fort, establishing the main eastern approach to Scotland's capital that had endured through the passing centuries.

Without a map, he needed directions for the address of this reward claimant. The sound of hammering and the smell of hot iron said that there was a blacksmith's forge near the riverbank.

The large, heavily muscled, sweating man paused in his exertions to greet him.

'Aye, down the High Street. Turn left and then right. Just across from Pinkie House.'

Faro thanked him and the blacksmith, now curious, said: 'You are welcome. This is your first visit to the Honest

Toun, sir?' Proud of its history, Faro was told that this ancient epithet dated back to the fourteenth century, when the Regent of Scotland died in the burgh after a long illness, cared for by the citizens. The new regent, the Earl of Mar, impressed by these good folk, rewarded them thus for their honesty.

Faro had a feeling that the blacksmith had only just begun on his story, that there was a lot more, but took the opportunity of a rider arriving with a horse to be shod to hurry on to his destination.

He found the tiny cottage that owed little charm to antiquity sandwiched awkwardly between two modern and rather ugly houses that managed to display by their closeness a feeling of hostility to their diminutive neighbour.

Already he had misgivings as he knocked on the door. A very old man, leaning on a stick, peered up at him. At his introduction in his official role, the man brightened visibly. His back straightened and his eyes gleamed. 'Aye, aye, we saw him right enough. Or at least, my lad did, my eyes aren't what they once were. But the lad recognised him immediately from the poster. Aye, it was him all right, no doubt about it, sleeping under the arches of the bridge.'

'Where is your son now?'

The old man shook his head. 'He's at work, on a farm, two, three miles up the hill yonder.' He pointed and Faro was less than enthusiastic about that prospect.

'It's a guid, long walk, ye ken, but the lad said if anyone came they were to give the money to me.' So saying, he held out his hand expecting fifty pounds to be poured into it. 'I'll see he gets it.'

Faro shook his head. 'I'm sorry, sir, I can't do that.

We need some sort of proof. That has to be provided and an arrest before the reward can be claimed,' he added, knowing that there could be none, that this man asleep by the river whose presence had been seized upon was likely some passing vagrant. And there would be more similar claims, lots more, of that he was certain.

The old man was not only disappointed, he was very, very angry and Faro left him shouting abuses about the police who cheated everybody, making promises they weren't prepared to keep.

Wearily now, but with some compassion for these folk who had been so misguided by Gosse's reward poster, since one could hardly blame them for believing that this was a unique opportunity to get possession of a pot of gold, an enormous sum of money in their impoverished lives, he headed in the direction of his next call, aware that a similar reception awaited him.

At Fisherrow the boats were just unloading, with good herring catches if the shrill screams of the clouds of seagulls were any indication. He approached one of the men and was told, aye, the house is up the hill yonder.

This looked a mite more prosperous than the old man's cottage. The door was opened by a servant girl who, when he introduced himself, said:

'Oh, you're too late. The master has gone into Edinburgh himself to claim the reward. You've just missed him,' she said, with a giggle. 'He'll be sorry. You could have saved him the journey,' she added, giving him the admiring look she saved for young and handsome men. 'But he'll reckon fifty pounds was worth the journey.'

Faro didn't feel that he was called upon to explain the

intricacies of the reward money offered, the proof that was needed, and with a polite bow bid her good day.

She watched him go, wishing she had offered him a cup of tea. A lost opportunity to ease her present dull life with a good-looking policeman in her kitchen.

A mile away lay Belmuir village. He thought gratefully of the inn with a pie and a pint of ale before going across to the poorhouse.

It was not to be. Just as he emerged after taking some refreshment, he saw a carriage heading down through the village. A moment later it stopped just yards away. The door opened and Lady Belmuir poked her head out and beckoned him. He could hardly ignore that.

He walked across, and smiling, she opened the door wider, pointed to the seat opposite.

'What are you doing here, Mr Faro?'

'A business matter.'

She smiled wryly. 'Is that so? Having seen you emerging from our local inn, I presume it is done.' He frowned and she added briskly, 'You can forget whatever business it is that brings you here. I have something very important for you.'

Here was a quandary. He could hardly tell her that he was heading to the poorhouse to look for a missing servant or give her that story about accommodation for a frail mother. Even as he was thinking up some more valid reason, she said, 'I will take you back to Edinburgh. In fact, you are the very one I am looking for.'

So saying she patted the seat. 'I am in desperate need of your assistance, Mr Faro.' Weakly he stepped in and sat down opposite, almost overwhelmed in a cloud of exotic perfume.

The laird of Belmuir was elegantly dressed as ever in a dark-green velvet outdoor dress, just short enough to display a neat silk-clad ankle as she moved the full skirt to let him sit down. The ensemble was completed by a matching feathered, large-brimmed velvet hat, which she removed, throwing back the mane of dark hair that had struck such a chord of Orkney and Inga at their first meeting. Would he never cease to be haunted by it, that painful reminder of a love lost?

From her reticule she took out not the usual feminine fripperies but a small, exquisite silver flask. She held it out and said, 'May I offer you a dram?'

'Thank you, no. I am on duty.' Perhaps she recognised his slightly shocked look and she smiled indulgently. 'I always carry my little flask. One never knows in carriages when something unfortunate may require the aid of a little refreshment.'

Tapping the roof for the coachman to proceed, she leant back against the well-padded upholstery and sighed. 'You are the very one I am looking for, Mr Faro,' she repeated. 'That fool of an inspector is really quite impossible. I want you to look into this important matter concerning the theft of our Leonardo from Moray Place.'

Faro interrupted. 'Inspector Gosse is giving this his full attention, ma'am.'

'Full attention, indeed!' she said scornfully. 'The wretched man hardly listened to me. Full of his own importance. Said it would be taken care of.' She shook her head and added scornfully. 'I have to tell you, I don't trust him.'

Faro was aware that he could not overstep Gosse in this enquiry, nor did he have any wish to add yet another mystery to his growing list while he still had to effect the urgent removal of McLaw from the scene, but he realised he had better humour this beautiful but formidable lady.

'I shall take you directly to Moray Place and you shall have the opportunity to look over the scene and consider how the thief got away with the painting. I will be indebted to you, Mr Faro,' she added with humility that surprised him. 'The Leonardo means a great deal to me personally.' So saying she began to describe it, the head of a young boy, the beautiful setting, the wonderful colours. 'Various people who viewed it were taken aback.' She leant forward, smiling into his face. 'They said it bore a truly astonishing family resemblance.' Pausing for this to be taken in, but observing no change in his expression, she sighed. 'Do you know anything of painting, Mr Faro?' It so happened that Faro knew a great deal and spent much time in art galleries. In no time at all they were discussing the merits of Raphael and Rembrandt and some of the more obscure early Italian artists. As this conversation between two knowledgeable people carried them towards Edinburgh, Lady Belmuir, or Honor as she wished to be called, considered the man sitting opposite.

Here she was sharing her carriage with a nobody, was it just because he struck a chord, reminding her of the love she had lost so long ago? And this man, as well as handsome, was also of humble stock, worth a hundred brother Hectors and his wasteful, dissolute life.

As he talked so animatedly, his deep voice stirred something in her soul. She liked looking at him, tall, strong, and her stomach gave a tiny lurch that had nothing to do with the carriage going over a bump in the road.

She wasn't used anymore to emotions like this, not for a long time had any man stirred her senses beyond the flirtations of undesirable, often old and ugly men at social gatherings. The young who admired her were too young and mostly without money. She thought of Moray Place waiting for them and again considered this man, a mere detective without any sort of background or breeding. Maybe an hour or two together – again that tiny lurch of desire. Now regarding him narrowly as he talked of additions to Edinburgh's art gallery, she smiled. Surely he would be flattered. Common men always liked the gentry women, or so someone had told her. Nothing serious, or lasting, of course, just an hour or two. His wife, if he had one, need never know.

CHAPTER TWENTY-TWO

As the carriage swung into Moray Place, Honor Belmuir felt the thrill of sexual excitement. Men had wanted her, but most men she found dull and boring. It was years since she had met anyone like Faro. That dreadful Inspector Gosse, she knew, would have been more than willing, trailing after her, devouring her with his eyes as he walked through the house. But he repelled her.

The carriage stopped. 'Here we are.' Stepping out, he helped her to alight. For a moment, deliberately, she leant against him and he felt the power of that exotic perfume, even as they walked up the steps, the door opened by the footman to whom she handed hat and gloves.

'Follow me,' she said and they walked together up the grand staircase winding up to the third floor. Turning, he looked away from the marble floor far beneath them and gave his attention to the few pictures adorning the walls and that blank faded space on the wallpaper once occupied by the Leonardo.

'We always kept it up here,' she said, 'away from the bright light.'

Faro nodded. He was well aware of her intentions, which had little to do with a stolen picture. Suddenly it was all very clear to him and he guessed why Gosse hadn't made much of this robbery. Carefully examining the space, he could have written the story relating to that theft and the insurance company's inevitable reluctance to pay to settle her claim. He was polite enough, however, to fulfil his duties and ask the relevant questions.

How had the thief entered?

'Alas, through a window. Come and I will show you.'

He followed her down the great staircase, across the marble floor and through a door, along dimly lit stone corridors and into a kitchen similar to that in Belmuir House but empty of activity, seeing that this mansion only became a hive of activity once the Belmuirs were in residence, holding court in their townhouse for the relatively short period of Edinburgh's recognised social season.

At his side, she sighed and pointed to a side window. 'Very carelessly left open by one of the kitchen maids. She has since been dismissed.'

'Do you have her address?'

She looked startled by the question and shrugged. 'It may be somewhere. I'm not quite sure, she was only one of several maids. We hardly keep a record of their addresses, or of their personal details of their lives. I believe she lives out country somewhere. I can't remember the exact place, if I ever knew it.' She paused and gave him a winning smile. 'Is this quite necessary?'

'It helps with enquiries.'

Another smile, rather arch this time. 'Are you not prepared to take my word, Mr Faro?'

Frankly no, would have been his reply but her answer was all he needed. That dismissal was what he had expected. No one must remain to be questioned about an open window. The maid would have been given money to keep her mouth firmly shut, a good reference and sent back home to a vague place in the countryside.

He had already heard enough, and having received well-planned and thought-out answers, he realised this was one theory he would share with Gosse, if the inspector ever got to know that Faro had been called in.

Lady Belmuir was desperate for money and it wasn't the first time a robbery had been arranged, an excuse to claim the insurance and a frequent reason for police time being wasted.

A tap on the door interrupted them. The footman entered, a murmured conversation ensued, voices raised. Lady Belmuir came back and said: 'Such a nuisance. I have a further engagement and the coachman has just informed me that there is a problem with one of the carriage wheels. He can get it fixed but it will take half an hour.' Sighing, she gave him a pleading look. 'Will you stay and take tea with me?'

Faro felt he could hardly refuse, especially when this rather extraordinary woman intrigued him and he was curious to know more about her. He did not have long to wait.

There seemed to be no maids in residence and the butler

brought tea on a silver tray with a selection of sweetmeats. Lady Belmuir apologised for the poor fare as she poured the tea and the door closed.

'Tell me about yourself, Mr Faro, you are not from these parts.'

He gave her a brief summary of his origins in Orkney and she seemed very interested. Finally, the information she really wanted. She smiled. 'Have you a first name?' When he told her, she was refilling the dainty teacups, her head down and she repeated: 'Jeremy, may I call you that?'

He inclined his head. 'If you wish.'

A pause, before what she most wanted to know. 'Are you married, Jeremy?' He said yes, and with her face still averted she handed him the cup and asked where did he live.

'I know it well. The little cottage near Solomon's Tower.' Again he nodded and she frowned. 'It is very small, surely?'

He felt like saying yes, by comparison to this vast mansion, but merely smiled. 'Large enough for our family thus far, ma'am.'

She threw up her hands in mock horror. 'Not ma'am, please. My name is Honor.' And coyly, 'If we are to be friends.'

Faro could not see himself as her friend or of ever being so informal as she went on, 'You have a family?'

'A stepson and my wife is expecting our first child.'

This was something of a blow but doubtless one that could be overcome for her purpose of a brief dalliance with this very attractive man.

'You are fortunate to have a family. I have only a brother,' her lip curled scornfully at the mention of Hector, 'who is intent on following the family tradition of leaving us penniless. That is why my clever father, when he knew he was dying, appointed me as the next laird. Hector is utterly worthless; he has already, without my knowledge, sold many of our antiques, he loves money to gamble away on wine, women and drunken orgies with his comrades, who are no better than he. His other love is the hunt. He should have lived in medieval times when the Belmuirs rounded up the stags to make it an easy day's killing for their guests. I believe even the women took part with a crossbow.'

She shuddered. 'Never for me. I love animals.' A shrug as she added, 'Better than people mostly. But he just wants to kill them.'

She was silent, frowning, and Faro wondered after this outburst of confidentiality if this would be an opportune time to take his departure. What were her thoughts? They would have surprised him. She had never forgiven Hector for shooting her horse because it declined a jump and threw him an ignominious fall on a Dalkeith hunt where, sure of a win, he had money at stake. If that wasn't bad enough, his host had mocked him.

That was when she began to hate him, remembering when they were both children and how he always enjoyed mercilessly teasing her little dog and even hurting him. One day the wee pug had had enough, and bit him. The next day the dog was missing, then found dead – poisoned. Hector just laughed and touching the bandage on his wrist said, 'Why not, he deserved it, little brute, for biting me.'

Worse was to come. The man she loved, so like the one sitting opposite and, like him, a nobody, was a beater out shooting with the guests. When he was reloading one of the rifles, it misfired and killed him. A terrible accident it was assumed, but not for his sister who was sure it was murder. There was nothing she could do, only grieve. Hector came to her bed that night, to console her. The rest was a nightmare, which even now she could not bear to think of, only that he had ruined her life and she loathed him with all her heart and she swore somehow, someday, she would get her revenge.

A tap on the door. 'The carriage is ready, m'lady.'

'And about time,' she snapped.

Jeremy rose to his feet, bowed. She did not want him to leave, she wanted to prolong the interview with this gentle, cultured man who she found it difficult to connect with violence, with surly men like that dreadful inspector who had attempted to flirt with her. What a horror.

She held out her hand. 'I hope we will meet again.'

He inclined his head, smiling, and said nothing. What was there to say, even if he had been single – worse perhaps – they would have had nothing in common apart from a knowledge of paintings and their lives could have no meeting place.

'The Leonardo?' she queried.

'I will do what I can.'

She insisted that the carriage take him to his next assignment.

'There is no need for that, it is a mere step away in the High Street.

'Then I will save you that step. I might call on your inspector and let him know that you are to take over the case.'

Faro froze at the suggestion. 'Please do not trouble, rest

assured I will do that.' And face the fury that would follow, the anger and humiliation.

There was no escape, the carriage would transport him to the door of the Central Office. She watched him descend, walk lightly across and disappear inside. Sighing, she moved on, determined in that moment, that married or no, she would certainly make sure that they met again.

CHAPTER TWENTY-THREE

Leaving the grandeur of Moray Place and a life that had scraped the fringes of his own, Faro returned to Central Office.

Gosse was not in a good mood. Standing at the window, he had seen the Belmuir carriage arrive. He had straightened his cravat, put on a welcoming smile, sure that the lady laird was coming to see him. Perhaps she enjoyed his company and doubtless found him very attractive.

And at that moment all his hopes were shattered as his hated detective sergeant descended from the carriage. Seething, he listened as Faro reported the results of his two interviews. The Fisherrow claimant had been in already, demanding the reward money.

Gosse scowled. 'That makes twenty so far and all with ridiculous stories. Just any man with a beard and unruly mop of hair suits their purpose.' He shook his head, not surprised but still hopeful that his reward, this last resort, would produce the missing McLaw. Faro knew better than most that it was a waste of time, a waste, however, that fitted his own plans.

'What did Her Ladyship want?' Gosse demanded.

'She was kind enough to offer me a lift back into Edinburgh. What she really wanted,' he added hastily, seeing Gosse's scowl, 'was to press for information on that stolen Leonardo.'

'And what are your thoughts on that?'

Faro gave him a wry look. 'The same as yours, sir. I got the impression that they are seriously lacking cash and that the brother is something of a spendthrift.'

Gosse rubbed his chin. 'Precisely. I have heard rumours. Certainly no insurance will ever look at it, and we have to regard it as an arranged robbery and in due course the picture will no doubt turn up in some odd corner of the stables, presumably left there by the thief. Case closed.'

Talking of stables jolted Faro back to McLaw. 'Are there more reports to look into, sir?' A long drawn-out sigh and Gosse indicated a sheaf of papers. 'See what you can do with these.'

Faro took them, hoping for one that would fit in with his plan. Somehow he had to get access to borrowing a uniform that would fit Charlie for their journey to the railway station and see him boarding a train.

'What about Moray Place meanwhile, sir?'

'I will deal with it, play for time. Say that the police are making a thorough investigation and have a possible suspect in mind, a local thief who has done this sort of thing before.' He grinned. 'That should keep the lady silent for a while. Meanwhile we have more important matters than a mock robbery. We have a killer to track down, and the longer he remains free, the more dangerous he will become.'

Home once more, the day with all its problems temporarily at an end, Faro stepped into what could have fooled him as a happy domestic scene, full of peace and goodwill. If only it were true. There were Lizzie and Vince at the table with his mother holding court, enthralling them with tales of Orkney. They had obviously hit it off very well. The only ghost at the feast was the presence of Charlie or Teàrlach McLaw, although no one would have guessed that this smiling happy man listening to every word was in fact a wanted killer.

Mary was very taken with him. She insisted on walking Coll that evening with Jeremy. 'I need the exercise. Mrs Brook's food and now yours, Lizzie, living alone I'm not used to eating like this. I won't be able to get into my clothes by the time I get back home.'

As they walked along the gentler slopes towards Hunter's Bog, Mary took his arm and said, 'I am so glad to have met your brother-in-law. What an excellent fellow and aren't those two alike? They could almost be twins. How did you get on with your day, dear? Any news of capturing that dreadful murderer?'

Faro gave a thought to the dreadful murderer sitting cosily back there in the cottage as he shook his head. 'Gracious me,' said Mary. 'The police are not doing very well, are they? A man like that roaming about. We could all be murdered in our beds.'

Faro permitted himself a wry smile at that.

There was a new moon, a shining crescent above the

211

hill, beaming down on them. Mary sighed. 'I love being here, dear, it has quite changed my ideas about Edinburgh. Your cottage is lovely. If only the countryside was not to be ruined by those awful buildings,' she added as he walked her towards Sheridan Place.

Would there be news at last of Tibbie, he wondered, as Mrs Brook opened the door. A sad shake of the head went unseen by Mary as they exchanged words about the good weather, with Mary eager to tell her what a splendid day she had had, and how it had been so good to meet Lizzie's handsome brother.

Mrs Brook said, 'I have had a postcard from the superintendent. This one is from London and he expects to be with us sometime next week. He hopes Mrs Faro has arrived safely.' Smiling at her she added, 'He is very much looking forward to making your acquaintance, Mrs Faro.'

'Is all in readiness for his return?'

Mrs Brook replied that the furniture was in place, with only a few ornaments and pictures to unpack, so all would look like home for his return.

Mary immediately offered her assistance in that direction and Faro left them with a sense of relief that Macfie would be home again. Once more he had an overwhelming desire to confide his problems in the superintendent but with his long experience of the law, Faro knew, alas, what the decision would be. Macfie would sternly insist that McLaw be given up, but he was also for justice.

Could anyone convince him that there had been a miscarriage of justice and that McLaw should be given a retrial? He pictured Gosse's fury at such a suggestion, especially as his detective sergeant had gone over his head about the whole thing. It was a forlorn hope, Faro realised, and opening the garden gate, he knew there was only one answer.

He had to get McLaw away before Macfie's return. Somehow he must get hold of a uniform tomorrow. While he and Lizzie prepared for bed, he told her of his plan. Lizzie sighed sadly but was aware that this was inevitable. Much as she and Charlie were devoted to one another, by keeping him under their roof she was putting him in terrible danger. She must see that? If she really cared for him she must see that he had to be away from Edinburgh, perhaps on his way back to the Highlands.

'They might pursue him there,' Faro added. 'It would be better if he left the country, lost himself in London or took ship from Leith to France.'

They agreed that going abroad would be safer and Faro said that even with the beard shaved off and the close hair cut, there was still a possibility that someone from the past might recognise him.

'With a constable's uniform, helmeted, we might get away with it. No one gives policemen a second glance. So that's what I need to get from the store tomorrow.'

Lizzie laughed. 'No, you don't, Jeremy. Yours is up in the loft stored with lots of other things.'

Faro stared at her in amazement and she smiled shyly. 'I know you said I was to get rid of it, but somehow I wanted to keep it. I remember you were wearing it when we first met. And you looked so handsome.' She sighed. 'I fell in love with you as a policeman – and I just wanted to keep it.'

For once, Lizzie's sentimental attachment to things from their past days together, their two years of marriage, and their lack of space in the cottage, had been a blessing.

There was one problem. 'It will be too big for him.'

'Only the trousers will need shortening. He will get away with the jacket – and the helmet.'

And so it was all arranged. Lizzie would make the alterations and they would leave immediately, go to the railway station at Waverley or to the port at Leith. Faro would consider which was safest.

Faro put the plan to Charlie. He listened, silent.

'We will go tomorrow morning on the earliest train, before I start work. There should be fewer folk about or in the station. Going back home you should be safe enough back in the Highlands.'

Charlie looked at him, shook his head and repeated. 'Going back home. Where is that? Our croft no longer exists, it is gone. The laird cleared the land for sheep.'

'What about England? London, then, or there are good railway connections at York, according to the newspapers.'

Again Charlie shook his head and said firmly. 'I am not going anywhere.'

Faro stared at him indignantly. 'Well, you certainly can't stay here,' he added slowly.

Charlie nodded. 'I can do just that. I am not going anywhere until you clear my name.' He paused. 'I am going to give myself up.'

'What! Are you mad? Surely you must realise that every minute of your presence here has put us all, particularly your own sister, in peril?'

'I have thought of that. I will never identify her as my

214

sister. No one knows that, I shall say that I held her hostage and that if you gave me away I would not hesitate to kill her and the boy Vince.'

The complications were beyond Faro, he had only a glimpse of the danger involved in such a plan. 'You will never get away with it,' he said weakly.

Charlie was adamant. 'Look, if I go now, I am running away. I am admitting to the murder and that the verdict was right. And by doing so I will be a fugitive for the rest of my life. Well, I would rather hang than that. I only want to go on living as a man freed from guilt.' He paused. 'All you have to do is to prove that I am innocent.'

'How am I to do that? The words are easy but you are putting me in a position of grave responsibility.'

Charlie laughed. 'Come along, sir. You are the clever detective, all you have to do is to find Annie's killer, somewhere in Fisherrow, bring him to justice and get me a retrial. Then we'll all live happily ever after.' For Faro, this decision made the nightmare of getting Charlie away worse than ever. He had never expected this. But no guilty man would have ever have made such a decision, a guilty man would have taken every opportunity to escape. All it proved was almost beyond reasonable doubt that the man they had sentenced to death for murder and knew as John McLaw was innocent. Faro was thankful that he was innocent of the bookshop murder, and only guilty – if that could be proved – of lifting Molesby's suit.

The burglary had been the work of the man mistakenly sighted as McLaw and held by the Glasgow police. Gosse would be incensed that that this was not the work of

McLaw but of another criminal who had confessed to it when arrested for the attack and robbery of Mr Price in Fleshmarket Close.

At least Vince was free from Gosse's further interrogations, one problem to be crossed off the list looming ahead, the worst of which, by far, was going to be proving Lizzie's brother innocent.

Where to begin?

CHAPTER TWENTY-FOUR

He had to begin somewhere and as a starting point, in which he had little faith, was the poorhouse; armed with the pretext of an allegedly frail mother, he might meet Annie's sister Nora, conveniently a nurse there.

Although he gathered from Charlie that the sisters were never on good terms, she might inadvertently provide information that would lead him in the direction of Annie's killer and also to Tibbie's connection with the poorhouse.

Aware of the need for a better excuse, he got it sadly that morning when he went into the police office to learn from the desk constable that the body of a woman had been found in the railway tunnel near the Pleasance.

'Nasty accident, sir. Lying there a couple of days, they think. Reckon she must have fallen off the train from Fisherrow. Inspector has gone to the scene of the accident but the body is in the mortuary. No idea who she is at this stage.'

As he made his way down the corridor Faro had an ominous feeling that he knew the woman's identity and wished that he did not.

The doctor looked up from examining the corpse. 'An accident, I should say, no evidence beyond injuries, cuts and bruises, accountable with falling off a moving train. Between thirty-five and forty.' He glanced up at Faro's solemn face. Replacing the sheet he said, 'Probably not as agile as she might have been. As you see, a club foot.'

Faro nodded sadly. This was undoubtedly the missing Tibbie.

Gosse had returned to the office and was bustling about with the papers on his desk. He glared at Faro. 'You will have heard by now, another body. Woman in the tunnel. Accident this time, thank God. The railwaymen said that two days ago – which would confirm the time of death – the train arriving from Fisherrow had a door open and a window pulled down.' He shrugged. 'It gets very stuffy in the tunnel, time they made a rule about folks conveniently using it to dump their rubbish. She must have tried to close the window, accidently opened the door and fallen out.' He looked at the papers again. 'No identity, nothing beyond a reticule containing a handkerchief and a few coins. Not even a key.' He paused. 'From what she was wearing, I would speculate without doubt that she was a servant, unless you have a better idea,' he added mockingly.

'She was a servant, sir.'

'Indeed, and how do you know that? We have your usual intuition to thank, is that it?'

Faro ignored the barb. 'I believe her to be the servant the housekeeper at Sheridan Place expected to arrive a few days ago. Mrs Brook was very concerned and about to notify us that she might be a missing person. However, as she knew little about her, she felt cautious about making such a statement.'

'Very wise, and a lot of use that would be. We get plenty of those. Mostly husbands who walk out on wives or vice versa, as you well know.' He sighed. 'Another waste of police time. I expect this housekeeper realised that servants often change their minds, get a better offer.' He paused again. 'Wait a moment. Sheridan Place, isn't that where Macfie has moved to?'

'Correct, sir. Mrs Brook is the housekeeper.'

Gosse sighed. The less he had to do with Macfie, the better and the happier his life.

'You get on to it, Faro,' he said briskly. 'The usual details for our report. Find out where she came from, family and so on.'

Faro nodded and as he headed for the terminus at the Pleasance, he remembered Mrs Brook mentioning that she might help Tibbie by offering her some employment. The railway guard stepping off the train recognised him and said: 'Sad business about that accident. We've been on about better lighting and getting rid of the rubbish. There have been complaints about a rotten smell, thought it was the rubbish, now we know what it really was. Dead body in that confined, airless state—' He was prepared to go on in some more detail when Faro interrupted. 'Did you know about the jammed window and the door?'

'Oh aye, that's the other thing. Needs fixing. I complained about it.'

'So you were on the train when the accident happened?'

'Oh yes, but I didn't see anything at the time. It was one of our busy days, the afternoon train that collects market produce every few days from the poorhouse gardens.'

Faro felt triumphant. Was this the connection with Tibbie he was looking for? Had she been trying to escape again, he wondered, remembering vividly the scene he had witnessed of her struggling with a man who was restraining her from boarding the train at the halt. 'Do you recall seeing anyone of the deceased's description boarding the train there?'

The man shook his head. 'I'm always too busy seeing the goods are being stored properly. Can't be expected to remember every passenger who gets on board.'

'You might remember this woman. She was lame, had a club foot.'

The man frowned. 'There were some women, one of them might have been her, but I couldn't say exactly,' he added reluctantly. 'Folk from the poorhouse often take the chance of a free ride into Edinburgh. We don't ask for a fare if they are travelling with the market produce van, gives them a rare chance of a change of scenery and a bit of novelty in their dull lives. Even them from the big house aren't too proud to take a free ride with us,' he added importantly.

There had been no mention of a rail ticket being found in her reticule, so that fitted.

'Were there other passengers from the poorhouse that day?'

The guard stared ahead thoughtfully. 'Couldn't say, really. The passenger coaches take six, three to a side. Just like the old-time stagecoaches, so there could have been others with her.'

'Was she accompanied by a man?' Faro persisted.

'I have no idea, sir.' The guard laughed uneasily. 'What makes you think that?' Faro had a suspicion that all these questions were making him uncomfortable.

'The open window that troubled you all?'

'Aye. It was closed when the train arrived at the station, although we thought it had been jammed open previously,' the guard said somewhat reluctantly. 'Can't say I took much notice. Too busy,' he added with a faint smile.

'We thought she must have been alone in the carriage, though, when the accident happened. She would never have fallen off the train had there been someone with her.'

'Possibly. That's it!' A quick response but not before Faro had seen not only eagerness but something more, fear in the guard's eyes.

At the sight of the driver walking down the platform, he looked relieved and, saluting Faro, he said: 'Have to get on with it, sir.' And climbed aboard, leaving Faro with the distinct impression that he knew a lot more than he was willing to admit.

Was Tibbie's possible companion the same man he had seen her struggling with before? If he was also from the poorhouse then he was probably well known to the guards.

This train was scheduled to leave for Fisherrow in an

hour, but first of all he had to go to Sheridan Place and break the sad news to Mrs Brook.

Opening the door, she was smiling and held up a card. 'It's from London, sir, the superintendent will be home in a few days.'

Suddenly aware from his grave expression that was not the reason for his visit, she put a hand to her mouth as he said: 'They've found Tibbie. She fell off the train a couple of days ago, in the Pleasance tunnel.'

'Poor soul, oh poor soul,' she sobbed and putting an arm around her Faro led her into the kitchen. Wiping her eyes, she said: 'What a dreadful thing, a terrible, terrible thing to happen. I knew all along when she didn't turn up. Lying hurt in that awful dark tunnel,' she wept.

Faro didn't want to make it worse for her by going over the details again, but he listened patiently as she began to blame herself.

'There was nothing you could do, Mrs Brook. She had no identification on her, nothing. I don't know what she was doing at the poorhouse but we'll need her Liberton address and arrangements for interment.'

Mrs Brook straightened her shoulders, dried her eyes. 'I'll take care of that, sir.'

'Thank you.' He paused. 'I hate asking you this, Mrs Brook, it is a most gruesome task. We will also need someone who knew her to identify her. Can you bear to do this?'

Mrs Brook shivered. 'Of course, sir, it is the least I can do for her.' As he was leaving, she said: 'Was it really an accident, sir?'

'As far as we know from the details.'

She nodded, her expression grim. 'I hope you are right, then.'

And there was something in the way that she said those words that Faro realised her thoughts were on a similar line to his own.

CHAPTER TWENTY-FIVE

As the train approached the halt at Belmuir, Faro had not yet composed in his own mind how he would extract any information about Tibbie, as well as having the interview with Annie's sister, Nora.

Poorhouses had a bad reputation as forbidding institutions whose powerful image cast grave shadows over people's imagination.

'Going to the poorhouse' was an awesome whisper, a last resort to be avoided at all costs. Not only poverty but also respectability was threatened by such a move. Even if one's finances recovered, it was never forgotten, the poorhouse stain remained. Folk would shake their heads and whisper and say he will never make good, he was in the poorhouse, you know.

As he left the train and wandered across the courtyard to the grim, tall, grey building, entering it from this angle must have put little hope into anyone's heart. For those inside possibly watching, stepping through those doors carried an enormous social stigma. For the elderly it was a place that you never came out of again, except in a coffin for burial in an unmarked pauper's grave.

Such was the fate of Agatha Simms. From that bungled burial had sprung the death of her sister who had, against all legal rules, taken the coffin from the grave to fulfil her sister's dying wish to be buried in the family vault at Gifford. To her horror the coffin, when opened for a last glimpse of her sister's face, revealed no corpse, only large stones. This had set in motion her indignant enquiry, followed by Celia's own death, accident or murder, by a runaway cab on the Mound, witnessed by her maid Tibbie who fell off the train in the Pleasance tunnel before she could reveal what she knew to the superintendent's housekeeper, Mrs Brook, who had offered her a situation as a living-in maid at Sheridan Place.

Looking round the gloomy entrance with a glimpse of rambling corridors, he guessed that he should have approached by the front door. He was lost and stopping the first person he met, he noticed that all wore an identical grey uniform. But they looked well fed, their expressions cheerful, not at all distressed or demented, with the appearance of ordinary folk he might meet any day in Princes Street.

This reality presented a very different picture from that supplied by the eminent author, Mr Charles Dickens' in his novel *Oliver Twist*, a great favourite of Faro's, which had coloured a succession of readers' ideas and accounts of middle-class 'social explorers, who clothed themselves in dirty old rags to gain admission for a night's stay and to witness conditions for themselves'. That was England, of course, and conditions in Edinburgh were certainly less grim he decided, waiting at a reception desk respectable enough for a hotel or a hospital, with people going about their own business, many clutching papers. Most had some connection. If they were not living under the roof, they were supplying it with goods, or buying the firewood the inmates had chopped.

'I got lost,' he explained to the man at the reception desk. 'I was looking for Nora, one of your nurses, and I took the wrong turn.'

The man pointed. 'Well, you've found her.' He grinned. 'There she is. Nora, a gentleman to see you.'

The woman who approached, walking briskly towards him, was in her late thirties or early forties and must have been at least a decade older than her sister. Thin, with pulled-back grey hair, a mouth of the kind described by his colleagues as like a rat-trap spoilt a face that even in its best days could never have been described as pretty. Before she spoke a word, he could see the perfectly natural reaction of why she must have envied and despised that young sister who had been a beauty and so desirable to men. Annie, he guessed, for all her faults, when she still lived at home must have needed a generous and forgiving nature.

'Well, what is it you want?' Nora was asking.

He decided his official role might be the one most acceptable and produced his identity card. She looked at it briefly and scowled. 'What has that to do with me?' This wasn't going to be easy, and looking around, he said: 'Just a moment of your time, if you please.'

With an impatient shrug she led the way into a small, glass-windowed office and regarded him defiantly. 'Well?'

'It is about your late sister Annie.' That was enough to make the scowl deepen. 'I have no sister Annie. I lost her long ago.'

'We are aware of the sad details.' The word 'sad' brought a mocking gesture.

'We all thought she deserved all she got, been leading up to that for a long time, sooner or later—'

Faro held up his hand. 'The police are aware of the details, Mrs Rickson,' he said patiently. 'There have been some slight changes—'

'We all know that. Charlie is on the run. And good luck to him is all we have to say,' she ended with a triumphant nod. 'If only he hadn't been such a soft mark and put up with her goings-on—'

As she ranted on the subject of unfaithful wives in general and how God punished Jezebels, he realised that here was one very unlikely person on McLaw's side, but he did not enjoy the prospect that he was related through marriage, by even the remotest thread, to this harridan.

When she paused to draw breath he nodded, he hoped sympathetically, and said, 'A terrible blow for the rest of the family. I trust her father and brother have recovered from the shock of all this.'

'Recovered? There was nothing to recover from. Our mother married Joe, it was his second marriage. He had Frank by then.'

'You got along well together?'

She thought about that for a moment. 'Pa was fine; he owns the local, the Coach and Horses, so we had a good life, that was why it was so sickening for Annie to go off as she did. If he had been cruel to her, anything like that—'

She was off again, he realised, and put in hastily, 'What about her brother Frank?'

'You might well ask. Idiot that he was, he worshipped her. Right from the beginning, he thought she was God's greatest creation. Even when he got married – he still couldn't keep his eyes off her. Miriam with their two bairns, and her a helpless invalid since the last one was born. It was a disgrace.'

'Did she respond to his attentions?'

'Anything in trousers would do for her. Even Frank, her own stepbrother.' She added in a shocked voice, 'He was always the one she wanted—'

Faro decided these revelations were casting a new light on the case. He wanted to know more when they were interrupted as the door opened.

A suddenly changed Nora dropped a curtsey. 'Excuse me, master. This man's a policeman, wanted some . . . some information,' she stammered.

The tall man Faro recognised from their earlier meeting as Sir Hector Belmuir turned his back on Nora and said sharply to Faro: 'Something we can do for you?'

'I met Mrs Rickson on my way to the reception area. I'm afraid I left the train at the back entrance and got lost. I am looking for information concerning accommodation for my mother. She lives in Orkney and is elderly now, and becoming frail. As we can no longer visit each other as often, I would like to have her somewhere near Edinburgh and your establishment has been highly recommended.'

The man addressed as the master nodded and without looking in her direction said: 'You may leave us, Mrs

Rickson.' She did so, with a sweeping curtsey.

'Take a seat, Mr . . . Faro, isn't it?' Sir Hector sat at the desk. 'I deal with such matters. Perhaps before allowing your mother into our care, you would wish to know something of our reputation.' A thin smile. 'Regard it as reference,' he added and opening a drawer, took out some booklets. 'To save you reading all these, I should explain that although poorhouses have gained a bad name, they are a valuable addition to the community and the poor would be much poorer without them.'

Faro found that hard to believe as he went on: 'A complete overhaul of poor relief administration came with the 1845 Scottish Poor Law Amendment Act, or the New Poor Law, of great assistance to able-bodied men, and a safety net for those in genuine need – the elderly, the sick, and orphaned children. Once taken care of by monasteries and religious houses, after their dissolution by Henry the Eighth, assisting such people became the lot of the better-off and the landowners like ourselves.'

Faro guessed he was talking about the Belmuirs as he continued:

'The Poor Relief Act formalised how the poor were to be provided for, revolving round the parish, the area served by a single priest and his church to which every householder was required to contribute, an annual tax based on the value of their property. The able-bodied were expected to work while a place evolved to accommodate the impotent poor – those too old, lame or blind who could not work.'

As he waxed eloquent on the subject, Faro had a chance to study the speaker, a more businesslike friendly version of the angry, frustrated rabbit-hunter flourishing a rifle at their first encounter at Belmuir.

Tall, good-looking, with the look of breeding that he shared with his sister, there was nevertheless a difference: although Sir Hector would be under forty, there were already lines that hinted to the dissolute life Honor Belmuir had indicated. Something about his eyes, a slackness in the mouth and a heightened complexion indicated that the master of the Belmuir's poorhouse had a less creditable side to his nature than goodwill to all mankind.

Faro hoped that the dire future his father, the last laird, had predicted, that had made him wisely leave all to his daughter, was being overcome by Sir Hector's enthusiasm and dedication to being master of his own small community.

'A hundred years ago almost one in seven parishes in the country was soon running a poorhouse, or a "workhouse" as they are more commonly called in England,' Sir Hector continued, 'and it was economic to house all their paupers under one roof, and offering what was called the poorhouse test resulted in many fewer claimants as life outside as a free man appeared more attractive, even for the lowest of labourers scraping by on meagre wages.

'The stigma remained, the fear that they were entering a kind of prison for life with no hope of ever getting out meant that it was often a last resort. Some were put off by the formality of an interview with a Relieving Officer, like myself, who regularly visited designated places in each parish and applicants would explain their circumstances, probably hoping for an offer of "out-relief". If this was refused, an "offers of the house" was provided for the applicant, together with any dependants.'

Pausing to fill a glass from the crystal decanter on the

table, Faro guessed its contents were whisky or brandy. Hector drank deeply before replacing the glass and continuing: 'Travelling can involve a walk of five or ten miles and after a lengthy admission process, new arrivals are placed in a reception area known as a receiving ward. Come, let me show you.'

Faro followed him out along one of the corridors where Sir Hector threw open the door into what bore a suspicious resemblance to a hospital ward in its austere appearance.

The master clearly did not see this as he continued cheerfully, 'Here their details are taken, their own clothes taken away and put into storage, and a uniform is issued. Then a bath is provided in the washhouse outside, which for many is a new and often a quite terrifying experience. Then they undergo a medical examination, in case they are carrying an infectious disease.' Glancing at Faro to see how he was taking all this, he said: 'As you can well imagine, living closely in large numbers, we live in constant fear of infectious diseases, like consumption, which spread like wildfire. In the last year several of our residents have succumbed and died,' he added sadly, leading the way back into the corridor and closing the door.

'Finally, all admissions have to be formally approved by the Board of Guardians, on which I also serve. We have weekly meetings. Come, Mr Faro, I trust you are not weary. We have more to see.' As they continued down the corridor he said: 'One of the most unpopular aspects we have overcome is the separation of male and female, children from parents and whole families living in separate sections with virtually no contact.'

Opening a door, a rush of fresh air and they were in a

three-sided courtyard with a succession of doors and small windows.

Turning to Faro he smiled proudly. 'As you see, there is none of that with us, we keep families together so that it is like living in their own familiar home. That is one reason why ours is so very popular. Our poorhouse is not a prison, Mr Faro, as you can see for yourself. Inmates are at liberty to leave at any time, merely giving us notice so that their own clothes can be retrieved and formalities carried out.

'As with entry, however, families have to leave together so that an uncaring man cannot abandon his dependants to our care. They are also, with permission, allowed to leave for a brief period to try and find work outside. We find this is often popular in summer when there are harvests to gather in and fruit to be picked. The old and infirm are merely content and grateful to spend the rest of their days being cared for.'

As he was speaking, Sir Hector opened yet another door into another corridor, an area larger than the rest. Near to the kitchens, judging by the smell of cooking.

'This building,' he said 'was once part of the castle, a modern innovation decided upon by Lord Belmuir some 150 years ago.' He shook his head. 'As you see, a rather plain and unattractive addition, which detracted from the original castle built in the sixteenth century. Our father, the late laird, disliked it intensely. It mostly lay empty and we can now provide for 200 persons, thanks to his great plans in transforming it into workshops, stores, a laundry, a bakehouse and even a mortuary.'

Mention of the mortuary made Faro think of Agatha Simms. How long had she lain there before being rushed off into a pauper's grave and how many suffered the same fate? Was the master aware of that or was it in the hands of some lowlier member of the administration?

Sir Hector opened double doors to reveal rows of tables and chairs. 'This is our dining room, a communal area which serves as a chapel where we have daily prayers, morning and evening.' And closing the door, 'No work on Sundays, when I myself officiate at divine service,' he added proudly. 'Cleanliness is vital with a large number living together. Daily ablutions from the hand pump in the yard is not for us, we have male and female washrooms and an earth closet, which provides excellent fertiliser for our garden produce. Chamber pots are still accessible for the staff, but there is a water closet similar to that inside the castle.

'Some of our board believes that we should decorate our plain but substantial building, but I am firmly against such a measure, with today's architectural weakness for turning every new building in Edinburgh into a mini Balmoral Castle.'

He smiled. 'As for daily duties, women do domestic duties, cooking, sewing or working in the gardens, with the men producing our extensive and may I say quite famous market produce. And then there is the farm. Pigs kept fattened on kitchen waste, two cows for the milk and chickens for our eggs, taken care of by the women.'

Pausing, he looked out of one of the passing windows. 'I would have liked to take you across, but alas, the weather!' A fine drizzle shadowed the glass.

Ushering Faro along the corridor, he opened a door and Faro found himself back in the reception area. 'I hope you have enjoyed our little tour. We like the anxious relative to feel that their loved one being relinquished into our care will be happy and content, and the elderly, if necessary, tenderly nursed to the end of their days with us. The demented, too, are well cared for. They need considerable sympathy and understanding.'

'I believe I saw one of them from the train when I was passing through the halt returning to Edinburgh.' That remark was safe enough, for the man he had seen with Tibbie that day was certainly not the master of the workhouse.

About to take his leave, Faro turned and said: 'There is one other matter on which perhaps you could assist me.'

'Willingly, if I can, Mr Faro.'

'It concerns a young woman, an orphan, whose early days were spent here. We have an acquaintance, a housekeeper, who had it in mind to take her on as a servant after her mistress died.'

'And this housekeeper wishes for a reference, of course.'

'Not exactly. The young woman wrote a letter of acceptance but failed to appear and the housekeeper was very concerned about her non-arrival—'

'Ah yes, sadly that frequently happens,' Sir Hector interrupted.

Faro continued: 'The housekeeper was so anxious that she asked my advice about notifying the police about a missing person enquiry.'

Sir Hector smiled. 'A little premature, I'm sure.'

'It was too late. The woman was dead, killed in an accident on the railway.'

'Ah,' said Sir Hector, shaking his head. 'That poor

unfortunate who died by falling off the train in the tunnel. Such an unfortunate accident. I read about it in the newspaper.'

Faro paused for a moment and continued: 'As the housekeeper identified her and is prepared to take on the funeral arrangments, perhaps you could assist by supplying some details, date of birth and so forth from your records.'

Sir Hector considered this, tapped his fingers on the desk and frowned: 'That would be before I took over the management and I'm afraid I cannot help you, as my predecessor was a little lax in such matters. I will do what I can to trace this Tibbie person but I'm very doubtful if any of our early records still exist.' He stood up. 'Now you must excuse me. It has been a pleasure meeting you, Mr Faro, and I look forward to welcoming your mother once the paperwork is completed.'

Sir Hector followed him out to the desk where he said the clerk would take details regarding Mrs Faro. With a slight bow, he departed, leaving Faro the unpleasant duty of giving information he had no intention of fulfilling.

Toying with the application form and wondering how he could decently escape without committing his mother as a prospective resident, the door burst open and a well-dressed man in his late fifties rushed in, red-faced and very angry.

At the clerk's startled expression, he shouted. 'My name is Mitchell and I demand to see someone in authority – at once.'

'How can we help you, sir?'

'It is too late for that. The matter concerns my father, who died a few days ago.'

'Our condolences, sir,' said the clerk smoothly.

'I'm not interested in your condolences, I want to know why he has been laid to rest without my knowledge.'

'A telegraph was sent to you, sir—' the clerk began.

'Without leaving enough time for me to make the journey from London to Edinburgh even on the fastest train.'

'That was most unfortunate—' the clerk blustered. 'We did all in our powers to delay matters.'

'You didn't do enough. I was not even informed that he was at death's door, simply that he had died and the funeral couldn't be delayed. I demand an explanation,' the man said, thumping the desk.

The clerk look scared and, leaving the desk, said: 'I will find someone, sir, if you will just be patient.'

As she hurried out of the room, the man became aware of Faro for the first time.

'How dare they do things like this, is it not bad enough losing a parent without finding that you were not given a chance to see them in their last hours or even see them to their grave?' The bluster had gone, the man looked almost tearful. 'It is dreadful, dreadful. I am the eldest, how am I going to break this awful news to the rest of the family?'

Faro was never to know, as the door opened to admit Sir Hector. He would have loved to stay and listen to that interview as Mr Mitchell was ushered into the private office. The clerk retired behind the desk and Faro pocketed the paper saying: 'I must take this with me, there are some details I need to check.'

As he left, there were indeed many details to check, not concerning the admission of Mary Faro but why the so efficient workhouse with the admirable testimonial, the impressive tour by the master Sir Hector slipped up when it came to keeping records up to date and arranging funerals. Celia Simms had received the same treatment regarding her sister Agatha and here was another. How many more were there going undetected, bodies disposed of with indecent haste. An accident in the procedure or something much more sinister?

He thought of his mother and how angry she would be if she knew how he had used her as his cover story, and he thought of the little time he had spent being given a tour by the master. There was only one discrepancy in that tour and he was to remember its significance.

CHAPTER TWENTY-SIX

He had one more call to make. At the Coach and Horses. He could take the train from Fisherrow after he had a chance to talk to the proprietor and his son Frank. It might prove interesting after Nora's revelations regarding Annie's relationship with her stepbrother. And he would be glad of the chance of once again sampling their excellent fare – a pie and a pint of ale would go down very well after the morning's work.

Both Frank and his father were serving. He had come at a busy time and there were workers, with the look of local labourers, enjoying an hour's break.

Frank served Faro, who was once again struck by his striking appearance. Tall, good-looking and strong, there was something undeniably honest about his smiling countenance and welcoming manner, very different to whatever had been troubling him on that first encounter, as was Ben Hogg's version of his relationship with Annie. The pair's devotion to each other hardly fitted with

Nora's account of Annie's relentless sexual pursuit of her stepbrother. However, it did offer up a grim possibility.

On the night of her death, had she been successful in seducing him, and when Charlie arrived home unexpectedly, Frank had been horrified at being caught in bed with his stepsister. In a panic that even though the room was in darkness he might have been recognised by Charlie, he had reacted violently by knocking him out. He was certainly taller and heavier built. Again Faro imagined the scene: had Annie threatened to tell his adored invalid wife in her desperation that he should not leave her, rushed after him, pleading? Had she tried to stop him leaving by seizing a knife and in the struggle that followed, she had died?

Faro was certain that was what had happened, but the sequel did not. He felt Frank would have faced the truth, that he would not have dragged her body back into the bedroom and placed it on the floor at the side of her unconscious husband so that when he awakened and found her dead, he would get the blame.

Frank, realising that this customer was a newcomer who should be politely welcomed, asked what had brought him to Belmuir and was he staying in the area? Faro shook his head and replied that he was just here on business and that he lived in Edinburgh. The young man smiled and wished him well and Faro could not think of any appropriate reason for raising the subject of his stepsister's murder, particularly given the rumours of their relationship.

So he left knowing that he was no further on with proving McLaw's innocence and that many men can have the face of angels and be devils inside, like the man he had just spoken to, and this also included Charlie.

239

He boarded the train with some misgivings. Nora was prejudiced, he had involved his mother in a lie and wasted Sir Hector's time and made no progress in the accident or murder of Tibbie. 'The unfortunate woman', Sir Hector had called her. He was not the man struggling to stop her boarding the train, and any connection with Frank Robson seemed unlikely. He stared out of the window at the passing countryside aware, not for the first time, that the killer might be a faceless resident of the village, or even a casual visitor and that, as such, tracing him was an impossibility and Charlie McLaw would have to live with the stain of a murder he had not committed, a fugitive from justice for the rest of his life.

The train entered the dark tunnel and the approach to home, and Faro was soon to learn how narrowly Lizzie and Vince had escaped disaster in his absence.

The door opened and Lizzie ran out to meet him.

'Oh, Jeremy. Thank God you've come. It was awful, terrible. You'll never believe how dreadful—'

He put his arms around her. Through the window he could see two figures sitting at the table, his mother and Charlie. At least the worst he had been dreading hadn't happened.

'Pretend to be helping me to take this in,' she pointed to the washing hanging on the line and took a deep breath. 'Gosse – Inspector Gosse was here.'

'What!' So it was worse than he had imagined.

'I was pegging out a few more things when I saw him coming from the hill direction. He waved and shouted a greeting. There was nothing I could do. I couldn't run inside and close the door and warn Charlie. He was asking me how I was, very polite, with that ingratiating smile of his.' She shuddered. 'Said he was on his way back to the office, taking the short cut.'

'What was he doing on the hill?' Faro demanded. Was he looking for McLaw?

'He'd been on a case, that's all he said. Something about the tunnel.'

Something to do with Tibbie's accident or murder. That was at least a relief.

'He was just being polite, I expect. But I was terrified. I could hardly talk to him. He kept chatting on and on, how was I? How were we enjoying the cottage? I knew he was hoping I'd ask him in, give him a cup of tea. But all I could think of was getting rid of him. I hoped Charlie had heard us talking and was hiding in the box bed. I had to keep him out at all costs. Fortunately, like a prayer answered, Vince appeared, just home from school.

'And that diverted him. He transferred his attention to Vince. I was sorry, as I could see by the gleam in his eye that my little lad was in for yet another interrogation, but I left them to it and dashed into the cottage, closed the door and whispered to Charlie to keep out of sight, and then to my horror, I heard footsteps. He was outside, still chatting to Vince. I opened the door, I had no idea what I was going to say, but I certainly wasn't going to ask him inside, manners or no manners.'

She paused for breath. 'And at that moment, your ma came back from the Pleasance shops with her basket. I had to introduce them, I said this was your boss, Gosse bowed.' She rolled her eyes heavenward. 'I wish you could have seen him kissing her hand. And she was thrilled. I could see she was going to ask him in. She might mention Charlie and I'd have to invent something about my brother here on a visit—'

'What are you two doing standing out there gossiping? It's chilly, that's a sharp wind.' Mary Faro appeared at the door, overcome by curiosity. 'I've made a pot of tea.'

'Let's go in, then.'

She took his arm. 'Your inspector was passing by. Such a nice gentleman,' she added, and remembering that bow and the hand kissing no doubt, with a sharp glance at Lizzie, 'We do things differently in Orkney, always invite a stranger in for a cup of tea. It's one of our strictest rules, as you know, Jeremy. Never keep anyone standing at the door. He must have thought us very rude,' said Mary with a sharp glance at Lizzie. She had clearly liked his flattery and would have enjoyed more of the same.

'We do things differently in Edinburgh, Ma,' said Faro solemnly. 'And the inspector wouldn't have expected to be invited in. He's a very busy man, Ma.'

'I know that and he was very reassuring.'

'About what?'

'About this terrible killer you're all searching for. It's in all the papers, he said, but the police were on to it and we were quite safe. "Don't you worry, madam," he said, "you are quite safe here and we will get him any day now."'

Late that evening, alone with Lizzie, Faro thought of the irony of it all, even as Gosse was speaking, the wanted man who was giving him so many problems was in the box bed just yards away, and any day mere seconds away from discovery.

Faro shuddered as Lizzie said: 'I've been thinking, I was

silly to panic. I could have introduced him to Charlie as my brother, he looks quite different from the posters.'

'Never you believe that. Gosse has seen McLaw many times, he would certainly have recognised him, shaven or no. And if so, instead of getting into our warm, comfortable bed this night, we would have been languishing behind bars in the city jail. I let your imagination provide what would be in store,' he said grimly and did not add, 'Or what sort of future there would be for our baby.'

He gave her a fond kiss and said, 'Goodnight, Lizzie dear, sleep well.'

CHAPTER TWENTY-SEVEN

Faro lay awake most of the night, there was much on his mind to make sleeping impossible. Indeed, as he moved from side to side endeavouring not to disturb Lizzie, and going over the events of the past few days, he wondered if he would ever sleep peacefully again. Just a little more than two weeks ago he had been a happy, though very slightly bored, detective sergeant, his main irritation the tiresome daily contact with Inspector Gosse. Their dislike for each other was cordial which did not add rich harmony to the situation, especially as the inspector was determined to make life as uncomfortable as possible for Faro.

On social occasions, people he met, who had nothing to do with the police, smilingly asked him if he enjoyed working on a murder case. Who could? For him it meant carrying a vivid impression at the front of his mind of the corpse of the murdered victim. The worse the case, the stronger his determination and the keener his focus, and although the word 'enjoy' had no place in the process, he had to admit that this was the most interesting and exciting part of an investigation. Thinking it through, detail by detail, the search for parallels, motives and method, the careful piecing together of every detail that might help him by letting the character of the murderer into his mind. What kind of a person did this? What was his background, his state of mind, his usual daily life, his work, his family and friends? And then, what triggered such violence for all the elements according to what McLaw had told him – if this was true – this had not been the impulse of a scared man, rather than a methodically calculated, planned act of anger or revenge.

Faro had made notes about everything from the details of the scene of the crime as recorded at the trial. Not enough to be interesting and all pointing to one of the many open-and-shut cases of domestic murder.

His mind switched back to other similar cases he had solved, killers he had brought to justice, recovering faces, conversations and what he had learnt in these few years as a detective.

'Think yourself into his mind. You are he, get into his shoes and walk around in them. Think like him, fear what he feared and, above all, remember Macfie's unfailing maxim: Think of the motive.'

He sighed as he went back to the beginning, the day he had returned to Edinburgh and McLaw had already been sentenced to death for the murder of his wife. Not an uncommon murder by any means. Case closed, or so he believed, scanning the report of the trial and picking up the list of duties for the day. Then to crown it all and infuriate Gosse, who had been in charge of the investigation, McLaw, on his way to jail to await execution, had escaped and was on the run, with police all over the country alerted.

Little imagining, as retired Superintendent Macfie joined them for their usual Sunday walk and supper at the cottage, that Vince, working on Saturdays at the High Street antiquarian bookshop, was about to be involved in the owner's death. And although it was plain to everyone that it was the work of McLaw on the run – although Charlie denied this – how Gosse had gloated over this chance of making life a bit uneasy for Faro by constantly interviewing his stepson and scaring the lad with the grim fact that he had discovered Mr Molesby's body and so that made him the prime suspect.

Then there had been the chance meeting on Princes Street with Mrs Brook, Macfie's housekeeper. Recognising her and seeing she was so upset, on an impulse he had invited her into a cafe, hoping to calm her with a soothing cup of tea, only to listen to a horrendous tale of warring sisters who left it too late for reconciliation and of a coffin full of stones where Agatha Simms's body should have been. The Belmuir poorhouse where she had been an inmate was clearly culpable, then her sister, determined to find an answer, was knocked down and fatally injured by a runaway carriage on the Mound. Could this be dismissed as coincidence? Celia had been an old friend of Mrs Brook and she attended the funeral to be met by the distraught servant Tibbie who had witnessed the accident and related the whole terrible story. And when that maid disappeared and also met a fatal accident on the Innocent Railway, he found himself with two possible murders while the search for the missing McLaw continued.

Then there was the attack on an elderly gentleman in Castle Hill and a description that fitted McLaw, sighted in Glasgow by the police, with the stolen wallet and money still on him. A jubilant Gosse went off to bring him back in person, no escape this time, only to discover that the recaptured criminal was not McLaw. Angrily, a frustrated Gosse had offered a £50 reward with posters of the wanted man displayed, the inevitable result being that people from everywhere claimed to have seen him and wanted that reward. And although this was a constable's job, Gosse had enjoyed the humiliation of Faro by sending him to interview them personally.

Worse was in store. Kindhearted Vince had given shelter in the disused stable beside their cottage to a gypsy allegedly fleeing from a forced marriage by his tribe. When Vince, providing him with food and hoping to help him escape, was not enough, this gypsy had decided to take matters into his own hands and when Vince's mother, only observed distantly, went out shopping, had entered the cottage to see what money he could find. He was not as safe as he thought. Vince came home early from school that day and Lizzie forgot her purse. He was caught in the act.

Faro suspected that Vince's gypsy was the missing McLaw and he was also on his way home only to find something so dreadful he could never have thought it possible. He knew nothing of Lizzie's early life before she left the Highlands aged fifteen, pregnant with a child by rape, and now Faro faced the shocking revelation that McLaw was her younger brother.

Bad enough, but even worse was the fact that he, Lizzie, and Vince were all guilty of concealing and sheltering a wanted murderer. For Lizzie, expecting their first child, her brother's fate might be disastrous. So Faro was placed in the terrible position of seeing the end to his career, his marriage and Vince's future.

While Faro was considering his options, Charlie McLaw had refused to escape, maintaining that he was innocent and that he did not intend spending the rest of his life as a fugitive. There was only one solution and that was for Faro to find Annie's killer and make McLaw a free man. Listening to McLaw's story, Faro had an intuitive feeling that he was hearing the truth; that Gosse had seized on the usual verdict, so easy to deal with that this was a domestic murder, a man comes home and finds his wife with another man and kills her, without knowing any of the facts behind that marriage.

McLaw had presented him with the proverbial needle in a haystack. Where was he to start without a clue to lean on? He had a suspicion that the poorhouse lay behind it all, and Agatha Simm's empty coffin hinted to a dark trade in selling cadavers to the medical school, a once grisly business begun by the resurrectionists and Burke and Hare, now legalised under a Parliamentary act by which bodies in the possession of workhouses – poorhouses in Scotland – could be donated 'to undergo anatomical examination by appointed organisations', in fact, medical schools.

There was more trouble on the horizon, quite unexpected and looming in his direction, in the shapely form of Lady Honor, laird of Belmuir, a very determined lady when she set her heart on something – or someone, in this case Detective Sergeant Jeremy Faro. She had decided to track him down in his lair, with the excuse of looking over the property at Solomon's Tower, the ancient tower house that was under her protection, while on her way to take up residence at her town house in Moray Place.

She had planned it carefully. There was no direct road except via Duddingston and that would not take her past the Faros' cottage. The carriage was to be left on the new Dalkeith Road and she set off on foot unaccompanied by her maid, her progress watched with some interest by the builders who, in awe of gentry, did not whistle, although they were curious about what she was doing and where she was heading at nine o'clock in the morning, fondly imagining that the upper classes let the day get well aired before they ventured out.

The weather was with her. It was a far from pleasant day, with swift-moving, dark clouds glowering down from the head of Arthur's Seat, and as the cottage drew near with its welcoming smoke rising from the chimney, the first drops of rain obligingly fell.

Her parasol was quite inadequate and it would make sense, she thought, for her to seek shelter. She walked up the garden path and knocked on the door.

Lizzie and Charlie, who had quickly retreated into his box bed, had noted her approach in a state of some anxiety, with no idea who this well-dressed, upper-class lady was wandering about on the hill with a parasol that was already dripping water.

Lizzie opened the door, curtseyed. 'Can I help you?'

Without waiting to be asked, Honor stepped inside and handed her the parasol. 'I wish to speak to DS Faro on a matter of extreme urgency.'

'I am sorry, he is not at home, madam. You will find him at the police station.' This was a bitter blow. 'At this hour?'

'Yes, madam. He starts at eight o clock,' said Lizzie and as the lady glared down at the ruined parasol and waited, she realised that refreshment was expected and some shelter from the rain, which they both considered with some deliberation.

'It is just a passing shower,' said Lizzie weakly.

'Um,' was the lady's comment. Lizzie gave one quick backward glance into the parlour and saw that Charlie was safe. 'Perhaps you would like—' she made a movement towards the room, at which Honor swept past her with a murmur that might have been thanks.

Both were regarding each other, Lizzie taking in the appearance of this grand lady, the elegant clothes, the beautiful shoes and that expensive perfume and wondering who on earth this could be and what was her business with Jeremy. She was being equally considered under narrowed eyes by the laird of Belmuir, a pretty, simple peasant, well-spoken, perhaps an upper servant, certainly not worthy of Jeremy Faro. The room, simply furnished but clean and tidy, reminded her of her housekeeper's apartment.

Then, as Lizzie walked across to attend to the kettle she saw that she was not just plump but pregnant. Poor Jeremy, what a life—

As Lizzie set cups on the table, the sun suddenly shone through the window, lighting up that glorious mane of golden hair, certainly a woman's crowning glory and never achieved by the laird of Belmuir, even with the daily application of curling tongs by her maid.

'The rain has stopped, I see.' And Honor stood up and with a gesture declined the offer of tea. 'You are very kind, Mrs Faro, but I really must go on my way. I have much that requires my attention.'

Lizzie didn't feel disappointment, just considerable relief. There was always the danger of Charlie having a bout of coughing or sneezing behind those closed doors. However, she was curious to know the name of this grand lady.

'Who shall I say called, madam?'

Honor had already reached the door. Seizing the dripping parasol and giving it an angry shake, she looked round briefly. 'Belmuir. But I shall see him in Edinburgh.'

As she disappeared down the path, Charlie looked over Lizzie's shoulder and said: 'I heard all that. Who was she, that lady with the loud voice?'

'I have no idea,' Lizzie shook her head. 'Something to do with the police, obviously.'

Charlie shuddered. 'And dangerous. Ealasaid, every time we get some unexpected caller, the danger becomes worse – not only for me, for all of us.'

'We will manage somehow.'

He shook his head and put his arm around her. 'We cannot go on like this forever.'

'It is only until Jeremy finds out the truth,' she said firmly. 'And he will, never you fear, and all will be well again.'

All being well again was a dream beyond Charlie's imaginings. He had little faith in Jeremy ever finding the real killer. It seemed a hopeless task.

* * *

'We had a visitor, looking for you, Jeremy,' said Lizzie when he arrived home that evening, quite unable to restrain her curiosity and keen to know who was the lady with the odd name who had given them a panic-stricken half-hour in her search for Mr Faro.

'Said she was called Belmuir.'

'A lady with the voice of authority, very loud,' Charlie put in before he could reply. 'These surprise visits – we can't go on like this. Someone will catch us out and recognise me sooner or later.' He shook his head. 'I'll never forget how scared I was, sure I'd be discovered when your inspector came. Talking to Ealasaid outside, I was terrified in case she had to ask him in.' He gave her a fond glance. 'She managed to keep him out, though. But I cannot subject you both indefinitely to this terrible danger. The last thing we need is a tide of visitors.'

Ignoring that, for she heard it from her brother many times each day, Lizzie looked hard at Jeremy and persisted: 'Who was the lady?'

'The laird of Belmuir,' he said shortly, with a calmness he was far from feeling. The presence of Honor Belmuir made him decidedly uncomfortable, especially that she seemed to have tracked him down to his cottage.

'Lairds are men,' said Lizzie firmly.

Faro made an impatient gesture, he hadn't time to go into all that explanation and said: 'They had a burglary in their town house at Moray Place that I've been investigating and she must have wanted to know the progress.'

'Then why come here? Surely the police station—' Lizzie began and Faro, pretending not to hear, asked: 'Where's Ma?'

'She didn't come today, sent a message that Mrs Brook had invited her to go along to the Woman's Guild meeting at the church.'

For which mercy, Faro silently thanked God. Had she been present when Belmuir called, her curiosity would have been boundless, her questions unanswerable. Muttering that he was glad she had found a new friend, with a sigh of relief he turned to Charlie.

'I know we're no further on finding Annie's killer, but I've just had another idea. As a last resort, I'd like to go examine the croft where you lived. Where it all happened.'

Lizzie yawned. She was very tired, this pregnancy as well as stress was draining much of her usual energy and by eight o'clock at night she needed her bed. Kissing them both goodnight, she said: 'I'll leave you to it. And I'll say a prayer for you.'

When the door closed on her, Charlie was looking very doubtful and Faro said: 'Often in what we call domestic murder cases, the answer seems so obvious that no one bothers to look for any clues. They've got the killer, case closed.'

Charlie shook his head, tried to look as if he thought going to the croft was a good idea. And failed. Whatever the outcome, he felt certain that he was a doomed man.

CHAPTER TWENTY-EIGHT

Inspector Gosse's foul mood was unconnected with the weather next morning when Faro arrived at the office. For a moment Faro thought his worst fears had been realised, that Gosse had suspicions from his visit to the cottage. Indeed, Gosse's anger was related to that short visit, but mainly because he had seen Lizzie taking in the washed clothes, the sun touching her golden curls, her bare arms . . . true she was less slender than he remembered, a certain thickness about the waist, but that did not matter. Gosse enjoyed a good armful in a woman but it was not until he got closer that he had realised the roundness signified that she was pregnant. This was the final straw, that his hated sergeant should have all the luck, a lovely wife and probably a son, the first of many.

He was a little put off that she did not seem anxious to meet him again, a more sensitive man would have put this down to her being distinctly scared – but what could be the reason for that? He lingered, making casual comments about the weather, hoping that the building workers with their all-day hammering were not disturbing her and also hoping that the estate house was as far as demolition went and that her lovely cottage would be untouched. He added, with a significant sigh and a glance at the table, that he had been out all day investigating the accident in the tunnel.

Lizzie ignored the silent plea, desperate to get rid of him, this in no small measure due to the fact that Charlie McLaw was only yards away from the man who was hunting him down. And so Gosse ended with a polite bow and departed, his resentment towards Faro increased considerably by the fact that Lizzie had failed to offer him a cup of tea, depriving him of the chance to exercise his charismatic charm upon her, even indulge in a little flirtation in the absence of her husband; and he determined to make Faro's life even more uncomfortable for his wife's lack of hospitality.

He pointed to a pile of papers. 'More sightings of McLaw and claims for that damned reward for your investigation.'

Gosse was realising, at last and too late, the effects that fifty pounds reward – a small fortune – was having on the population and Faro said: 'It is proving to be a waste of time, sir. Don't you think we should ignore it? McLaw is probably out of the country by now.'

Gosse wheeled round, glaring at him and thumping his fists on the desk, Faro stepped back hastily, fearing that the inspector was about to attack him as he shouted:

'Ignore it, should we? When did you presume to know better than your superiors what is the law and what is a waste of time and how they should deal with a wanted man on the loose and dangerous? Every day makes it more likely that he will claim another victim.'

'We have no evidence, so far. The only questionable death of the woman found in the tunnel, you said had been explained to your satisfaction. That it was an accident.'

'All evidence from the railway would substantiate that,' Gosse growled.

Faro did not think so. This was another case that he was trying to solve, the details of which Gosse was ignorant, all leading back to the poorhouse at Belmuir, which he was increasingly certain also had a link with the murder of Annie McLaw, the reason for McLaw's conviction, which, Faro believed, was a miscarriage of justice. If only he could prove it.

Gosse's hand trembled with rage as he pointed to the papers. 'Now get on with your work, Faro, and stop wasting any more time in arguing. I am certain that McLaw will be taken, and by my efforts with or without that fifty-pound reward. Even if the claims are useless, each person must be contacted and interviewed – we cannot have the population believing that their police force is not a hundred per cent efficient.'

As Faro left the office he pocketed the papers with their new claims, which he didn't bother to read. Charlie McLaw would probably be still asleep in the cottage, his breakfast being prepared by his devoted sister, so he would seize this opportunity of visiting McLaw's shack on the edge of the Belmuir estate and carry out a careful search of the scene of the crime, as he had done with Vince at the bookshop.

In their haste to arrest McLaw it was possible there had been no search for clues. Then he would return to the office, hand the papers to the constable at reception to send the usual polite reply that the sightings had been investigated and the results were negative, but thanking them for their efforts.

Faro wished he could have had McLaw to accompany him on the search of the croft. When they discussed it last night he even considered for a wild moment methods of taking him. But that was too foolhardy, especially as local people who knew him in his beardless days, even without the poster, would most likely recognise him.

Boarding the train, he was recognised by the railway guard as becoming quite a regular traveller. The guard's name was Jim and, as he was inclined to be friendly, Faro decided to put a few more questions his way, the conversation instigated by Jim enquiring about that poor lass who had died in the tunnel and hoping Faro would notice that efforts had been made by the railway to get rid of the debris therein, with a penalty fine for those who continued to dispose of their refuse there.

'Seems no time at all, since we got rid of the last notice,' Jim smiled. 'That one was for when we still had horses and were forbidden to stop the train in order to feed them. A long time ago, that was; steam made such a difference, changed all our lives.'

Faro said: 'I was somewhat surprised that the lady was travelling alone that day. The poorhouse are not inclined to let their residents out alone on a journey into Edinburgh.' He paused to see the effect this was having, but Jim merely stared out of the window, regarding the passing scenery as though it might have something to offer. 'On a previous occasion she was running to catch the train; it had just started and I asked the guard to stop it. She was very keen to escape from the man who was struggling to restrain her.'

257

'Is that so, sir? It wasn't me,' said Jim hurriedly. 'Although we have strict orders about the loonies who might be making a break for it.'

'Was she travelling with someone the day of her accident?' Faro asked again and received the same answer.

'It isn't likely she would have fallen out, sir, if there had been someone with her. And I don't recall anyone else getting on the train at the workhouse halt that day. Oh, excuse me, sir.' They had come to the first halt on the line and Jim made his escape, very thankfully, Faro decided. He was almost sure that for some reason Jim or even the railway company did not want to become involved in what could be safely dismissed as an unfortunate accident caused by one of their jammed windows, which had now been repaired.

On this bright, sunny day, he would have relished this train journey had he not been so preoccupied, and as the train gathered steam, he took out his notebook, checked the deep pockets of his greatcoat for candles, needed for searching dark corners, and most of all his magnifying glass. This was a matter of some amusement to his colleagues, but an essential for revealing minute details invisible to the naked eye. Replacing them alongside Charlie's map of directions to the croft, he remembered his request for a description of Annie, which was included in the notes.

'She was a great beauty,' Charlie had said. 'We had a painting done by an artist who told her that a hundred years ago when courtesans to the royal courts came from humble backgrounds she would have done very well. She loved that, always felt that she deserved a better life than had been her lot.' He shook his head sadly. 'I fell in love with her at first sight, but I don't honestly know why she chose to marry me.'

Faro left the train at the Belmuir halt and with the poorhouse and the castle clearly visible he made his way across the wooded estate grounds. Charlie's map had few landmarks, and soon feeling lost, he was fighting his way through overgrown gorse bushes, which caught at his clothes. Someone before him had not been so lucky – he detached a fragment of fine cloth with a button attached, torn from some garment.

At last a small clearing and a tiny, ivy-covered croft emerged. From the great chopping block and piles of wood that still remained, this had been the woodcutter's cottage. It looked sad and desolate, swamped by the enormous trees, which cut out most of the sunlight, its walls overwhelmed by the ivy that threatened to block out the windows. Charlie had laughed when asked about a key. 'We never had one, if it ever existed then the Belmuirs would have it. Besides, folk like us never lock our doors. What have we to steal?'

He pushed open the door; there were two rooms, he had been told, a kitchen and, through it, the bedroom. He walked through to the bedroom, a bleak place, indeed, with little in it. The once handsome half-poster bed, possibly inherited from the castle at some clearance or discarded by its previous owner due to a change of fashion, seemed out of place in such humble surroundings. There was a shabby, well-worn mattress from which sheets and blankets had been removed.

Lighting a candle and crawling beneath, his magnifying glass revealed no bloodstains on the floorboards, all pointing to his theory that Annie had not been killed in that bed.

The room's only other furniture was a mirrored dressing table with a few drawers, all empty, and a wardrobe. At first glance this was also empty, but in its depths there was a large picture frame, the portrait of Annie.

He sighed and replaced it. He doubted Charlie would want this painful reminder, which confirmed that she had been a beauty. A final, minute search of the floor and then into the kitchen. Untidy, unclean, it offered little but dust. In the poor light from the window he set two candles into the wall sconces and set to work searching cupboards, which were empty. Kneeling, magnifying glass in hand, he began searching inch by inch the wooden floor surrounding the table and near the kitchen sink.

Then his first find. The minute remains of two once bloody footprints, the first barefoot and small and undoubtedly female, the second, a man's shoe or boot, faded and invisible to the naked eye. But as he looked further, there were traces in between the surrounding floorboards, dark stains that were undoubtedly dried blood and those led into the bedroom.

He sat back on his heels. Annie had been killed in the kitchen and her body dragged back into the bedroom and placed beside Charlie's unconscious body.

His theory had been right but it was small comfort. Although this was evidence, it was doubtful that the kitchen premises had been searched at the time of the murder. The killer had already been decided upon. It was an open and shut case, just another domestic murder with the husband swearing that he was innocent.

Evidence, but where did it lead him? Certainly, now one thing he knew about the killer was that from the footprint, it had been a fine shoe, not a policeman's issue boot – those he knew well – nor a working man's nailed boot. Annie's last client had not been a local man, and that stretched the search into the impossible.

Suddenly the door opened behind him. A dog rushed at him, a man with a rifle silhouetted in the doorway.

As Faro leant back against the wall, pushing away the dog, a man shouted. 'Down, Rex. Down.' And moving closer, a cold voice said, 'Are you aware that you are trespassing? Give me your name and I'll have the law on you.'

Then, as the candles Faro had placed in the sconces to give extra illumination revealed the intruder, the voice exclaimed, 'Mr Faro! What in God's name are you doing here?'

The man was Sir Hector. There had to be an explanation and no time to think of any that would be convincing. 'I was told at the poorhouse that there might be cottages to let on the estate and I was interested in perhaps renting one.'

'Then you should have gone there first and got someone to accompany you. You could get lost, and as we have very strict laws about trespassing,' he indicated the rifle, 'you could have got yourself shot, mistaken for one of our deer.'

'My apologies, just an impulse, I find this a very attractive area, a good escape from the city.'

'Indeed, but I assure you this cottage is quite unsuitable,' Sir Hector eyed him coldly, a slight twitch of his eyebrows indicated that this was a poor story and he wasn't believing any of it. Ushering him from the croft and closing the door he said:

'I will put in your request to the proper authority and they will no doubt get in touch when some place suitable for renting comes up. Meanwhile, you should be able to get the train back to Edinburgh. If you head in that direction,' he pointed towards the workhouse, 'they will halt for you.'

And that was the end of the conversation. An inclination of the head and a less friendly Sir Hector than on their previous encounter walked away, the dog at his side. Faro went across to the railway halt and waited for the train. He had made a sorry mess of that, and did no favours by involving himself with the Belmuirs, who would not take kindly to this inquisitive policeman roaming around the poorhouse, especially if he suspected there might be more in those boxes of market produce than vegetables from the gardens of the estate making their way into Edinburgh – or more appropriately to the medical students at Surgeons' Hall.

He sneezed and searching in his pocket took out a handkerchief and a piece of cloth fell to the ground. He picked up what he had idly pocketed caught by a piece of gorse; it indicated someone in a great hurry to escape from the McLaws' croft. That someone could be the killer. He looked at it again, a piece of evidence perhaps, but useless. His mission had failed.

CHAPTER TWENTY-NINE

It was late when he returned, the cottage in darkness. Everyone had gone to bed. He was thankful for that, although movement above his head hinted that Vince was still awake. He saw little of Vince these days, busy at school he spent most of the evenings after supper up in his attic room doing his homework and reading, only emerging to take the faithful Coll for his evening walk. He didn't seem to have need of their company any more and Faro felt that he was losing the bond they had once shared. He had been sorely tried by Gosse's persistent questioning and Faro realised that he felt alienated from these adults, and the complications of the dangerous situation into which he had been unwittingly dragged were too much for his understanding.

For a moment, he was tempted to climb the ladder and talk to his stepson, but what was the use? To be honest, Vince was not the most important issue and he was very tired, weary, wanting only to lay down his head, sleep and end the long day.

In the morning on the way to the office he would look in and find out from Mrs Brook when Macfie was arriving. After some hours troubled by a nightmare, he awoke knowing he would not sleep again. He got out of bed carefully so as not to disturb Lizzie and the slight snoring from the box bed indicated that Charlie still slept. A scratching above his head, there was a whimper from Coll; opening the attic trapdoor, the dog leapt down into his arms.

It was a brisk, cloudless dawn promising a sunny day, and they would have a fine walk together. That would clear his head and prepare him for whatever the day had in store. As Coll raced ahead he remembered so many days just like this, when life seemed so good before the terrors of the past weeks had changed all their lives. He would have given much to even imagine that their lives could ever be the same again.

The cottage was stirring when he returned. Breakfast was always a silent meal and as Lizzie bustled about preparing porridge and cutting bread, Vince and Charlie appeared, both yawning and with little inclination for conversation.

'Yes, a fine walk,' Faro said, kissing Lizzie, 'clears the head.' She smiled at him and made no mention of the events of yesterday or the mysterious lady laird of Belmuir.

Preparing to leave, he said, 'I'll call in at Sheridan Place and find out from Mrs Brook when Macfie is arriving.'

The Pleasance was astir with activity, steam rising from the train about to leave for Fisherrow and market stalls abounding, the smells of cooking, the laughter of children, dogs barking, it was living up to its name, despite the crumbling properties, the tall tenements sadly in need of

264

upgrading. He wondered how the new road with its long terrace would affect the district as he walked into Sheridan Place.

Mrs Brook opened the door and whispered excitedly: 'He's back, Mr Faro. And there's a lady with him. She collected him in her carriage from the railway station—'

As she ushered him into the dining room, he was taken aback, to say the least, to find that Macfie was indeed home, eating a hearty breakfast with a lady at his side, a lady Faro recognised but was not at all pleased to meet again.

With no opportunity to tell Mrs Brook what was happening regarding Tibbie, they could say no more as Macfie jumped up and took Faro in a hearty embrace.

'Good to see you again, lad. Come away in. And you're just in time for a bite with us. Food is splendid abroad, but not much of it is as good as Mrs Brook's. How have you been? You're looking well.' All this as Faro took a seat at the big dining table.

Mary Faro was already seated there, looking very pleased with herself. She beamed. 'Good morning, Jeremy.'

'Your mother and I have already become acquainted,' Macfie smiled with a bow in her direction.

The other woman seated had her back towards Jeremy. A dark-green velvet hat, a now familiar fragrance. The last woman in the world he wanted to meet at that moment.

Macfie beamed. 'This is Honor Belmuir, Faro.'

If Macfie had had Lucifer himself seated at the table, Faro could not have been more taken aback. He bowed. 'Your Ladyship.'

'You two know each other?' said Macfie, also taken by surprise at this encounter.

'We have met already,' said the laird of Belmuir coldly. 'I was unaware that you knew the superintendent.'

'We are old friends,' said Macfie delightedly. 'I have known Honor since she was a wee lass.' He looked at her; there was great affection in that glance and something else, a touch of sadness. 'Sit down, Jeremy. You'll eat with us.'

'I have breakfasted already, sir, but a cup of tea would be most welcome.'

Faro took the seat next to his mother, facing Belmuir, while Mrs Brook set another place and hovered in the background.

'Mr Macfie has made me very welcome, what a very nice man,' whispered Mary. 'Are you sure you don't want some more breakfast, dear, it's delicious.' The smell of cooked bacon was almost irresistible and Faro weakly allowed Mrs Brook to serve him from the silver dish on the sideboard.

Looking across at Belmuir and Macfie, who were talking quietly, Mary said: 'And such a nice lady – for one of Them, I mean. No edge, so charming.' He could have told her about the other less agreeable side of the laird of Belmuir as she said: 'And she sent her carriage to the station to meet his train.'

Faro wondered about that, all the way from Belmuir to meet a train. How did she know? Then Macfie said: 'It will be good to have you at Moray Place, Honor. We will see more of you.'

And for the first time she looked at Faro as if some explanation was necessary and repeated what he knew already. 'We spend the season in our town house. Much more accessible for concerts and social occasions. And,' turning to Macfie, 'I am also hoping that Brandon can help you discover who stole our painting and if possible get it back.'

'If it has not been sold already, my dear,' said Macfie, patting her hand. 'That is often the way with such robberies, stolen to order.'

Having now been included in the laird's conversation, Faro's thoughts were less on the problem of the stolen portrait than how he could get Macfie alone, as soon as possible, and confide the details of the horrendous situation in which he found himself. He had no doubts that Macfie's affection for him would provide sympathy, but as to approving of his deliberately breaking the law, that was another matter. However, he had no alternative, if he could not track down Annie's killer in a few days, McLaw was going to give himself up and take the consequences. Without revealing his relationship to Lizzie, which must for ever remain a secret, Charlie intended to claim that in a chase across the hill Faro had recaptured him. Gosse would be furious at Faro having whipped the prize from under his nose. His only consolation.

The clock struck the half-hour. 'I must go,' Faro said. 'If you will excuse me.'

'I must also leave you,' said Honor Belmuir. 'I have a busy day – so many things to attend to before Moray Place is ready to offer hospitality to our many friends. My brother is already there making arrangements for a welcoming party.' She paused and smiled and looked at Macfie, 'You shall come.' And to Faro, 'We would be delighted to have your presence too.' A gesture. 'And of course, Mrs Faro.' Did she mean Lizzie? Mary clearly thought the invitation was to her.

She almost curtseyed and said. 'I would be delighted.'

Honor regarded her critically. 'It will depend, of course, on how long you are staying here.'

Mary looked anxiously at Macfie who laughed. 'She can stay as long as she likes, Honor, so I am sure we can persuade her,' he added, and escorting Faro and Honor to the door, he said to her: 'Dinner this evening, my dear,' and to Faro, 'Drop in on your way home, lad. Bring me up to date.'

The Belmuir carriage was not waiting outside. Before Faro could comment, Honor said: 'Perhaps Mr Faro would be good enough to escort me to Moray Place.'

Faro bowed, cursing silently. It was not on his route to the office and he had little desire to spend a further session in this disturbing lady's presence.

CHAPTER THIRTY

Walking towards Sheridan Place later that day, he was aware that Macfie was his last, his only hope. It was vital that he confided in this experienced crime officer who might recognise something he had overlooked in his own futile attempts to track down Annie McLaw's killer.

Mrs Brook opened the door. As always, she looked at him hopefully and he shook his head, feeling guilty that he had to admit to another failure regarding her suspicions regarding Tibbie's death being officially dismissed as an accident.

She shook her head sadly. 'You did your best, sir. No one could have done more.' It was scant conciliation. 'The superintendent is expecting you.'

At that, the door from the room already book-lined and destined to be a study, opened and Macfie came out with a beaming welcome. 'Glad to see you, lad. Come in, come in.' Mrs Brook lingered awaiting orders. 'Tea? Or something stronger, perhaps.' Thanking her, the sideboard was already set up with an imposing line of decanters and he pointed Faro in the direction of two handsome leather armchairs by either side of a good-going fire. Taking the seat opposite, he leant forward.

'Well, what is all the latest news? What's been happening in my absence? Has McLaw been recaptured? The place is thick with unsightly posters – and what's all this nonsense, this rumour about Gosse personally offering a reward? Incredible!' He paused to pour them both a generous dram, while Faro told him of Gosse rushing to Glasgow to find that the man the police held was not McLaw at all.

Macfie shook his head. 'Such folly thinking a reward would help. Was he not aware from long experience of the human race what the result would be? An endless tide of folk alleging sightings from all over the countryside.'

'And it was my duty to track each one down and interview them,' Faro said grimly.

Macfie made a face. 'Surely that task should have been allocated to the constables? Hardly a fitting role for his detective sergeant.'

Faro shrugged. 'I obey the inspector's orders, sir. That's my duty.'

Macfie smiled ruefully. 'Gosse doesn't do well in hiding his dislike – or is it envy of you, Faro? We all know that.' Pausing, he placed his hands together in a characteristic gesture. 'But that is not what is troubling you, is it? I know you well and I've sensed from the moment you came through that door while we were at breakfast that there was something seriously wrong.' He leant forward. 'Not Lizzie, I hope – this baby? Or Vince?' he added anxiously.

'No, sir. All is well with them.'

Macfie nodded. 'Thank God for that.'

Faro decided that matters were complicated enough and he'd save the bookshop burglary and the owner's death for another time as Macfie, refreshing their glasses, gave him a quizzical glance.

'Like to talk about what's bothering you – all in confidence, to an old friend?'

Faro doubted if even this old friend, once a chief superintendent of the Edinburgh Police, would find what he had to say acceptable, or be able to offer sympathy on a situation that went against the principles of a lifetime's service.

He sighed deeply and began the story, without revealing names. 'A domestic murder, one that is well known to all of us. Husband returns home one night, rather drunk, and finds his wife in bed with another man.'

He heard Macfie's sigh. 'And of course, he killed him.'

'In fact, he did not. He said that the man leapt on him, knocked him out and when he recovered consciousness it was daylight, and his wife was lying on the floor beside him with a knife in her chest. He was covered in her blood and knowing no one would believe his story and that he would be blamed, he went to his stepfather, who instead of helping him, told the local constable and who had him arrested.'

'And this was the story he told them,' said Macfie doubtfully.

Faro nodded. 'Gosse refused to believe a word of it. Arrested him immediately on a charge of murder.'

'Could he put a name to his assailant?'

Faro shook his head. 'It was dark, sir. And he was very drunk—'

Macfie held up his hand. 'Excuse me interrupting, Faro, but isn't this the McLaw case?'

'It is, sir. But I have every reason to believe that he was speaking the truth, that it was the other man who killed her and set up the scene so that McLaw would be blamed.'

'From what I recall of reading about it, one realises it was outrageous and criminal to cast the blame on the husband, but according to the evidence, this woman was a known prostitute.' Macfie looked thoughtful. 'Obviously this was not a planned murder, perhaps it was even manslaughter rather than homicide. And all you have told me suggests that this was not one of the lady's casual clients, but rather points to a local man with some very good reasons for concealing his identity.'

Faro went on to say how he had visited the croft, the scene of the crime, and after a very careful examination with the aid of his magnifying glass had found minute dried bloodstains leading from the kitchen to the bedroom that had confirmed his own theory that Annie had been perhaps knifed in a struggle and the man had dragged her body into the bedroom, putting her beside her unconscious husband to let him take the blame.

Macfie listened, nodding in occasional agreement. 'A distinct possibility. Continue.'

Faro sighed and ended with his visit to the Coach and Horses.

'Do I take it that you have her stepbrother as your prime suspect?'

'I have no other – not one that was immediately feasible, I mean, after my examination of the croft. The question is, how to proceed, get a confession and so forth.'

Macfie put down his glass and eyed Faro shrewdly. 'A stepbrother hardly comes under the list of incestuous relations, although as a form of marriage it would be among the Church of England's rules of consanguinity.' He sat back and smiled wryly. 'This is all very much a theory, you know, and one you cannot hope to prove. We can never know the truth, it is still only McLaw's word, circumstantial evidence and, I fear, all very thin.'

Pausing, he gave Faro a shrewd look. 'You have taken this man's case very much to heart, that you believe his version of events, however unlikely. Quite remarkable.' He scratched his ear thoughtfully. 'May I ask, is there some reason you've a personal interest?'

Faro took a deep breath. 'McLaw is Lizzie's brother.'

A moment's silence to take it in before Macfie exploded. 'Dear God! Dear God!'

The superintendent was shattered at the enormity of Faro's family being involved. He had suspected something personal, but nothing – nothing like this. He leant across the table, seized Faro's hand, and asked sternly. 'And do you know his present whereabouts – where he is hiding?'

Faro nodded miserably. 'I do indeed, sir. We have been keeping him concealed in our cottage.'

'This is getting worse and worse.' Trying desperately to remain calm, Macfie exclaimed, 'You and your family could be arrested as accessories, concealing a murderer. I suppose you have thought of that?'

'We've thought of everything, sir. The idea was that he should stay safe until I tracked down the real killer.' And he went on to explain how he had found out the details of Lizzie's early life in the Highlands as a girl. 'I felt I was living with a stranger, sir, that I had never known her background or even that she had a brother. She avoids accounts of my police activities, never reads murder reports in the newspaper and even if she had done so, that name John McLaw would have meant nothing to her. His Gaelic name is Teàrlach – Charles – and McLaw is just a clan name.'

'How did you make this discovery?' Macfie asked grimly.

And Faro told him about Vince and the refugee from the gypsy camp, how Vince's strange behaviour had alerted him and, going into the stable where he was asleep, he realised that this gypsy was none other than McLaw, the man they were all searching for. 'But before I could arrest him, Lizzie was on the scene greeting her long lost brother – in the Gaelic—'

Macfie interrupted shortly: 'You realise that whatever your personal feelings, you are breaking the law and you have told me enough for you – and Lizzie – to both be locked up?' Eyeing him sternly, he added: 'It is beyond belief that you should have taken this step above the law, regardless of the consequences.'

Faro looked at him. This was not the Brandon Macfie that he had known, the old friend, this was the face of the man he might face across the courtroom. 'In your defence you have only this man's preposterous story.'

Feeling rather sick, Faro's reply, 'Which I believe', was met by scornful laughter.

'Try telling that to the jury. You have been incredibly gullible is all I can say in your defence. Does this wretch know what he is subjecting his sister and her family to by getting them involved?'

'Indeed he does. He is now threatening, as I have failed in my attempts to find the real killer, that he will go to the police and give himself up, without involving any of us.'

Macfie sighed. 'A noble gesture for a man on his way to the gallows. But not unknown. Even a guilty man would not wish to see a beloved sister suffer.' He shook his head. 'And in the circumstances, this is the only action that can save you. You must not restrain him – he must do it – and immediately.'

'Not immediately, sir. Let him have a couple of days. I think I may have something I picked up at the croft, frail perhaps, but the only other incident also involves the poorhouse at Belmuir.' Briefly he told him Mrs Brook's story of the two sisters, the sinister accidents to Celia and Tibbie.

Macfie listened and smiled thinly. 'You'll have some difficulty proving anything to their discredit – a very highly thought-of organisation. And popular – do you know they have a waiting list for relatives of very sick and elderly persons to spend their last days there?'

'I believe so, sir, but there have been two accidents involving Belmuir, which to me look suspiciously like murder. I suspect they do a lucrative trade in dead bodies, which instead of being reverently buried, are being sold in large boxes under cover as market produce and sent direct to Surgeons' Hall for dissection by their students.'

Instead of the shocked surprise Faro expected from this announcement, Macfie merely laughed. 'My dear lad, you haven't discovered anything new. That trade has been going on for years. Unpleasant, I grant you, especially for relatives of the dead, if any. Distressing, but not illegal.

Something had to be done after the notorious Burke and Hare scandal and let me quote you from the bill that was passed. Went something like this: ". . . that it should be lawful for executors and or another party in possession of the body of any deceased person to permit and allow body of said person to undergo anatomical examination." And that included the administrators of workhouses. It stretched further, the poor could now sell the bodies of their sick and old relatives to the medical school as long as there was a written document and two witnesses. It also included – and this is where the poorhouses came into it – many residents who were illiterate or had no relatives. There was no law saying that they could not take money for their bodies which became the property of the poorhouse.

'It is just a few years ago,' Macfie went on, 'in '59 remember, that medicine became a regulated profession, requiring a formal education, and the dissection of three bodies was compulsory for all who wished to qualify. So whatever your finer feelings, this is not only legal but also necessary if medical science is to progress. At one time we were forced to rely on the gallows but there weren't enough criminals to satisfy the demand and that's how the resurrectionists came into being.'

He tapped the table, smiled. 'Time for another drink, lad.'

'No, sir. I must go. We have early supper.'

'Very well.' Macfie sighed. 'I'm afraid you will get no further with your attempts to prove that Mrs Brook's friend was killed by a runaway carriage and that the servant who witnessed the incident did not fall out of an open door in the railway train, trying to close the window.'

He shrugged. 'There is too little evidence and you are not likely to find any more from the poorhouse. Honor would be appalled. It was her father's brainchild and she is very proud of his efforts to help the community – which indeed has spread in all directions. She is an excellent laird and is having problems keeping Belmuir going, losing money. Not much help from her brother who is in charge of the poorhouse but has a lifestyle that is, to my mind, rather deplorable.' Pausing, he added ruefully, 'I've known Honor since she was a girl. A good lass. Pity she never married, a bit past that now.'

A tap on the door, Mrs Brook looked in. 'Her Ladyship's carriage, sir.'

Macfie laughed and said. 'Ah, yes. The Café Royale.'

Waiting for Mrs Brook to bring down Macfie's evening cloak, Faro said: 'About my visit to the poorhouse, sir, there was something I think you should know.'

A few words about what had been troubling him and as they descended the steps together, he said: 'I'll give that some thought, lad, but my best advice, and indeed my only advice, is that you let McLaw give himself up – and as early as possible.'

Honor looked out of the carriage and seemed surprised to see Faro. Her look at Macfie was a question and he laughed. 'No, my dear, he is not coming with us. Besides, I like having you all to myself.' And to Faro: 'My warmest regards to Lizzie and to Vince. Tell them I am looking forward to resuming our Sundays together.'

Faro watched the carriage depart and wondered whether those Sundays would ever be the same again. Worst of all, once McLaw walked into Gosse's office and gave himself

277

up, what had he left behind? A ruined marriage, for he could expect Lizzie never to look at him again with respect and admiration. Nothing in his life could ever be the same.

As he approached that once welcoming cottage, with the lamplight shining in its window, he thought of the task that lay before him and the emotional scene that must inevitably follow next morning when he said yes to Charlie, this is the best thing for you to do; when he watched him kiss his sister and, taking him firmly by the arm, they walked out past the builders with their scaffolding and their hammers, across the Pleasance and up the High Street to the police station. And what lay at the end of it?

For Charlie, his brother-in-law, who he had failed so badly, a hangman's rope.

CHAPTER THIRTY-ONE

At the cottage, while they were having supper, PC Oldfield handed in a note. 'Sorry to disturb you, sir, the lad said it was urgent.' It was from Honor Belmuir, that he was to meet her at Moray Place at nine o'clock as there had been a discovery concerning the stolen painting.

He guessed that if Gosse had been around when the message arrived, he would have been delighted to go to Moray Place, but the inspector had a strict rule of not working after hours.

Faro sighed deeply. He had problems enough at present without this lady who seemed intent on believing he had magic powers to find the thief, which, for Faro, was as impossible as finding Annie McLaw's killer, especially as he did not believe the painting had been stolen in the first place and that it would turn up eventually as having been 'mislaid'.

It was not until he reached the New Town and climbed the steps to the imposing town house that he remembered

Macfie and Honor were having supper together.

He paused on the threshold, had he made a mistake in the date? Was it tomorrow evening?

To his surprise it was Sir Hector who smiled and opened the door: 'Servants' night out. We don't need the full staff here until we officially move in, when we will bring them from Belmuir.' Seeming equally surprised by finding Faro on the doorstep, he asked: 'What can I do for you, Mr Faro?'

'I had an urgent message from your sister.'

'Oh, yes, of course. She has an engagement, been delayed and sends her apologies. Said I would do just as well. Come in, come in.'

As Faro followed him into the hall he said: 'The good news is that the Leonardo has been found. If you will follow me,' and leading the way up the lofty staircase, three flights leading to the top floor where Hector, walking ahead, now leant against the balustrade. 'Quite a climb. I'm out of condition, I fear!'

His face was flushed by the exertion, the toll of a hearty lifestyle that didn't include a great amount of exercise beyond trailing round the estate grounds of Belmuir Castle shooting rabbits and drinking rather heavily when he was not thus engaged.

'You seem remarkably fit, Mr Faro.'

Faro made no comment, he was looking up at a remarkably fine portrait of a boy's head that was undoubtedly the one that had been reported as stolen.

'Here it is. Yes, we have it back again. Have to apologise for an unfortunate mistake. Our parlourmaid discovered while she was dusting that the frame was cracked' – he shook his head – 'the other explanation, which we did not pursue, was that she dropped it. Anyway, that put her in a panic. It had to be repaired before its absence was noticed, so she took it to the picture-framers in the High Street. Her mother is quite ill and as she is easily distracted, she forgot to collect it.

'Well, well, that's all past,' he added with a cheerful grin while Faro decided that it was a very thin explanation and that somehow the Belmuirs had realised that the burglary story would not go down with the insurance people. As this was a quite a sudden volte-face, perhaps Honor had mentioned it to Macfie who was in her confidence and he had warned her off.

'We keep it up here as the sunlight is disastrous for old masters.' Hector was still leaning against the balustrade. 'You need to stand back here for a better look.'

Faro moved cautiously. After that steep climb, he had a fine view of the marble floor in the hall sixty feet below. He shuddered; it would not do to have vertigo, he thought, as he stepped back.

He was not prepared for what happened next. Sir Hector said: 'Have a good look, Mr Faro. For this is the last thing you'll see on earth.' So saying, he raised his fist, struck out at his face. Faro ducked, his back against the balustrade. Cursing, Hector seized him and tried to throw him over bodily. He struck out again, but with only a bloodied nose, Faro dodged, recovering from the shock of this attack. If there was to be a fight then they were of equal height but Faro was an experienced fighter who had tackled many criminals, many desperate men. This was not one he had expected to encounter.

And Hector had the advantage: Faro's back was against the balustrade and with the weight of the two men there were ominous sounds of creaking and as Hector tried to grab him by the throat and push him over, the wood began to crack and Faro knew that they would both crash to their death on the marble floor far below.

Hector's grip was relentless. He was choking. Slipping, slipping – nothing to hold on to, Hector's red, grinning face above him.

Then another face, a woman's. Hector shouting: 'Help me, help me with him. You took your time getting here. Help me, damn you.'

So she was in it too, Faro thought sadly. His last thought. No escape from death now. But suddenly he was free, staggering against the balustrade. The fight had moved on, and now it was Honor with her arm around Hector's neck. Pulling him down, off balance.

'You bitch!' he was screaming.

Footsteps and another arrival, Macfie breathing heavily, behind him a couple of constables.

Macfie gasped out: 'You all right, Faro? Saw it all on the way up. Thank God I got here in time.' Out of breath he said: 'Took me an age to climb all these stairs. I'm an old man, you know, a bit out of condition,' he added as the screaming, blustering, swearing Hector was handcuffed.

Macfie, while out of breath, had enough left to say: 'I am arresting you, Sir Hector Belmuir, for the attempted murder of a police officer.'

'I think you might include the murder of Annie McLaw,' said Faro.

'That wasn't murder.' Hector yelled. 'She was a prostitute

and it was self-defence. Started screaming at me, thought I had killed her wretched, drunken husband, and as I tried to leave, she went for me with a knife, a knife – damn her.'

Honor watched silently as Hector, screaming obscenities at her, was escorted down the stairs. Her first thought was not Faro but Macfie. 'Are you all right, Brandon?' And taking his arm while he protested that he didn't need any help going downstairs, she led the way back down into the dining room and indicated the table.

'We need fortification, gentlemen,' and while she went to the sideboard and poured out three very substantial drams, Macfie turned to Faro: 'With your information that Hector had let slip, I told Honor.'

Handing them their glasses, she raised hers. 'I already knew that he had killed the McLaw woman. Stabbing is a messy business and he gave me all his excuses and his bloodied clothes to burn. It was our carriage that knocked down that poor woman on the Mound. He was terrified that she might reveal his dealings with Surgeon's Hall and that her servant might recognise him. So he kidnapped her. But it was too difficult to keep her locked in the poorhouse, so he let her go – an accident on the railway train with an open door.'

Macfie took her hand, kissed it gravely. 'You're a good lass, Honor. Always were – despite—' A shadow crossed his face, and she finished it for him.

'Despite my obnoxious brother, you mean?' With a shrug she went on. 'Naturally, he expected me to help. He always was a coward.'

She sighed. 'I've waited for this moment a long time, Brandon. A very long time. And the only way to give him what he deserved was to go along with his plan, catch him in the act. I told Brandon, and here we are.' She took a deep breath. 'My revenge, you could call it.'

And as if aware of Faro for the first time. 'He ruined my life once and after the incident with the McLaw woman, which I am ashamed to say he persuaded me to overlook, for the sake of the scandal, the family name dragged through the courts.' She stopped and regarded them both sadly. 'But I don't care about that now. What have we to lose – we have lost almost everything. What use is a damned name? We are the last of the Belmuirs and that won't save us from extinction. That painting upstairs, that we were trying to pass off as a burglary, was our last resort. But I knew, somehow, that the insurance people wouldn't oblige – despite the family name,' she added bitterly.

'The day I called at your cottage, Faro, the carriage had to stay on the road, and I saw all those wanted McLaw posters, everywhere, even on the builders' scaffolding.' She took a deep breath. 'Suddenly I couldn't take it any more, I couldn't stand by and let an innocent man hang. I knew how desperate you must be to prove it when Hector came to me and said: "They're on to us. I found that damned policeman crawling about the croft on his hands and knees. Well, he was wasting his time. I'll see to it that he won't be long with us. Accidents can happen."' Pausing, she looked at him. 'I knew he intended to kill you. And I told Brandon, about the return of the Leonardo and how easily a man could fall to his death down all those stairs.'

Macfie said, 'Thank God we got here in time. An overturned cart delayed us. And he was wrong about Jeremy here not knowing. Hector had let slip some clues—'

Faro interrupted, 'Such as reading all the details about the woman Tibbie's fatal railway accident when they had never been reported in the newspaper—'

'Really,' Honor interrupted. 'How clever of you, Faro.' But there was no warmth in her voice as she added to Macfie: 'What will happen next? To him – apart from a great scandal to shake the walls of Edinburgh. Our final humiliation.'

Macfie shook his head, said firmly. 'A confession before witnesses, which will clear McLaw.' He touched her hand. 'I will do everything I can, my dear, use my influence where it matters most to prevent your humiliation, but your brother must pay for his crimes. He'll get by on manslaughter, I shouldn't be surprised about that. You can be sure that a jury will see to it. He killed a prostitute in self-defence, the very idea of hanging a titled man of a great family for that is preposterous. And McLaw will get a pardon – I'll see to that. A free man.'

Honor sighed and the old man put his arm around her. She took a deep breath.

'Brandon, Brandon, I've waited a long time, many years now, for this. When I was a child he killed my horse for throwing him, my dog for biting him and . . . and—' she stopped, 'something more important.' In a voice hardly audible she looked at Faro and added, 'He took away my great love, the only man I ever wanted, and destroyed my life.'

Macfie listened impassively. 'Revenge is one thing, the law is another.'

'And seldom do they meet,' she said bitterly.

Suddenly weariness struck them. It had been a long

and terrible end to the day and Honor saw them into the carriage that would drop off Macfie at Sheridan Place and take Faro to his cottage. She watched Faro climb in and held out her hand.

'I owe you a great debt, Mr Faro.' And suddenly that warm hand in hers was not enough. She leant inside and kissed his cheek. 'Alas, a debt I can never repay,' she whispered.

Macfie was silent as the carriage moved away and Faro, feeling embarrassed, had to say something. 'Pity she never married. This man she wanted died in an accident, I take it?' There was a silence, so long he wondered if Macfie had heard him or had fallen asleep.

And then a sigh that was almost a sob. 'Aye, that was Sandy, my Sandy. Too poor, a policeman's son.' He shrugged. 'Not from the right class.'

There was jubilation at the cottage. Charlie would give himself up. He would remain on bail in Macfie's custody until his case was heard. What of the future? Lizzie would have begged him to stay. She had it all worked out. They could leave their beloved cottage, move to a larger house. Terraces were growing up everywhere, such as one of those tenements being built on the road outside.

But no, Charlie had decided. He would go abroad, where no one had ever heard of him, and begin his life anew with two friends from his schooldays, brothers who had great hopes of America. He would keep in touch with his beloved Ealasaid, of course, and who knows, maybe they would meet again, with that wee boy, who would be his nephew.

'My wee girl,' said Lizzie firmly, patting her stomach. 'I am to call her Rose.'

Vince, too, felt very grown up now. The events of the last weeks had changed him, especially his regard for his stepfather. One evening he said to Lizzie: 'Ma, I have to tell you this. I feel very disloyal.' And taking her hand, 'I hope you will understand, but you know, of late, I don't feel the way I used to about my father. I know he was a hero, and I've always cherished his memory, but somehow all that is fading. He doesn't feel real any more. Not like Stepfather. He feels much more like my father. I hope you understand.'

They stood at the window. He was coming home, walking up the path. Supper was ready and Lizzie smiled.

As Faro waved to them, she understood perfectly.